A PLUME BOOK

FALLING UNDER

DANIELLE YOUNGE-ULLMAN is a novelist and playwright from Toronto, Canada. She studied English and theater at McGill University, then returned to Toronto to work as a professional actor for ten years. Her one-act play, *7 Acts of Intercourse*, debuted at Toronto's SummerWorks Festival in 2005. *Falling Under* is her first novel.

Danielle Younge-Ullman

falling
uNder

A PLUME BOOK

PLUME
Published by the Penguin Group
Penguin Group (USA) Inc., 375 Hudson Street, New York, New York 10014, U.S.A. •
Penguin Group (Canada), 90 Eglinton Avenue East, Suite 700, Toronto, Ontario,
Canada M4P 2Y3 (a division of Pearson Penguin Canada Inc.) • Penguin Books
Ltd., 80 Strand, London WC2R 0RL, England • Penguin Ireland, 25 St. Stephen's
Green, Dublin 2, Ireland (a division of Penguin Books Ltd.) • Penguin Group
(Australia), 250 Camberwell Road, Camberwell, Victoria 3124, Australia (a
division of Pearson Australia Group Pty. Ltd.) • Penguin Books India Pvt. Ltd.,
11 Community Centre, Panchsheel Park, New Delhi – 110 017, India • Penguin
Group (NZ), 67 Apollo Drive, Rosedale, North Shore 0632, New Zealand (a division
of Pearson New Zealand Ltd.) • Penguin Books (South Africa) (Pty.) Ltd., 24 Sturdee
Avenue, Rosebank, Johannesburg 2196, South Africa

Penguin Books Ltd., Registered Offices: 80 Strand, London WC2R 0RL, England

First published by Plume, a member of Penguin Group (USA) Inc.

First Printing, August 2008
10 9 8 7 6 5 4 3 2 1

Ⓟ REGISTERED TRADEMARK—MARCA REGISTRADA

LIBRARY OF CONGRESS CATALOGING-IN-PUBLICATION DATA
Younge-Ullman, Danielle.
    Falling under / Danielle Younge-Ullman.
        p. cm.
    ISBN 978-0-452-28965-9 (trade pbk.)
    1. Self-actualization (Psychology)—Fiction. 2. Friendship—Fiction.
3. Psychological fiction. I. Title.
PS3625.O98F35 2008
813'.6—dc22   2007039766

Printed in the United States of America
Set in Horley Old Style

PUBLISHER'S NOTE
This is a work of fiction. Names, characters, places, and incidents are either the product
of the author's imagination or are used fictitiously, and any resemblance to actual per-
sons, living or dead, business establishments, events, or locales is entirely coincidental.

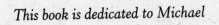

This book is dedicated to Michael

Acknowledgments

My deepest thanks and gratitude to:

My agent, Emmanuelle Alspaugh, for falling in love with this book in the first place and going on to be the most dedicated, hardworking agent I could wish for;

My editor, Alexis Washam, who is smart and flexible and has such clear vision; she has been a total joy to work with;

Marie Coolman and the fabulous publicity, art, and sales departments at Plume, plus Melanie Storschuk and the great people at Penguin Canada;

Early readers who gave me invaluable feedback and encouragement: Joel Hechter, Shelley Saville, Edna Saville, Laura Adamo, Suzanne Fitzpatrick, and Lori Delorme, plus my writing group, Maia Caron, Heather Wardell, Joanne Levy, Bev Katz Rosenbaum, and Maureen McGowan;

Kristy Kierman, Tish Cohen, and the other founding memebers of www.thedebutanteball.com for inviting me to dance, and my fellow Debutantes: Gail Konop Baker, Jenny Gardiner, Lisa Daily, Jess Riley, Eileen Cook—a hugely talented, generous, funny group of women that I've been blessed to share this journey with;

My friends and family, from whom I have had immearsurable love, support, and inspiration, in particular: Cindy and Gary Ullman, Brett Younge, the Saville and Ullman families, Brian Younge, Kimber Stevens, Nicholle Russell, Laura Adamo, Gillian Stecyk, Miranda Stecyk, Leslie Zacks, the Kleinberg family, and the McGill Girls;

David Rennie, for setting me on the path,

And Michael and T, for whom I live and breathe.

falling
under

Chapter One

Ask Santa for a new bike, and you might get it.

But Daddy might leave on Christmas Day.

When you reach out to touch your shiny new bike, Mommy might start yelling at Daddy about how dare he spend their money on a new bike and how you're only five and what do you need a new bike for anyway?

You play your invisible trick—the one where you pretend you are a small rock—and hope that no one will notice your heart thumping so loud and your ears burning and your eyes blinking again and again.

Daddy yells back at Mommy and soon they are yelling in each other's faces.

You take your hand off the bike.

You wish, instead of asking for a bike, you'd asked Santa for no more yelling and no more breaking things and slamming of doors. You wish you'd asked for Daddy not to walk out the door and say he's never coming back and stay away until Mommy calls and begs him to come home like she has four times already.

The yelling gets louder and the words get meaner and then it all stops. A blast of freezing air gets in when Daddy opens the front door. You shiver and the door slams shut with Daddy on the other side.

In the long silence before Mommy starts her crying and her kicking at the door, you think about what she said about the bike.

How come Dad and Mom had to pay Santa?

Oh.

It doesn't matter what you asked Santa, you realize, because there is no Santa. There's no Santa, and Daddy's not coming back this time. Somehow you know it.

Chapter Two

When all else fails I go to Erik. Tonight, all else has failed.

He answers the door, eyes bloodshot, unsurprised. And then the hitch in my breathing that comes, that always comes with Erik.

"Can't sleep?" he says.

"No."

He steps aside to let me in, shuts the door behind me, slides the bolts, and chains the locks.

"Drink?" he says.

I refuse, as always.

There is no bar, just a huddle of bottles on top of a giant, long-broken stereo speaker. He pours himself a Lagavulin, neat, as always.

"You painting?" he says.

"All day."

"Good."

"You breaking the law?"

"Not at the moment," he says with the ghost of a smirk.

The couch is clear of its usual technological detritus. I follow him there, and sit.

I shouldn't be here.

I should never have been here. But it was too late years ago, and now it doesn't matter so much.

We try small talk but soon run out of easy things to say. Our ill beginnings surface quickly, so it's really better not to converse.

"So," he says.

"So."

I feel his eyes on me. He knows if I'm here, I've done everything I can to still the storm inside, to put all the demons back into their boxes and seal the lids. But sometimes they won't go. Sometimes my ears are full of screaming, and sometimes, like tonight, the voices are mine.

Erik has them too—demons, voices, nightmares seared on the soul—I knew it the first time I saw him. And sometimes, when there are large, dark spaces inside that you cannot escape, sometimes someone can meet you there, keep you company. Sometimes they can break you out.

I turn my head and let his eyes in. We search, and accept.

There can be no love here; we don't want it and we don't have it to give, especially not to each other. No love, but there is something else.

"Mara," he says. A question, a command.

"Yes."

We both stand.

I know the way to the bedroom, I know his mouth will taste like Scotch. I walk ahead and listen for his footsteps behind me. Just inside the door his arms wrap around my waist. He swivels me around and pulls me closer. I let him.

I come here because I know Erik will drag me to the edge. He will drag me there, push me over, and then leap after me, to a place beyond pain, beyond loss, beyond the things that haunt us in the empty spaces of the night.

When all else fails, I have this.

Chapter Three

Spring comes.

You want to ride your bike, but maybe if you don't, then Daddy will come home and Mommy will get out of bed in the mornings and this time nobody will shout or throw hot cups of coffee at each other.

You walk to kindergarten and hope, every day, to come back to a house with both Mommy and Daddy in it.

Then Mommy notices you not riding the bike.

"We could have used that money," she says. "We can't just go buying bikes that we don't ride. We'll end up in the poor house."

"Where is the Poor House?" you ask.

"It's nowhere you want to go," she says.

"Is that where Daddy went?"

"I told you not to mention his name."

"Sorry, Mom."

She will never understand why you're not riding the bike, and if she did it would only make her cry, so the next day you get on it and ride down the block. As soon as you're out of sight, you get off. You hope Daddy will understand that you had to ride it, just a little bit, and will still come back. He doesn't.

In June, Grandma and Grandpa come to visit. You tell Grandma about Daddy being gone and Mommy sick and crying every day.

"I know, sweetheart," Grandma says, and pats your shoulder. "But it will all be okay, you'll see."

You don't think so. In case she doesn't know, you tell her about Santa too.

Grandma looks at you, very serious, and tells you about God, who is like Santa, only without the presents and the red suit.

"He gives more important presents," Grandma says, "like listening to your problems and helping you out when things are hard."

You're not sure about this, but you start talking to God sometimes. You ask Him to stop Mommy from crying and eventually she does, only now she's grumpy instead and has to go to work and comes home after your bedtime. You realize you liked it better before, because even if she was crying, at least she was home.

You also talk to God about Daddy coming back and you practice being small so you won't bother him when he does. Grandma promised that God would answer your prayers, but when you turn six and Christmas comes again with no Daddy, you start to doubt.

Then one day in February, like a miracle, he's back.

Only he smells funny and you have to visit him in an ugly place downtown. And he hardly ever smiles, and doesn't talk, except to ask you why you don't eat very much and why you're such a quiet little thing. He doesn't realize that you understand about money and you understand about mess and noise. You don't need much and you can be very small and quiet. You hardly ride the bike and you'll never ask Santa for anything else.

You sit next to him on his stinky couch every other weekend while he watches television and smokes cigarettes.

You're not so sure you like the daddy God sent back and you're not so sure you like the way He has been answering your prayers in general.

I leave Erik sprawled and vulnerable, and steal away into the predawn light.

I've never liked seeing him asleep, never wanted to wake up with him, share breakfast, read the newspaper together or whatever it is that people do.

Erik and I are too intense, too different, and the things we have in common are the wrong things. We should never have spoken, never have touched, much less the rest of it.

On my way back across town I ask the taxi to stop so I can get myself a large black coffee.

Once at home, I stand under the shower and scrub him from my skin. I stay until I am pruny, but I will never be clean.

I am disgusting, pathetic, and weak. But what else is new? I wash my angst down the drain and turn the water off.

In the bedroom, I put on my customary uniform: pants, T-shirt, and cardigan, all black. Every item of clothing I own is black, navy or beige. Everything coordinates with everything else in my closet and each day I put on the next pair of pants in the row, the top T-shirt on the pile, and so on. Simple.

In the kitchen I make more coffee, force down a granola bar, and then walk out the kitchen door to my back-porch-turned-studio. I put on my smock, mix my colors, and sit down to work.

It's 6 a.m. I start work every day at 6 a.m. If I haven't slept because I was surfing the net, out late with Bernadette, or getting my brains fucked out by an emotionally damaged computer hacker, tough shit.

Up.

Showered.

Dressed.

Caffeinated.

Working.

Period.

The east-facing windows bring the morning light in threads. Later it will be so bright I will turn my easel backward.

I face the work before me and sigh. I would love to feel I am changing the world. I would love to think my work transfixed people, changed their perceptions of reality, moved them to tears, heroic action . . . any action.

It might have, once. In the early years of art college, I painted to express the depths of my soul. I wanted to be Frida Kahlo, with maybe a little Jackson Pollock thrown in.

I painted like it mattered, like I could create something unique. People who knew about these things thought I had a Future.

Now I paint to soothe. I paint to banish the very emotions I used to channel because somewhere during my final two years, I got jaded and stopped believing—in art, love, happily-ever-after . . . and mostly in myself. All those feelings became too much for me; they began to burn me up. And so, here I am—far from Frida, or any other kind of greatness.

But I make a living. I crank out circles and squares, colorful geometrics that people buy to match their furniture, shapes with a logic that quiets my mind. Someone might be kind enough to call my paintings "Zen" and they might be moved to change the position of their couch, but that's all.

By 4 p.m. I have finished the piece. Sapphire circles intertwine with smaller yellow and purple circles, all floating above a forest of sharp, triangular shapes.

I look at it with the satisfaction that it's finished, but no other feeling, no opinion on whether or not it's "good." Done is what it is. I'll call Sal to pick it up, and never think about it again.

"Five done, and it's only mid-October," I say to Sal's voice mail. "Whatever else, you've got to admit I'm fast!"

There's a message from Bernadette saying she's coming over at 5:30. She never asks, just informs me, but she's one of my few links to the outside world, so I don't mind. As it is, I have my groceries and my art supplies delivered; payment from Sal comes via direct deposit. I can hole myself up for weeks if I so desire.

"Do you think you might be agoraphobic?" Bernadette asked me once.

I shrugged, looked away.

"Honestly, do you ever go out when I'm not with you?"

"Sometimes," I said.

"Like when?"

"I don't know . . . Like if I run out of toothpaste. And I go to Dad's sometimes."

"That doesn't count," Bernadette said. "I'm talking about going out, on purpose, to do things. Social things."

"I'm social enough."

"Right."

"Bee, I'm fine."

"If you say so."

Of course, she was right. Not that I'm agoraphobic, but something is wrong with me. Something is wrong and it's not getting better.

A trip outside, to the world beyond my front door, is fraught with peril for me, especially if I'm alone.

First, I don't like crowds. Too many colors, too many smells and noises, too much being jostled, poked, looked at. Too many potential lunatics who might be carrying knives, guns, anthrax, who might have little girls locked in their basements, or be carrying the next SARS or avian flu virus.

Whenever I leave the house by myself, my mind assaults me with images of disaster. I see myself falling into manholes, being crushed by a falling building, tripping on concrete stairs, tumbling down. I imagine the doors of vans opening as I walk by and stocking-capped thieves or kidnappers grabbing me, hauling me inside. The van is soundproof and they torture me with pins and matches and don't even ask for ransom—not that anyone would pay it.

I have a car, but I hate driving it. I just know I could lose control and mow down someone's cat or dog, or worse, their child. Or I might crash into a telephone pole because the brakes have failed, have been cut. Arms broken, fingers mangled, lungs collapsed, death imminent.

And then there's skin cancer, an expanding freckle caught too late, one week to live. Bug bites, malaria, smog, second-hand smoke, rabid raccoons, tainted beef.

And then, always, always, the tape plays where I step out in front of a car, a truck, the—

Oh, please not the streetcar.

Yes, the streetcar.

The streetcar going too fast, can't stop in time, my legs frozen, body seized up, the thunk of metal on flesh, the trajectory of the body, airborne, the sickening sound of a skull cracked open, the smell of blood, the sight of it mixing with oil on the street, with hair, fragments of—

Stopstopstop!

But I see it all. I imagine it all, and know that it is possible. These things happen every day and they could happen to me. The proof is there, in my own life and on the news, which I probably shouldn't watch.

I watch the news and read three newspapers online daily, and my fears expand outward, touching the people I love, tearing them away in senseless, violent tragedies while I stand, helpless, and watch.

It makes for a tense life.

I did look into agoraphobia. I called a hotline, spoke to a counselor. I agreed to join an agoraphobic support group she was starting, with fifteen others who had similar issues.

They offered to send someone to pick me up for the first meeting, but I declined. On a good day I can drive myself places, on a moderate-to-bad one I prefer a taxi.

I was the only one who showed up.

"I don't think you're agoraphobic," the counselor said, and looked at the circle of empty chairs. "I guess there was a flaw in my plan."

"Maybe. So, uh, what do you think is wrong with me?"

"An anxiety disorder of some kind," she said. "But I'm not qualified to diagnose you. You should see a therapist."

I went to see a therapist.

"Ego problem," he said.

"What?"

"You think the world revolves around you, that you've been singled out for something special by God."

"But—"

"Polluted animus," he said. "You need to come twice a week, and I'll try to clear you."

"Sorry?"

"We'll regress you and then do separation therapy."

"Um . . ."

"I sense resistance, I sense confusion. Believe me, that's the animus," he said.

Right.

"Polluted," he said.

Huh.

My giant ego, polluted animus and I went home and never came back.

———

Bernadette rings my doorbell at precisely 5:30. I open the door and she comes in and looks hard at me. She often looks at me like this, presumably making sure I haven't flaked out, started drinking, lost my mind, etc.

"Have I grown an extra set of ears?"

"Funny," she says. "How are you?"

"Fine."

"Good," she says, and then breezes past me into the front room. "We're going out."

Out. I haven't been anywhere except to Erik's in over two weeks. He should not be my only reason for contact with the outside world. It will be good for me to go out. That's what I tell myself, anyway.

I grimace at Bernadette, which she correctly interprets as a "yes."

"Get dressed," she says.

"I am dressed."

She gives my outfit a disparaging once-over.

"Right, I forgot, you're Banana Republic's answer to Goth."

"You're looking lovely," I say.

Bernadette is looking lovely, actually, if you discount the bright green furry vest thing she has on. It looks like a psychedelic rat has landed on her chest and died there. Her wavy red bob has been tortured straight, and the rest of her ensemble—lace-up boots, tights, and a short dress—are all in a shade of periwinkle that makes her dark blue eyes seem purple.

Dress, makeup and knee-high combat boots . . . uh oh.

"Bee?" I raise an eyebrow.

"I'm over it," she says.

"That's what I was afraid of."

"Can't pine forever."

"I hope not," I say. "It only lasted three weeks."

"It was an intense three weeks," she says.

"Sure. So what's the plan?"

"We need to stop by the Struggles for Justice and Dignity fundraiser and then—"

"Oh no!" I say. "That sounds a lot like the Peace, Justice and Vegetables group."

"No, no. This is *Struggles* for Justice and Dignity—no peace, no vegetables, totally different gang."

"But . . ."

"This group is nice."

"Yes, but—"

"And nobody will chuck tomatoes at you," she says.

"Promise?" I ask. I rub my collarbone and recall being whacked by a juicy beefsteak.

"You should never have admitted to eating that hamburger," Bernadette says, and starts to giggle. "You were really asking for it."

"Hey, I thought those people were about tolerance."

Bernadette snorts with laughter.

"Thanks for the support!" I say.

"Anytime," she says. "Oh, can you sign something?"

She whips a petition out of her purse and hands it to me. I peruse the page, making sure I agree with the cause, and am not committing myself to painting banners for the Left-Wing Used Book Sale or jogging for European Mobility Week like I did last year. *Support the Toronto Humane Society*, it says.

"Hard to argue with that," I say, and sign my name.

Bernadette's activism is an inspiration, but sometimes I wish she'd narrow her focus. I sign petitions, write letters to my member of parliament, and donate as much money as I can afford, but some of these organizations are seriously whacked. On top of that, my tolerance for rallies, fundraisers, and the singing of folk songs is nonexistent.

Bernadette is saving the world.

I can barely save myself.

"I promise we won't stay long," she says. She knows I dislike crowds. She doesn't know they make me want to crawl out of my skin. "You can even stay in the car while I pop in."

In the car alone or stuck in a crowd. Great options.

"I promise I'll be, like, two seconds."

I breathe. "Okay." I'll be fine. I'll be with Bernadette.

"And then I'm buying you dinner, and don't tell me you've eaten, because you never do."

"I do so."

"Whatever you say, Bones."

I wince. I hate that nickname. It's not my fault I've always been skinny and it's been years since I was *that* skinny.

In the bathroom, I pull my long, black hair into a ponytail, do a quick check to make sure I don't have paint on my face and consider myself ready.

I find Bernadette in the studio, looking at my finished painting.

"What?" I say. "You don't like it?"

"It's fine," she says. "It's good."

I shrug. "As long as Sal likes it."

"And what if he doesn't?" she says. "You get cut off?"

"Of course not, we have a deal."

"What if I wanted to buy a piece from you?"

"You'd have to buy it from him. You know that."

"Humph," she says. "I don't like it, the guy owns you."

"Not me, just the work."

She shakes her head and walks out of the studio.

"Forget it," she says. "Let's get going."

"Okay."

We get our shoes on and leave the house.

"Ready?" Bernadette says when she sees me standing at the door, not moving.

I give myself a shake and reach for the doorknob. "Ready."

"Where are we having dinner?" I ask in the driveway.

"I thought we'd start with a cocktail at G-spot, go for dinner at Byzantium, and then see."

I groan. "That's not dinner, that's barhopping."

"Don't worry, it'll be fun."

I sigh. Just what I need, another tour of the bars of Toronto in search of a soul mate for Bernadette.

Chapter Four

"Quick! Flirt with me!" Bernadette hisses in my ear.

"What? Why?" As if I don't know. Some ex-girlfriend or other must be nearby. Being a decoy-slash-stand-in love interest is one of the dubious honors of hanging out with Bernadette.

"Come on!" she says.

"Flirt? Are you sure?" I say. "What for?"

I like to play dumb just to bug her.

"It's Janet!" she says, and bats her eyelashes at me while simultaneously stepping on my foot. "Please?"

I don't know Janet, but I have infinite patience for the foibles of my best-and-only friend. I smile down at her and move closer, which is the extent of my ability to flirt—with men or women.

"Thank you," she says.

I spot a vaguely familiar woman over Bernadette's shoulder—blond hair, close-set hazel eyes, and the tightest white T-shirt-without-a-bra I've ever seen.

She approaches.

I know my job. I move in closer and start talking to Bernadette as if I don't see the braless wonder sidling up to her.

"So, Bee, I'm thinking you should quit your corporate job and dedicate your time to your causes."

Braless taps Bernadette's shoulder.

"Hi," she says.

"Just a sec," Bernadette says, and turns to the woman. "Hi."

"I saw you at Pope Joan a few weeks ago," Janet says.

"Right, right." Bernadette says, and smiles. They start in with the small talk.

Janet, Janet . . . I'm trying to remember the scoop. Ah ha! Janet was the one with the double life, the husband and kids in Oakville and the girlfriends downtown on the weekends. She lied to Bernadette for four months before the truth, ahem, came out. That breakup was bad, and now that I remember, I'm motivated.

"I love your vest," Perfidious Janet is saying when I tune back in.

"Thanks," Bernadette says. "Feel appeal, you know?"

Janet reaches her treacherous hand out toward the vest. This is definitely my cue.

"Excuse me," I say. "That feel appeal is for my benefit, not yours."

"Mara!" Bernadette says, and looks at me like she's shocked.

I put my arm around her waist.

"What?" I say. "I don't want some woman touching you." Possessive I can do.

"I'm sorry about this," Bernadette says to Janet, and tries to push me away. "We're having a misunderstanding here."

"Hey," Janet says. "It's okay, I'll leave you two alone." And she walks off.

Ha! Mission accomplished.

I grin at Bernadette. "How was that?"

"Awful!"

"Hunh?"

"We've seen her in three bars so far tonight!"

"And?"

"And she finally gets up the nerve to approach me and you drive her off!"

"But isn't Janet the one with the husband?"

She frowns, then starts laughing.

"What?"

"You would make a terrible lesbian," she says.

"No, I wouldn't!" I say. "Why would I?"

"You can hardly distinguish one woman from another."

"Oh. Uh oh. That wasn't Janet?"

"No. Janet already walked by."

"Oh."

"And that," she says, and looks in the direction of the retreating woman, "was supposed to be the love of my life."

Oops. "You better go after her."

Bernadette bites her lip and looks over her shoulder. "Are you sure?"

"Of course," I say. "Go."

"You'll be all right? Just for a minute?"

"I'm fine. I'll sit right here at the bar."

She beams. "Thanks!" she says, and starts off into the crowd.

I sit on a stool and order a diet pop. I swirl the ice cubes around in the glass and take small sips. In my peripheral vision, I notice someone hovering. A large woman with hockey hair is staring at me like she either wants to kill me or fuck me. Considering the locale, I'm guessing it's the latter.

I sigh. Not my type of lesbian. That is, if I *had* a type of lesbian.

I make the mistake of meeting her eyes, and she winks. I smile, but shake my head.

She lifts her eyebrows, *You sure?*

I nod. She shrugs and ambles off.

I try not to stare at Bernadette, who is now on the other side of the bar. Hopefully she'll work her mojo fast—get a phone number, make a date—so we can get out of here.

"Hello," says a deep voice to my left.

Uh oh. "Yes?" I say, and turn to look.

"Hi," he says.

It looks like a he, but around here you can never be sure.

"Hi," I say.

"How's it going?"

"Um . . ."

"Hey, I'm not trying to—"

"It's okay."

"—hit on you or anything," he says.

Definitely a he, which is good news, all things considered.

"That's fine," I say.

"You looked kind of bored," he says. "And I'm kind of bored, so I thought—"

"We could bore each other?"

He laughs. "Just figured we could pass the time with some conversation," he says.

Relax, I tell myself. Gay village equals gay man.

"All right. What are you passing time for?" I say.

"I had to get out of my apartment. You?"

"My friend is chasing down the woman of her dreams."

"Important task."

"Maybe, maybe not," I say. "Regardless, I'm left holding down the bar."

"My name's Hugo," he says, and holds out his hand.

I shake it. "Mara."

"Hello."

Hugo is not your typical gay boy with the spiked hair, fake tan, and tight shirt over buff abs. He's got regular skin tone, slouchy preppy-guy clothes, ear-length corkscrew curls, and lovely big eyes. He's rather cute, actually.

"So," I say, "how come you're hiding from your apartment?"

"Oh, I'm not hiding, it's just that I have a new puppy and I'm trying to train him."

"Train him?"

"To be alone for a couple of hours without chewing the furniture, peeing on the floor, howling nonstop, that kind of thing," Hugo says. "You see, he has separation anxiety."

"Oh no."

"He's a rescue and he's had a rough time."

"Aww. What's his name?"

"Pollock."

I laugh. "You're kidding. Like the artist?"

Hugo nods.

"Why?"

"His coat. It has this crazy speckled pattern. I brought him home and I was sitting there trying to think of a name, and I'd just seen *Pollock* the movie, so . . ."

"So it was in your mind."

"Yeah. I said the name out loud and he stopped, looked at me and cocked his head. I said it again and he gave just one woof, and that was it."

"It's a good name."

"Thanks."

Hugo and I sip our drinks and continue to talk. I'm not great at talking about myself, so I ask him questions. I discover that he is a vet but started out in insurance, and that he moved to Toronto two years ago to open a practice.

"Why the change?" I ask.

"I hated the industry I was in, didn't like the people I worked with, started not liking myself."

"Ah."

"And I always wanted to be a vet."

"It's funny, you seem like a people person."

"I am. I'm a people person and an animal person."

"Hmm."

"My turn," Hugo says. "You are . . . let me guess . . . a stockbroker."

I snort.

"Okay, wait, don't tell me. I swear, I'm really good at this."

"Sure you are."

His eyes scan my face and then slide down and back up my body.

Something happens in my belly: a zing, a jolt.

Whoa.

He looks at my face again and his eyes narrow.

"A painter?" he says.

"What?"

"Are you a painter? An artist?"

"Yes! How did you . . . ?"

"I'm right?"

"Yeah, but how . . ."

"Ha!" He raises a victory fist. "I told you, I'm a people person."

"Come on."

"And you lit up when we were talking about Jackson Pollock."

"Okay."

"Plus, you have paint on your thumb."

"Ah. Crafty. I'm impressed."

He grins. "And I'm naturally lucky."

"Lucky you."

"So, Mara-the-painter," he says, "what do you paint?"

He's flirting. I swear he's flirting. Not gay then. Bi? If so, I can direct him to the bisexual support group I gave money to last month, but I don't want to sleep with him.

Who said anything about sleeping with him!

No one. Right. Whew, close call.

Bernadette materializes at my side.

"You all right?" she asks, and darts her eyes toward Hugo.

"Sure," I say. "Fine."

"I could use a few minutes more," she says.

"No problem," I say, and she leaves.

"Your friend?" Hugo asks.

"Yeah."

"Not your girlfriend?"

"Nope."

Uh oh, I like him. I may be a hermit, but I know chemistry when I feel it.

Hugo . . . looking at me.

Yep.

Me . . . looking back.

"I like you," he says.

"Oh," I say.

"No really, I like you."

"You just met me."

"Sure, but I trust my instincts," he says. "Tell me you're not gay."

"Nope."

"Nope, you won't tell me you're not, or nope, you're not?"

"Not."

"Me neither," he says.

"Really," I say. "Why are you here then?"

"I live nearby, and I have no issues with the neighborhood."

"Okay."

"And the bartender makes a great Bloody Mary."

"Fair enough."

The air between us is suddenly thick. I understand nothing about love, but I know what to do about lust.

"Let's go then," I say.

"What?"

"Your place. Let's go."

His eyes widen. "You're kidding," he says.

"No."

"I was thinking more along the lines of your e-mail address and then maybe dinner."

"No."

"Hmm," he says, an odd smile on his face. He sips his Bloody Mary and studies me. I become conscious of every limb and every breath.

"So what you're saying is that you'll fuck me, but you won't have dinner with me?" he says.

"Essentially."

"Interesting."

"And I wouldn't mind meeting Pollock."

"No deal."

"Why not?"

"I try not to expose him to people who aren't going to stick around."

"You mean . . ."

"Because of the separation anxiety."

"Why don't you think I'll stick around?"

"'I'll fuck you, but I won't have dinner with you?'" he says.

"Oh, that."

"Yeah, that." He waits a moment, and then says, "Oh come on, just give me your e-mail address."

"I can't."

"You have a boyfriend?"

"No."

"So, what's the problem?"

Problem? Like *one* problem?

Love always starts out well. There's the chemistry, the lust, that gushy, dizzy, cuddly, brunch-eating phase, the wonder, the miracle of togetherness. And then familiarity creeps in, followed by disappointment, disillusionment, fear. Inevitably there is silence, screaming, betrayal, the wrenching, ugly truth when you look at each other and know that your love has turned to disgust, despair, boredom, hate. All happiness gone, all rotten, all rotting.

That's one problem.

Hugo and I, we could be happy. Maybe we would be happy. But happiness is dangerous, is treacherous, and one day I would lose him. I would pull out my soul and serve it to him and then he would be gone, murdered, kidnapped, felled by cancer, a heart attack. I see it: five in the morning, me answering the doorbell, police on the doorstep, Pollock or a baby in my arms, and then the news that Hugo is gone. Gone forever and my heart gone too.

I see it, I can't help seeing it. And that's another problem. I cannot trust him, but worst of all, I cannot trust myself.

That's a real problem.

Hugo is looking at me, his gaze open.

Terrifying.

What was the question?

"What's the problem?"

Right. I can hardly breathe.

"Uh . . ."

"Are you all right?" he asks.

"Um . . ."

I'm dizzy, ill.

"Hey, it's just dinner," he says. "Or coffee. People do it all the time."

"I know, but . . ."

"Okay, okay, I'm not some creep who can't take no for an answer."

"Sorry," I say.

"You know what, though?" he says. "I'm here a lot. I'll probably be here every night this week, so . . ."

"Right."

"So we could do this again, just casual."

"Mm," I say.

"Just you helping me pass the time while I train Pollock."

"Maybe," I find myself saying.

I can't manage "no thanks" but I can say "maybe"? I've got to find Bernadette and get out of here.

"Um, it was nice to meet you, Hugo."

Miraculously, Bernadette shows up at this exact moment. One look at me and she is all concern.

"You all right?"

"Fine."

She glares at Hugo, who throws his hands up in a gesture of innocence.

"Let's go," she says, and pulls me by the arm.

I look over my shoulder one last time, but Hugo has receded into the crowd.

Outside we hustle toward the car.

"What did he say to you?" Bernadette asks.

"Nothing."

"Hello! You look like you're going to cry and your skin is pasty. What happened?"

I open the passenger door and get into the car.

Bernadette grips the keys and stares at me.

I sigh.

"All right. He asked me to dinner."

"And?"

"Said he liked me."

"And?"

"And that's it."

"Oh," she says. "That's heinous."

"Bee, don't."

"What?"

"You know."

"I didn't say anything," she says.

"But you know I can't . . . I mean, I'm not . . ." I reach my fingers up to massage my temples. "Plus, I offered to go home with him," I confess.

"Before or after he asked you out?"

"Before."

"Ah ha! You like him." She starts the car. "Mara?"

I look out the window.

"Mara, listen, you've got to get over this."

We drive to my house in silence. We disagree on certain issues. And some things are not meant to be gotten over.

Chapter Five

In second grade, Clarissa Samuel un-invites you to her birthday party at Ontario Place even though she's already invited the whole class and your mom has already called her mom to say you're coming.

You tell Clarissa that amusement parks are for babies anyway and you bite your lip and make it bleed so you can go to the nurse. No way are you going to cry in front of Clarissa Samuel.

Instead of going to the nurse, you dash into the girls' bathroom and lock yourself in a stall. You squeeze your eyes shut and grit your teeth. You will stop crying.

Stop, stop, stop—you are tougher than this.

At recess, Clarissa and her friends start a chant.

"Mara i-is ba-ad, Mara's got no da-ad . . ."

Arm in arm, they march around the playground.

You can't be the only girl in the world with divorced parents, but that's how they act. That's how it feels.

"Mara's got no da-ad, no-o da-ad!"

No dad? You can't stand it, can't bear it, can't just swallow it.

You will kill her, you will crush her, you will rip her hair out and . . .

You must have flown, because you land right on top of her. You land on her and kick and punch and holler.

"I do so have a dad! I have a dad! You shut your mouth! I have a dad, I have a dad, I do so have a dad! You liar, you're such a liar, take it back!"

She hoofs you in the stomach and her friends pull at your arms, but you scratch her face and punch her in the nose and scream and scream.

There is blood on both of you by the time they separate you and drag you to the infirmary. You're hurt—your stomach aches and your knee is skinned.

You're also in trouble.

Clarissa has a broken nose and needs stitches on her elbow. Everyone says she did nothing wrong, they say you started it.

Liars, they're all liars. They just want to go ride roller coasters at Ontario Place.

The principal calls Mom, but she can't leave work.

Dad doesn't pick up his phone and you don't know the number of the restaurant where he works, and anyway he probably wouldn't come. You wish he would, because then you could show him to everybody.

The nurse fixes you up with Band-Aids and stinging red stuff and tells you that real ladies don't fight. You don't care much about being a real lady, but you're in enough trouble already, so you don't say so.

You stay in the infirmary for a long time, and the principal tells you to write a letter to Clarissa saying you are sorry. You grip the pencil, stare at the paper. Nothing comes out at first. Then you write:

> Dear Clarissa,
>   Mrs. Sedgwick says i have to say sorry to you but you shud say sorry to me too for saying i dont have a dad. i have a dad and his name is HENRY and he is a very nice dad. i dont think it is good to say that to someone just because you have lots of friends and cloths. and that is why i got mad and had a fight with you
>   MARA LINDSEY FOSTER
>   Ps. i also have a Mom in case you wonderd and her name is CAROL so dont say i dont have a Mom too
>   Ps again. i heard Ontario Place stinks and has lots of seeguls pooping. I hop they poop on you.

You know it's not the letter they want, and you're not sure about some of the words. You're about to cross out the part about the seagulls pooping when the nurse comes back in and takes the letter from you.

She takes you to Principal Sedgwick's office and makes you sit in the foyer. You're in bigger trouble now, because poop is a bad word and everybody thinks Clarissa is such a perfect girl, so nobody except you would like to see birds pooping on her.

Your knee is going to have a big gross scab. But if you stay awake late enough, Mommy will be home and you can show it to her and maybe she will rub the back of your neck with her hand and say "poor baby" and kiss it better. Maybe she will. Maybe you could get into more fights and then Mommy will feel sad and kiss you and let you come to work with her instead of sending you to school where nobody likes you.

You hear a sound like laughing and then voices behind the principal's door. Someone says your name, and then they stop laughing. You hear the words "broken home."

"You have to understand, she's from a broken home."

"Shh."

The nurse comes out and checks your Band-Aids one more time, then Principal Sedgwick brings you into her office.

"Mara, are you all right?"

"Yes."

"Are you . . . are things okay at home?"

You look at your shoes. "Yes, fine."

For the rest of the day you hear the words "broken home" in your head. You start to worry. When you get to your house, you stand in front of it and look for cracks. There are none. You take out your key and go inside. You check the walls, turn on all the lights and the water, inspect the ceilings. Nothing.

You sit at the kitchen table and think about the house. With all the fighting and breaking of doors off their hinges, and Mommy and Daddy hating each other, you're surprised something isn't broken. Then you think of Mommy telling you what a shitty life it is and Daddy downtown on his couch, staring into space.

Suddenly you understand what the broken part is. There is a crack in your house, a crack from top to bottom. And it runs straight through the middle of you.

———

6 a.m.: showered, dressed, caffeinated, etc.

Acrylics ready. Butt on chair. Blank canvas.

Yuck.

I've looked at a blank canvas hundreds of times, so my stomach shouldn't be in knots. All I have to do is choose: circles, squares, or rectangles? It's not like the future of the world hinges on my choice.

Right. Exactly.

I shut my eyes and see what comes. A happy face with big sweet eyes, and corkscrew curls springing from its head. Hugo.

I open my eyes to banish the image, but it won't go. It winks.

"Get lost, I don't do faces." I haven't done any kind of portrait since my last Life Drawing class in school, actually. And besides, last night is better forgotten. Much better.

I blink a few times and imagine a square. Perfect. Large, symmetrical, clean.

I begin. And if I'm painting over possibility, too bad. Squares calm me. Shapes with logic, with beginnings, middles and ends, soothe me. They numb my mind.

4 p.m.: check nonexistent voice mail.

5 p.m.: eat.

6 p.m.: pace.

7 p.m.: stare into space.

9 p.m.: ache to see Hugo again.

10 p.m.: put on coat.

10:01: take off coat.

10:30: get ready for bed. Stare into darkness. Think of Erik, Lucas and why I can't go out with Hugo.

3 a.m.: dream of being in a plane that is about to crash. Wake sweating, tears on cheeks. Carefully, carefully, breathe in and out. Four counts in, eight counts out. Banish nightmare. Breathe in, breathe out. Insert logic. Four in, eight out.

Sleep.

6 a.m.: work.

7 a.m.: groggy, grumpy, thirsty.

11 a.m.: daydream.

In the evening I leave another message for Sal, who hasn't come by yet to pick up the new paintings.

I call Bernadette and find her still at work.

"What's up?" I say.

She groans, and I can imagine her rolling her eyes.

"At the moment, I'm shaving off Bianca Lacey's shoulder blade."

"Hunh?"

"For the Ice Shade promo package," she says. "The shot is perfect, she looks beautiful, but freaking Mitchell sent it back because her shoulder blade looks too sharp, so I'm shaving it."

"You can do that?"

"Of course," she says. "We do it all the time. Usually I'd send it back to the art department, but we're behind."

"Want to come over when you're done?"

"Sure, why not?"

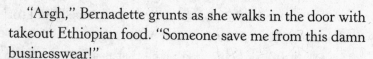

"Argh," Bernadette grunts as she walks in the door with takeout Ethiopian food. "Someone save me from this damn businesswear!"

She passes me the food, tosses her coat on the bench by the door, and kicks her heels off with more energy than is strictly necessary. I'm guessing she's not in the best mood.

"Fuck," she says and stomps to the kitchen with her over-sized purse in hand.

Uh huh. "What's wrong?"

"I hate my life," she says, and plops down on a chair.

"Ah."

"The traffic sucks, this frigging skirt is . . ." She unbuttons the skirt and wriggles it off, "digging into me, cost me a fortune, and I feel like a whale and a corporate drone at the same time." She digs in her purse and pulls out her Kiss My Ass sweatpants and Riot Grrrl T-shirt.

"And I didn't make it to my lunchtime yoga class." She pulls on the sweats and T-shirt, presumably her version of yoga wear.

"That's better," she says, and then crumples her work clothes and shoves them into the bulging purse where they are likely to be stained, stabbed, or ripped by the paraphernalia that she lugs around. "But I do hate my life."

"Yeah," I say. "You mentioned that."

"I brought wine, I hope that's okay."

"Of course."

She passes me the bottle and I open it, pour her a glass, and set the food out on the kitchen table. Bernadette gulps her wine. I rip off a piece of injera bread, start on the lentils, and wait for her to mellow.

"Not only did I digitally shave off a woman's back today, but I helped launch a completely useless product and sat in a meeting where an ad campaign was rejected because the model looks too 'dykey'. And it would have been bad enough if I'd just said nothing, but what I actually did was *agree*."

"Why would they be so . . . ." I say, "I thought you told me your coworkers knew."

She looks down at her lap. "Actually, only a few know," she mumbles. "You know I'd never lie about it, but I've stopped volunteering the information."

"This is news to me," I say, surprised at the revelation. "I don't get it."

"Well, you never know when one of the higher-ups, you know the old-boys-club types, will decide to hold something like that against you. And then there are guys like Mitchell who find out and then want to share locker-room talk."

"Eew."

"Yeah. He comes into my office and tells me what he did with some girl the night before, asks me questions like why don't some women like their nipples touched and how do we decide who pays for dinner on the first date."

"Mitchell is a caveman."

"Just one of the many delights of my work life."

"Maybe you should quit."

"Hello!" she says, and throws her hands up. "Student loan? Car payments? Rent?"

"Sure," I say. "I know."

After dinner, we decide to watch a DVD, and I let her choose. We wind up watching *Pet Sematary* for the eleventh time, and for the eleventh time I will have nightmares. When she leaves, the house is far too empty.

I turn on all the lights, the radio, the TV, and pace. Monsters in every corner. I can't escape my own head, can't stand to be with myself, won't be able to sleep.

Erik answers on the first ring.

I decide to call a cab so I don't have to drive at night. Parking will be impossible to find anyway, I reason.

The taxi driver is uncommunicative, unfriendly, possibly hostile. He probably hates his job, hates Toronto, hates women. Maybe he's not a real taxi driver, doesn't even have a driver's license, has somebody stuffed in his trunk, is high on crack or painkillers, plans to take us to the Scarborough Bluffs and drive right off the edge. Maybe next time I'll drive myself. If there is a next time.

Twenty minutes later I stand outside Erik's door and take a minute to compose myself. I knock and he opens. I look at him and the ride over is forgotten. Long, powerful legs, wide shoulders, and dark eyes that seem to know all the sad ugly secrets of the universe. I could stare at him for hours. Forever.

"Let me guess," he says. "You've baked me cookies and are here to declare your undying love."

"Funny," I say.

"Hysterical," he says, but he doesn't laugh.

I look away.

"I didn't expect you again so soon," he says. "You must need it bad."

Ah, that's better. I look back up at him and smile. "Up yours."

"Well, if that's what you want."

I laugh, let my coat slide off me. He takes two strides forward, closing the distance between us, and soon his lips are burning mine. When our mouths part, we are breathing fast. I bring my teeth to his lower lip and bite, just hard enough to make him flinch.

"Bitch," he says, softly.

"Cocksucking motherfucker," I say.

He laughs.

My hands go to the buttons of his shirt and he presses his hips to mine.

"Careful," he says. "I might decide to be nice."

He brings his fingertips to my cheek, and trails them down, passing my jaw line, then my neck, my collarbone. My mouth hovers centimeters from his and then I shove him back. He slams into the doorframe and grunts in pain.

"Go ahead and try," I say.

His hand whips out, grabs my hair, and this time I am trapped before he puts his lips on mine.

He slides down me, lifts my sweater just far enough for his tongue and teeth to find the skin of my belly. My eyes close and I shudder.

Suddenly I'm airborne over Erik's shoulder, then flying backward and down, onto his bed. He crawls on top of me, his shirt half open, and slides his hands up over my sweater.

"Take this off," he says.

"Make me."

I buck my hips and we tumble. Off the bed, we kiss and swear and yank at each other's clothing. Face down, shirtless, moaning, I feel the floor, cold against my hot skin. He strips my jeans off and I roll to my back, naked but for the bra around my waist. I tug at his shirt and the fabric rips.

"You're rough on my wardrobe." He tosses the shirt aside and stares at me. "Rough on my everything."

"What?"

He looks away, but not before I see something in his eyes. Something I don't want to see. It's only a moment, a flash, and then his usual look is back and we can both pretend I imagined the other.

"Nothing. Forget it," he says.

I'll certainly try.

He pulls the shirt off, throws it on the floor behind him and stands up. I watch his hands. They move to his belt buckle, and then the belt, thick, black, and leather, comes free of its loops. I swallow, then slide my eyes up his body and settle on his face. He keeps hold of the belt, unbuttons his pants, slides them down, and steps out of them.

"Nice cock."

"No talking."

He moves to stand over me, one foot on either side of my thighs. The leather tip of the belt snakes its way up the center of my torso, along the side of my neck, and stops at my earlobe. It slithers down to my breast, lingers there to tease me, then comes to hover at the junction of my inner thighs.

I clench my legs together and look up at Erik.

"No," I say.

He sits on me and grips my legs between his. His hand reaches up to cover my eyes and my mouth parts as he traces my lips with a finger. He pushes the fingertip between my teeth and I swirl my tongue around it and take it deep into my throat. Erik growls, shifts his weight.

I hear a clinking sound and feel cold metal at my clavicle. The buckle. He pulls it down, circles my nipples, trails along the line of my waist. The metal gets warm and my breathing comes faster.

The second I forget to clench my thighs together he slides a knee between them.

I scrape my nails down his back and say, "Fuck you."

His fingers dig into my hip.

"What do you want?" he asks.

"Nothing."

I fake compliance then grab the buckle and roll out from under him. I scramble to my feet on the other side of the bed. Erik groans and pulls himself up from the floor. His eyes gleam when he sees me brandishing the belt.

"I dare you," he says.

"Likewise," I say.

I snap the belt in his direction and then he's on me. Arms and legs locked in battle, we fall onto the bed. When the cool linen of the sheets molds to my ass and I feel both Erik's thighs planted between mine, I know I've lost. He is on me, over me, all around me. Hard mattress at my back and everything in me wants to beg.

"What do you want?" he asks.

I bite my lip, shake my head.

"Say it."

He wraps his arms under my knees and yanks me up onto his legs. I feel him hot and close . . . and say it.

I say it and he does it. Long, hard and fierce, until I can't see, can't think. There is no room in my head for voices, no room in my heart for pain. I am reduced to the elemental. I give everything up to Erik and, for a few minutes, he frees me. He takes from me past and future. His body pummels mine, punishes, drives out all fight, all sense of self. And finally he gives me what I need: he gives me silence, he gives me nothingness. He obliterates me.

Chapter Six

Daddy smells better, but he has a new friend who thinks you do stupid things like play with dolls and listen to Olivia Newton-John.

You don't.

Mom has a new job and she tells you it's important to get good grades so you can have gainful employment and independence when you grow up. You say your grades are fine.

They're not.

Dad won't come to parent-teacher interviews if Mom is going to be there, and Mom won't come if Dad is going to be there. You hope Dad comes, but he doesn't.

Mom finds out you are close to failing and might have to do fourth grade again. Her face turns red and in her scariest voice she says, "I hold up my end, Mara Lindsey."

The whole way home she ignores you. She slams the door on the way into the house.

"Is your father enforcing homework hours?"

"Mom, it's not his fault."

"That's not what I asked you."

She picks up the phone and stabs at the numbers. You edge out of the kitchen and hover at the bottom of the stairs.

"You're missing some important facts about our daughter," you hear her say.

Pause.

"About her *education*. She's about to flunk out of grade fucking four, asshole!"

One second . . . Two . . .

"I'm saying you're a pathetic excuse for a father. You expect me to take care of everything? You donate your sperm and figure you've made your contribution, well let me tell you—

"Don't raise your voice to me, you son of a bitch, you expect me to raise our child by myself, well it's not an easy burden!

"That's right, she's fucking up in school. She's not fine, she's a goddamn disaster and I hold you responsible, do you hear me? I hold you responsible!"

You should be used to it by now. You should not still shake and feel like throwing up. You want to run but there is nowhere to go that would be far enough. You tiptoe up the stairs and hide in your room with your eyes closed and your hands over your ears. But you can still hear them. You will always, always hear them because they are in your head, permanently screaming, stuck in your head, so loud, so loud and screaming inside your ears and mind, and you cannot escape.

Bitch and ball-breaker and liar, he calls her. Shut her up for good, wipe the smirk from her face, leave for good, disappear forever, and then she'll see. Never understood a single fucking thing about me, he says. And she calls him lazy, good-for-nothing, dreamer. Loser and a drunk, always will be. Piece of shit, go ahead and disappear, wish you would, wish you'd never been born, she says.

And you hug your knees and rock back and forth.

Out of control, they are always out of control. They are not themselves. They lose themselves and you lose them too. You lose them every time and you don't know, you never, ever know . . . if they will come back to you.

You squeeze your eyes shut, and close your ears, and try to make your heart smaller. It is so loud, the way it pounds. You want to scream, but what would they do? What would they do if you started screaming? If you did you might never stop. You would scream and scream and then run forever, and how would they feel?

They would not care because you are a burden. You are a disaster. You heard the words and you know they're true and you don't have parents like other people anyway. Solid one day, they slip through you the next.

~

While I'm in his bed, Erik eclipses all, but when I leave, I banish every thought of him. Except the memory of the strange look in his eyes when he said I was "hard on his everything"—that one is tougher to push away.

By the time I get home, I'm thinking again of Hugo. Stupid. I've had exactly one conversation with the guy. I fall asleep with Erik in my skin and Hugo on my mind.

The next evening, I pace my kitchen. It is the third night since I met Hugo, and I wonder if he's actually waiting there at the bar, thinking I might show up. But I acted like a freak, so he's probably not there. Or maybe he hangs out in lesbian bars because there's something wrong with him, like he's impotent, masochistic, afraid of commitment.

Who said anything about commitment?

Who said anything about anything? It's not like I even want to leave the house. I need my sleep. I cannot go out.

Who said anything about going out?

Who said anything about putting on lipstick and changing into a clean shirt and brushing my hair and grabbing the car keys and walking out into the dangerous world?

No one, that's who.

But that's what seems to be happening.

Because maybe I have a chance at something. Maybe it's been long enough since Lucas. Maybe I don't have to live like a hermit for the rest of my life.

So he might reject me. Will I break?

Of course not.

Probably not.

Hopefully not.

On the other hand . . .

On the other hand he might not reject me. He might like me and then like me more, and then maybe . . . then maybe he might love me, and this time . . . this time I might not screw it up.

And even if I do, will I break?

Well, I might.

Oh God, I really might.

But I might not.

And so I am driving. I'm in my car and I am driving. I want to turn around and go back home because I'm sure my brakes are going to give out, or I will crash into a telephone pole and meet with a grisly end, my innards spilling all over the seats, my life wasted, the upholstery ruined, all because of a guy.

But the steering wheel has a mind of its own and I keep going.

I make it to the bar alive. I take a moment in the entryway to calm myself, but it doesn't work.

He's probably not here.

I hope he isn't.

I hope he is.

I'm nauseous and I might puke on him when I see him.

I hope, I hope . . .

There he is, coming out of the bathroom.

Oh my God, oh my God, he sees me.

He smiles. Oh, boy, it's a deadly smile—worse, better, than I remembered.

"You came back!"

"Yes."

He takes me by the elbow and leads me inside.

"Just so you know," I say, "this isn't a date."

"Really."

"I just came to apologize, for, you know, acting like such a weirdo the other night."

"I like weirdos," he says. "Should we get a table?"

"Aren't you supposed to say, 'No, you're not a weirdo'?"

"You are kind of strange and I'm not a liar, so I won't contradict you. What would you like to drink?"

"Diet soda."

He orders. We talk. He asks me questions and I answer them. I ask him questions and he answers them. Not so hard, actually.

"So why are you so determined this can't be a date?" he asks.

"Because I don't date."

"Ah. So, we're just . . ."

"Hanging out," I say. "Having a drink."

"All right."

The minutes pass. Hugo makes me laugh, puts me at ease. Mostly.

"Are you going to give me your number this time?" he says when we've finished our third round of drinks.

"No," I say. "Are you going to take me back to your place and have sex with me this time?"

"Not this time," he says.

"All right. I'm guessing you have to get back to your puppy."

"Soon, yeah."

"Okay. It's been fun."

I stand up and put some money on the table.

"No, let me," Hugo says, standing. He places bills on the table and pushes my money back toward me.

I shake my head. "No chance."

"Then the service should be great tomorrow night," he grins. He touches my elbow and we exit the bar.

Hugo walks me to my car and waves as I drive away. I speed on the way home.

For five consecutive nights, I make myself get in the car and drive to Sappho. It's not easy, but, perhaps, *easier*. When the fear comes I picture myself driving through it, running it over. I see Hugo's face, remember his laugh and somehow I get there. Each night, I find him in the same place, Hugo at the same table. We sit and we talk. Every night he asks for my number and I ask him to have sex with me. Every night we both say no.

Chapter Seven

It's an easy solution: you get better grades, Mommy has less reason to fight with Daddy. You should have thought of it before. Also it really would be gross to repeat fourth grade and be in a class with a bunch of babies.

The librarian, Mrs. Stone, lets you have your own cubicle and you stay at school working until five every night. You pass after all, and Mommy smiles and smiles and takes you to the Golden Griddle for a special brunch to celebrate.

Grandma and Grandpa come to visit in June when school gets out. Grandma cooks real meals and you go for walks together and Grandpa talks to you about golfing and his handy cap.

When your weekend with Dad comes you don't want to go, but nobody asks for your opinion. You are packed up, shuttled off. When Dad brings you back on Sunday night, Mom gives him one of her looks.

"What?" he says.

"Late again, Henry," she says.

Oh, please, oh, please, not in front of Grandma and Grandpa!

"Excuse me if I'm not on your exact schedule," Dad says.

Mom's face starts turning red and you grip the straps of your knapsack.

"God forbid you hold yourself accountable," she says.

"God forbid you give me a fucking break once in a while."

No, no, no, no, no . . .

"Listen, you goddam cretin—"

"You tight-ass bitch—"

"Don't you swear at me, don't you start with me!"

"I'll start with you, I'll start with you anytime I want!"

And they're off.

Dad's eyes get big and his lips practically disappear. Mom's hands are in fists and she turns bright red all the way down her neck.

Grandma and Grandpa stare, their jaws hanging open.

You stand there wishing you had a ring like Bilbo Baggins to disappear with, or wings to fly away on, a hole to burrow into, a place to go where you never had to go through this again.

Because every time you feel like you're dying.

You're dying, or something else, something terrible, is going to happen. Mom and Dad's heads are going to explode, the house will be struck by lightning, the Russians will come in their fast planes and drop bombs, and none of you will make it to the basement because the yelling is so loud that you don't hear the warning sirens. Or they will burst in the door and find you and send all of you together to Siberia where there are no toilets and long lineups for moldy bread, and you will be stuck in a small room with Mom and Dad forever.

You would prefer Siberia alone.

You might prefer Siberia period.

The shouting continues. It is about nothing.

You stare down at the floor, afraid to see Grandma and Grandpa's faces. They never yell. After this they will probably never come back. Maybe when they go, you could go with them. Ha. Fat chance.

"Stop this right now!"

Everything stops. Everyone stares at Grandpa.

"That is enough," he adds. "It's a disgrace."

"Mara, dear," Grandma says, "why don't you go up to your room?"

After that, Mom and Dad stop screaming. At least, they stop screaming out loud. Mom tries to smile when Dad comes to the house, only she looks like she wants to bite someone. Dad smiles back. On the weekends he says, "And how's your mother?"

"Fine," you say.

"Oh, well," he says, "that's good."

It's almost funny. And they must think you're stupid, because they think you can't see them both, still screaming. They think you're still five years old, waiting for Santa Claus, but you are not. You know all about life and the things people really think and do.

⸺

"You don't drink," Hugo says on this-is-not-a-date number five.

"You're observant," I say.

"And you're sarcastic."

"Touché."

"So? Answer the question."

"You didn't ask one."

"You're funny." He laughs. "Why don't you drink?"

Here we go, getting personal. Ugh. But he's looking at me with those smart, sweet eyes and I can't dodge everything forever.

"You're wondering if I'm, perhaps, an alcoholic?"

"Or religiously opposed, or allergic, just don't like it? I'm wondering, that's all."

"All right," I say. "I could, at any moment, descend into soul-crushing, mind-numbing, self-pitying depression."

"Ah."

"Plus, I made a deal."

"That you wouldn't drink?"

"Yep."

"Who'd you . . . ?"

"My patron, Sal."

Hugo's eyes get wide and one side of his mouth twists up into a smile.

"You're kidding," he says. "You have a patron? Isn't that sort of medieval?"

"More Renaissance, actually, but no, I'm not kidding. When we started working together, I was a bit of a wreck. Sal made sobriety part of our deal because he knows I can get . . ."

"Depressed?"

"Yeah."

"And is that what you're afraid of, Mara? With me, I mean?"

I meet his gaze. "Did I say I was afraid?"

"Only a hundred different ways," he says.

So much for my brave face.

"I think it's kind of normal," he says.

"Being afraid?"

"Yeah. Everybody's afraid of something. People don't get to this point in their lives without some baggage, right?"

"I guess not," I say.

"And hey," he says and grins, "given the state of things, we should all be depressed."

"You think?"

"Oh yeah. The world's a mess. We've got religious fanatics, poverty, human rights abuses, global warming, poisoned water, bullshit advertising, mad cow disease . . ."

"All right, all right!"

"Assassinations, kidnappings, polarization of left and right, discrimination, tsunamis, genocide, cell phones, bad wages for strippers . . ."

I'm shaking my head, but somehow also laughing.

And he continues.

"Genetically modified broccoli, un-muzzled pit bulls, smog, the breakdown of family, puppy mills, gridlock, identity theft, loss of privacy, the Asian longhorned beetle killing our trees. It's endless!"

"Okay, stop, stop!"

He leans forward and takes my hand and gets serious on me again.

"So tell me, Mara, what's the deal?"

"Okay, Dr. Phil."

I could. I could tell Hugo that sometimes I am paralyzed trying to cross the street, that I have nightmares that bleed into the daytime, that it's more than depression, more than anxiety or alcoholism or compulsion.

And then, even with his accepting nature, his positive attitude, the wisdom I've seen in him these past few nights, he would still wreck it. He might want to save me, or tell me to pull myself up by my bootstraps, start jogging, do yoga, be logical, take medication, meditate, forgive myself, free myself, be stronger, braver. And I will hate him for it and it will be over.

And I really, really like him.

And so . . .

"It's no big deal," I say. "I had a relationship crisis a few years ago, and I got depressed, drank too much, couldn't paint. I turned it around and I'm making a living as an artist, which is an accomplishment. It's not to put you off at all, but I think it's more important to live in the present, don't you?"

"Sure," he says.

"So talk to me about today. What's going on with you today?"

And so, crisis averted, we talk. And talk. And keep talking. But it's not the words, or not just the words, but what happens alongside and between the words. It's my eyes, drifting over his body, and our hands and lips and the sounds that come from our mouths.

The bricklike pressure I carry around on my chest lightens, gets pushed aside, if only for a while.

The crowd is thin in the bar tonight.

Pauses filled with warm air, the touch of Hugo's fingers on the back of my hand, the thrumming of my heart as it squeezes against the wall of the box I've been keeping it in since . . .

I won't think about that.

Since . . .

Damn.

Since Lucas.

I shut my eyes.

"Mara?"

I open my eyes, try to smile, to recapture the mood.

"Sorry," I say. "Hey, what about that mindless sex?"

"Not a chance," he says.

"That's what I was afraid of."

"See you tomorrow night?"

"Probably."

Chapter Eight

"I'm not going to be dependent on some bastard," Mom says. "And neither are you."

It's not like you're telling her to marry him, but the nice man from down the street keeps calling and you feel bad telling him that Mom's out when she isn't.

"But, Mom, he might make you happy."

"I'll be happy when I know I can put you through university."

"I'm not going to university."

"That's what you think."

"I'm going to stay here and take care of you."

"Don't. You. Dare," she says in the voice that isn't supposed to be screaming, but really is.

"But, Mom, who'll make sure you eat? Who'll rub your forehead and pick up groceries and help you with your filing?"

She needs you. She has to need you. Your stupid lower lip is quivering and you hate that. You need to *not* need her.

Mom stares hard at you, pushes an oversprayed chunk of brown hair behind her ear.

"Of course I need you, kid. But you're going to grow up, and then what I need is for you to be able to take care of yourself."

"Okay . . . I'll go to university. I'll be a doctor."

"Let's just get you through the fifth grade."

"Okay," you say. "Mom?"

"Yes?"

"D'you think I'll have a husband ever?"

"I don't know, sweetheart. Do you think you'll want one?"

"Well . . ."

Will she take it the wrong way if you say yes?

"Only if we don't fight and he promises not to interfere with my career."

Mom throws her head back and laughs and laughs, then she grabs your shoulders and dances you around the room.

It's a good day. A day you hold close and relive on all the other days when you come home to an empty house or a mom buried in paperwork who shushes you for making too much noise washing the dishes.

You never complain that you're lonely, or that the kids at school don't like you—you know she can't do anything about it.

One month into junior high (where you still have no friends), Mom buys a house in North York and you have to move.

Being the new girl doesn't turn out to be the great fresh start it was supposed to be—instead, it sucks. You're not a girl who takes piano lessons or ballet or plays on a soccer team. You are not a girl who gets a new fall wardrobe and fancy pencil cases. It's not the divorce—lots of kids' parents are getting divorced now—it's that something is wrong with you. You don't look right in your clothes, you don't laugh at the things other girls laugh at, or, if you do, it's a beat too late, too loud. You don't have a record collection or watch *Falcon Crest* or have a crush on John Stamos. You have nothing that says Esprit or Benetton on it, and you don't perm your hair. You're rotten at sports and you live in a serious world—a mom in night school with two jobs, a dad in an apartment that reeks of cabbage and cigarette smoke. You are alone.

But alone is fine. Alone is perfect, as long as nobody bugs you. You doodle nasty cartoon versions of your classmates in the backs of your notebooks and practice glaring in the bathroom mirror at home. You're getting tall, so the glaring works, and soon the only people who talk to you are your teachers.

One day after Thanksgiving, someone sits beside you at lunch.

"I see you drawing," she says.

You say nothing.

"What are you drawing all the time?"

"Nothing," you mumble.

"You're new."

"No shit."

"I'm Bernadette. We're in Geography together."

"I know."

"Sometimes I skip."

You take a bite of your sandwich.

"I skip class, and I hang out behind the 7-Eleven and smoke."

"Good for you."

"You could come."

"No thanks."

"You don't have any friends," she says.

"And?" you say, and ignore the wobbly feeling in your gut that her observation brings.

"Well, you want one?"

"One what?"

"A friend, dipshit."

"Oh."

"I have some friends already," she says, "but some of them are so immature. You seem . . . smart. Different."

It could be a trick.

"Maybe," you say.

"Maybe, huh?" she says. "Okay. We could do, like, a trial period."

"All right."

"Cool."

"I'm Mara."

"Sure, I know."

"Oh. Okay."

"One thing . . ."

"Yeah?"

"Call me Bernie and I'll fucking deck you."

Of course you say yes.

You say yes to the first boy who wants to "go around" with you too. All at once you have a best friend and a boyfriend—if getting stoned and giving someone a hand job makes him your boyfriend. But he's clumsy and boring and soon you break up with him. Bernadette, though, her you keep.

Suddenly going downtown to Dad's for the weekend is very cool. Bernadette comes with you sometimes, and you can always sneak a couple of beers.

Dad catches you taking one once, when you're there alone. He tries to have a heart-to-heart about it, but he doesn't do so well considering he's on his sixth.

"Dad," you say, "it's really no big deal. I know what I'm doing."

"But, sweetheart, it's not . . . Your mother would . . ."

"Never know."

He blinks.

You sit down next to him on the couch. "Dad, I'm very mature, and I know how to handle it."

"Hey, I'm not so old, I get it, but . . ."

"It's just a beer now and then. I like the taste."

"Me, too, honey. Me, too."

"How 'bout I just sit here with you and finish it while you watch the game."

"Just this once."

"Okay."

"And don't tell your mother."

"Never."

He smiles.

You smile back. "Our secret," you say.

And that clinches it. Beer and baseball become a tradition for you and Dad, except when he has a girlfriend, which he often does. Then your weekends are spent going to lame amusement parks and the zoo. You sneak the beer into your room at night and try not to hear them screwing in the next room. You're twelve, so it's not like you don't know about these things, but seriously, it's gross.

⚊

Hugo and I find the bar too noisy on our sixth meeting. He suggests we walk.

The word "walk" has a slightly sickening effect on me, but I can't exactly say I don't walk. Obviously I walk; it's a basic skill. I roll my shoulders and breathe. I focus on Hugo, on wanting to be with Hugo.

"You okay?" he asks.

"Fine," I say, and grip the edge of my chair.

"You look a little . . . dizzy or something."

I swallow, then nod. "Yeah, I was for a second. I'm fine though."

I stand up and reach for his hand. The warmth of his grip grounds me.

"Let's walk," I say.

He gives me a cute, shy smile, squeezes my hand and we're off.

The air is crisp and smells of fallen leaves and wood smoke. I take full breaths. I'm okay. Air has never smelled so good.

"So," Hugo says, "what about your family? You said your parents are divorced. Are they both still in Toronto?"

Something always wrecks it.

I try to relax my jaw.

"Yeah, my dad lives on Jarvis. He, um, works in the restaurant industry on and off, he's got an on-and-off girl-friend, and generally he's . . . either on or off."

"I'm not sure if I should laugh at that or not. Are you serious?"

"Dad's got issues," I say. "He's all right though, he's . . . we're friends."

"And your mom?"

I sigh. "She's here too. I don't see her very much."

"Why not?"

"I used to know."

"Is this another one of those off-limits subjects?" Hugo asks. "Should we talk about . . . I don't know, particle theory, musical theater?"

There is an edge to his tone, which makes me feel sick in addition to tense.

"No, it's fine," I say. It'll have to be. I can't shut him down on every personal subject and expect him to keep hanging around. "I'm sorry, I'm just out of the habit of talking about any of this."

"Okay . . ." he says, and waits.

"Um . . . my mom and I . . . it's been a rocky relationship since I was a teenager, even before that. For a long time I was angry but now . . . we're just different. It doesn't work very well between us."

Again, he waits, just watching me.

I take a deep breath. "My dad was a bit of a flake, in terms of child support, reliability, all kinds of things. It's not really his fault, he's just always been a mess. To be fair though, my mom was on her own supporting us, raising me, etcetera. I was made very aware of what a strain it was for her, how disappointed she was in how her life turned out. And she wasn't exactly the warm and fuzzy type—still isn't. She wasn't around a lot because she had to work so much and when she was, her parenting strategy was about making me tough and independent."

I pause and glance at Hugo, who is now looking far too sympathetic.

"She succeeded," he says.

I make a sound that's almost a laugh.

"You don't think so?" he says.

I'm flattered, but he has obviously confused prickly and paranoid with tough and independent. What would he think if he saw me hiding in my house, painting the same thing over and over, running to my lover to get my fears fucked away? Would he think I was tough if he knew that the closer we get to a relationship the more terrified I am?

"I'm glad you do," I reply.

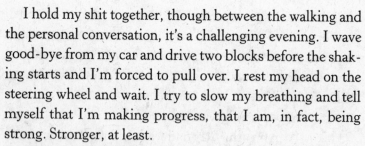

I hold my shit together, though between the walking and the personal conversation, it's a challenging evening. I wave good-bye from my car and drive two blocks before the shaking starts and I'm forced to pull over. I rest my head on the steering wheel and wait. I try to slow my breathing and tell myself that I'm making progress, that I am, in fact, being strong. Stronger, at least.

But when the shaking subsides it leaves a chasm of loneliness and doubt. I find myself driving, but not in the direction of home.

I park the car, take out my rarely used cell phone and dial. I usually give him more warning. I usually manage to stay away longer. But there is a strange safety in Erik and I need that safety right now.

He's waiting in the open doorway, a lit joint in his hand.

"Hey," I say, and brush past him.

Maybe it's because of Hugo, or maybe I'm more of a mess than usual, but I start babbling about the weather and then the mayoral race and finally about an editorial piece I read online this morning. Erik leans back on the closed door and squints at me through the haze of smoke until, finally, I trail off.

"What's going on?" he says.

"Nothing," I say, but I have trouble meeting his eyes.

Regardless, he sees me. Even stoned, even though we never talk much, he sees.

"Bullshit," he says. "Try again."

"Oh," I say. "You know I'm always a little fucked up. Nothing new."

"Really?" he says. He moves to stub the joint in an ashtray and then walks toward me. I take a step back and bump into the side of the couch. He comes close and stands inches away, never breaking eye contact. "Then how come you can't shut up? How come you look like you might break if I touch you?"

"I'm fine. Touch me all you want."

He reaches out and draws a line up from my throat, under my chin with his index finger. The still, dark look in his eyes and the delicacy of his touch send shock waves through me. I swallow and somehow hold his gaze.

"I don't think you're here for the usual, Mara," he says in a whisper. "Though, of course, I'm all for it, if you are."

"Yes, I am," I say, but my voice sounds strangled.

He lowers his head and brushes his lips across the skin of my neck. The shaking starts again and quickly spreads to my legs. I lock my knees to keep them still.

"Liar."

I reach for his shirt, but my fingers can't manage the buttons. He takes my hands in his and presses them against his chest. I feel his heart thumping. His eyes search my face.

"Ah," he says.

"What?"

"Not running fast enough, are you," he says. It's not a question, he just knows. He knows because he has his own past to run from, his own ghosts to flee. And of course, there's always Lucas. We both know more than enough about that.

As always, he sees right through me, right into me. It makes me feel obscenely naked.

I try to pull away, but he's got my hands trapped.

"Let me go," I say and jerk backward.

"I don't think so," he says. "Did something happen?"

I shake my head. If I don't get out of here I'm going to turn to mush. I'm going to fall apart and blubber like a fool and I really, really don't want to do that here.

"Please. I have to go."

He lets go of my hands, but only to wrap his arms around my waist, pick me up and carry me to the couch. He puts me down and kneels on the floor in front of me, between my legs, effectively blocking me in.

"*You* came to *me*," he says. "And I get it, all right? I fucking get it."

I can't hide the shaking anymore. I'm gasping for breath, holding my arms crossed in front of my chest.

"Okay," he says, his voice warm and calming. "Okay."

He climbs onto me, straddles me so his legs brace mine.

"Hold on," he says. "Just hold on."

Erik presses his forehead to mine and puts his hands over my cold fists, slowly opens them and twines our fingers together. I grip his hands and his body absorbs some of the shaking.

He holds me and murmurs soothing words. When the tension starts to ease, I reach under his arms and wrap mine around his back. He pulls my head to his chest and presses me closer. A few tears fall, but I don't turn to mush. Eventually my breathing slows to match his and I feel the heat returning to my limbs. I should really pull away, but I can hear his heartbeat and he is so warm . . .

"Better?" he whispers.

"Mm-hm."

"I'm not crushing you?"

"Mm-mm."

In another few minutes we shift so that we're lying side by side. The couch isn't quite wide enough, but we squeeze together anyway. We close our eyes and listen to the hum of the computers and the sounds of the city.

It should feel weirder than it does.

It should feel much weirder when he leans over and kisses the corners of my eyes, my cheeks and then my lips. It doesn't feel nearly weird enough.

"Erik," I say.

"Sorry, I didn't mean . . ."

"No, it's not that."

Our faces are inches apart. His breath is on my face and his eyes look huge.

"What then?"

"You're just . . . not supposed to kiss like that."

"You don't like it?"

"Um . . ."

He does it again.

"You can stop me anytime," he says.

"You'd think so, wouldn't you?" I slide underneath him and bring my lips back to his.

He moves slowly, watches my face and parts of me unravel with every touch.

"Jesus," I say, even as I slide a hand into his pants. "You're scaring me."

"Don't worry," he says and moans as my fingers close around him. "I'm still the same old Erik."

He is and he isn't. We're both too far gone to care. Just for now, just for this night, I close my eyes and arch against him, letting the tender mix with the fierce . . . and pretend it doesn't matter.

Chapter Nine

You are fourteen and nobody fucks with you anymore. Your best friend is awesome, you can drink without puking your guts out, and your mother has a Master's degree.

Never mind that she's become a feminist and stopped wearing a bra to the grocery store, which is seriously embarrassing.

You say "fuck" these days and sound like you mean it.

You wish your dad were more like Bernadette's, though. Bernadette's dad takes care of the yard, helps with meals, plays tennis and golf, and discusses the Political Situation at the dinner table. Bernadette's dad would never go a week without changing his clothes or cry to Bernadette about how his life stinks.

Your dad does.

You never know, when you arrive on a Friday night, if you're going to get Hyper-Fun Dad or My-Life-Is-Over Dad, and nothing you do seems to make a difference.

At first with Bernadette, you try to pretend nothing is wrong, but she goes to his place with you, and it gets hard not to notice.

"It could be his apartment," she says one sticky Friday afternoon when you're on the subway toward Dad's.

"What d'you mean?"

"Well, no offense, but . . ."

"Yeah . . . ?"

"The place is ugly."

"Ha. True. You think it—"

"Bums him out, yeah."

"I don't think he can afford to move, Bee."

"Hello, budding artist? I'm not talking about moving."

Dad is totally agreeable and even lets you paint your bedroom walls purple with silver moons and stars, in honor of Prince.

On Saturday morning, while Bernadette covers the kitchen walls in Sunlight Yellow, you prepare to begin your first mural. Dad is hanging out watching you while he waits for the first coat of Romanov Red in his bedroom to dry.

"So you're big in art class," he says. "I didn't know that."

"I don't know about big." You shrug. "I just like it."

"Well, Bernadette says you're big. Talented."

"I just look good compared to everyone else because they all took it to have an easy pass, Bee included."

You pick up a medium-size brush and step back from the wall. What kind of scene would cheer Dad up when he's here by himself?

"Does your mother know?"

"About art class?"

Would a baseball field look good? Hm. No.

"No. About me being, uh, a little bummed out some-times."

"What? No. No, I don't talk to her about you."

"Oh. Okay, good."

"Besides," you say, "you're okay. Managing a bar is tough. You just get tired, stressed out. Right? I mean, every-body gets stressed out."

"Does she?"

"Who?" you say, like you don't know he means Mom.

If you say Mom is having a hard time, then you'd be lying. If you say she's doing well, it makes him jealous, bit-ter, sends him down. Because the battle rages on still. Under the thin crust of civility is all kinds of bad shit. Mom baits Dad with her vocabulary, her education, and her success. Somehow everything she achieves takes something from Dad—she knows it, he knows it, she rubs it in.

Dad strikes back with his puppy-dog eyes, his handsome smile, the carefree pose. And he hurts her with you—with the fact that you love him. Why he uses this, how he knows it works, is a mystery, but it makes her crazy. As if your love is a possession, a weapon, a reproach.

Your mom doesn't want you to love your dad. He rubs it in that you do. Their war continues past the marriage, past the divorce, past any logic that you can see. And you hang out in no-man's-land, your white flag tattered and shot through.

You ignore Dad's question and decide to paint a beach.

By Sunday morning, there is blue sky, the sun, waves lapping at the shoreline and pale, pale sand. It's not bad, but you decide to add Dad, or a hint of him, to the scene.

"Dad?" you call out.

"Yeah?" he replies from the kitchen where he's helping Bernadette with the trim.

"Come in here, I need you to model your legs."

He laughs as he comes in. "If I had a dime for every woman who—"

"Ew, don't say it."

"Kidding, kidding."

You add Dad's legs and feet, plus the bottom of a lounge chair, low on the wall, so it looks like he's there on the beach. As an afterthought, you add your own legs, in the chair next to his. And then . . . maybe some girls in bikinis? He'd love that, but no, too gross.

You'll call it *On the Beach with Dad*.

You take a few steps back to get perspective.

Uh oh. The beach and water look fine, but the legs on the chairs . . . They look like stumps in striped boxes growing out of the sand.

Yikes. *On the Beach with Severed Legs* is more like it. You could add Mom's legs in there too and call it *Family of Legs*.

And then there could be the corresponding mural: *The Legless*.

Family Without Legs.

Ha.

Walking on Stumps While Your Feet Relax at the Beach.

Shiver.

You're getting creepy in your old age.

"Let me see it," Bernadette says, and comes to stand beside you.

She tries not to, but she starts to giggle, and then it becomes a roar, and then Dad runs in and looks and laughs until he has to sit down on the floor.

"I'm going to paint over it!" you shout over the cackles, snorts and slapping of legs.

"Don't you dare," Dad says. "That thing'll crack me up every time I look at it."

And that's as good a reason to paint as any.

Bernadette comes back with you two weeks later. On the subway, you lug a large duffel bag containing the fabulous curtains you sewed together in Home Ick. They have palm trees on them.

Dad's not home yet, so you let yourselves in, put the curtains up, and admire your work.

Then there's a knock at the door.

"Dad? You forget your keys?" you call out as you walk to the door.

It's not Dad on the other side of the door, but his landlord, Chuck.

"Hi, Chuck, what's up?"

"Sorry, kid, but I saw ya comin' in and I gotta tell ya, yer dad's not gonna be home tonight, likely."

"Why not?"

"He's, uh . . ." He shuffles his feet and rubs a hand across his comb-over.

"He's what?"

"He's in jail, kid."

The doorframe spins, but you grab on to it.

"Hey, nothin' serious," Chuck says, "just another drunken disorderly. He was causin' a disruption."

Bernadette comes to stand beside you and puts a hand on your arm.

"Where is he?" she asks.

"I told ya, in the slammer. Since this afternoon. Look, he tried to take a p—to urinate in the damned lobby. Can't have that kinda behavior, so I called the cops."

"Oh my God. Where . . . We have to . . ."

"What. Station. Did they. Take. Him. To!" Bernadette says.

Chuck tells her. She closes the door in his face.

"You okay?" she says.

"Shit."

Not okay, not okay, NOT OKAY!

"My dad can't be in jail."

"I know. Let's go get him."

"Bee, you don't have to come."

"Shut the fuck up," she says. "Let's go."

I collapse into a chair in a downtown coffee shop and wait for my head to stop spinning.

Bernadette slides in across from me. "Thanks for playing hooky," she says. "Sorry things got out of hand."

I let Bernadette convince me to attend a gay rights rally this afternoon. When she called, I was in my studio staring into space, disturbed by memories of my encounter with Erik and more disturbed that it happened on the heels of an evening with Hugo. A few hundred screaming people suddenly seemed a paltry challenge compared to sorting out my personal life.

But it was a bad idea. Bernadette and I got separated and I was nearly trampled to death by the right-wing zealots who were all hot to equate homosexuals with pedophiles, polygamists and people who fuck sheep. Bernadette found me, grabbed me by the arm and hauled me out, but by then I was so freaked I thought my head would burst open.

"Hey, no problem," I say and take a sip of my steamed milk. No more caffeine for me today. Maybe a lobotomy. "I like a near-death experience every few days. Keeps me sharp."

"Ha," she says. "Seriously, thanks. I know you get a little wiggy in crowds."

"I'll be fine."

"So . . . how are you?" she asks. "What's new?"

This is usually a ridiculous question and we both know it, but she keeps asking. Today though, I wouldn't know where to start. Erik is an impossible subject and I'm not ready to talk about Hugo.

"Same old," I say. "Changing the world one rectangle at a time. You? What about that woman you met?"

Bernadette is about to reply when something or someone behind me catches her eye.

"Holy cow," she whispers.

"What?"

"Turn around slowly, and tell me who that is, standing in front of the biscotti."

I try to act casual, and do as she says. Oh my God. I turn back.

"Is it who I think it is?" Bernadette says. "Is it Faith English?"

"I think so," I say, and slide down lower in my chair.

"How do I look?" she asks, and starts putting on lipstick.

"What? You're not going to . . ."

"Are you kidding? I've been hoping to run into Faith English since, well, since high school. How's my hair?"

"Fine, but Bee—"

She gets up, yanks her sweater down.

"I'm going in," she says. "Wish me luck."

I don't.

Chapter Ten

The subway makes that awful screeching sound and you don't even cover your ears.

"Have you ever seen a jail?" you ask Bernadette.

"Only on TV," she says.

"Same here."

At the station, after sending you from one person to another, they finally say you can see Dad, but that he can't get out unless you post bail.

Bail!

It seems like a lot of money just for getting drunk and trying to take a pee. You and Bernadette empty your wallets, but between you, you've only got fifteen dollars.

"Well, here's my case for a bigger allowance," you say, and Bernadette covers her mouth to hide her laughter.

"You're nuts," she says.

"Can you blame me?"

She says she'll wait, and soon you are walking in. Doors are opened before you, then locked behind you as you pass.

Under the disinfectant are the smells of sweat, cigarette smoke, and urine. Gross.

Cold, cold concrete everywhere and Dad cries when he sees you.

"Oh, sweetheart," he says, "I'm so sorry. Promise me you'll forget this ever happened."

"I'll try."

"Please?"

All these moments adults expect to wash over you without effect—such bullshit.

"Sure, Dad, I promise."

No big deal, just another day when you see your father surrounded by criminals, unable to cope with anything, including leaving his dick in his pants until he can get to a bathroom.

"It's not my fault I couldn't find it," he says.

"Find what?"

"The can, I couldn't—"

Ew, ew, ew!

"Shh, that's okay, Dad."

"Please don't tell your mother," he says, and looks at you with those big eyes.

"Of course not."

He shakes his head back and forth and whines. He's still drunk, obviously, and a pathetic sight.

"So, Dad, I don't have enough money for bail and I don't know how else to get you out."

"It's okay, I called a friend and she's coming in the morning," he says. "They'll probably drop the charges anyway, but I have to wait till tomorrow."

"But . . . will you be okay here?"

"Sure, sure. You go to Bernadette's house for the rest of the weekend, all right?"

"Okay."

His face crumples and he grips your hand in his.

"I'm sorry, I'm a bad father. I'm a terrible father."

"No you're not, you're fine."

Lots of fathers get hauled into jail for being drunk in the middle of the afternoon! Don't worry about it!

A guard comes to tell you your time is up.

"I love you," he says.

"I love you too, Dad."

"Don't ever stop. Please don't ever stop."

As if you could.

It might be easier if you could. In fact, it might be better not to have parents at all. The thought feels like a stab in the belly. Shame on you.

You walk back to the waiting room and Bernadette. There is a grapefruit-size lump in your throat and you try to swallow it as she gets up to ask how he is.

"Tanked. Pathetic," you say. "As expected."

"And you?"

"Well, it's nine o'clock on a Friday night and other teenagers are watching a movie, going to a party, or grounded and doing their homework. And I'm here."

"Yeah," she says, and puts an arm around your shoulders and squeezes.

You are stretched, singed, raw.

"I feel old," you say.

"I know," she says.

Bernadette's family is great, but you don't relish explaining why you're showing up there late Friday night when you're supposed to be at Dad's. Back in his living room, about to repack and leave for her house, Bernadette seems to read your mind.

"Why don't we just stay here?"

You nod. "There's vodka in the freezer."

She grins. "Right on!"

It's a good night to drink.

Bernadette is wise and sweet and knows not to pry, knows you're not a fan of "letting it all out." Letting it all out is bullshit. You can cry and scream and let it out, but it will still not BE out.

Vodka and orange juice. Cigarettes.

You stick your legs through the balcony railings and swing your bare feet. Bernadette blows smoke rings and you look up at the sky.

"No stars," you say.

"City's too bright," she says. "Something about . . . I dunno, they told us in science class, didn't they?"

"Dunno. Doesn't fucking matter."

"Nope, doesn't."

Your blood is sluggish as it moves through your body. You feel a slow, achy thrum in your legs as they swing. You down the last of your glass.

Bernadette eases down onto her back and you join her.

Things are starting to spin.

"Whoa," she says.

"Yeah."

"Well, at least we got a good grade on the curtains," she says.

"Waste of fabric," you say.

"Nah."

"We should've done prison stripes instead," you say, and laugh even though it's all starting to hurt again. "And instead of a beach mural, I should've done graffiti."

Bernadette snorts.

You need more alcohol, because it's not working anymore. It's worn off.

"Come on," you say, and get up.

Inside, your eyes land on a paint can. "BEE!"

"Shh, not so loud," she says, and leans on the wall. "What?"

"I think there's still some . . . what's that color?" You point.

"Purple."

"Yeah, still some purple."

It's funny, it'll be so funny, fucking hilarious.

You pry the lid open and find a brush. Bernadette wobbles along beside you. You dip the brush in.

"Wait," she says, "you're not actually . . . don't wreck your mural, Mar, that's not—"

"Shh, don't worry," you say, and walk carefully toward the front door.

"Okay," she says, and tips then catches herself.

"Lush," you say.

"You should talk, chicky."

On the wall beside the door, you paint: →
And then, a few feet farther: →
And again, down the hallway: →
"Ooohh," Bernadette says.
On the bathroom door:

→ TOILET ←

Ha.
Ha, ha, ha, fucking ha.
And then . . . in the bathroom . . . above the toilet . . .

GET OUT OF JAIL FREE!
(piss in your own toilet)

Excellent.
You are standing with the brush in hand and you are laughing. Bernadette isn't.

"What? It's so awesome!"

"Yeah, but maybe too . . . too much?" she says.

But "much" comes out sounding like "mush" and that's funny too. And funny is good, funny is great because you would rather laugh than cry.

"It is definitely too *mush*," you say. "That's the point. It's all too fucking mush. Musshhh. Muh-muh-muh-mmmuuuussshhh."

She just looks at you.

Another laugh bubbles up, but it comes out sounding like a shriek. Too loud. Too loud and everything is a bit . . .

"Fuzzy brain," you say. "Fuzzy."

"Me too," she says.

"Fuck it all anyway. T's'all too musshhh. But I'm fine, fine, fine, always fine. My job to be fine. Too mush to be fine, but I am FINE!"

"Shh, shh, I know."

All fine, except . . . except for the mush.

The mush, which is

too

fucking

MUCH!

Paint can and brush waver on the cracked toilet seat.

Shitfuckdamn . . .

Eyes crying, nose running, both traitors.

Nose and eyes damned traitors.

Well, then, let the traitors drip. Let them run and drip right out. Bernadette is here and also . . . also dripping from the eyes and nose.

"Hang on," she says. "Just hang on to me."

And you do.

Someone must be hammering nails into your skull.

You blink, then hear the sound of a key in the door.

Owwwwww.

You hear a moan and turn carefully, and see Bernadette on the floor next to the couch.

"Oh my God," she says.

"Shit . . . he's home." You sit up on the couch and blink your eyes.

Dad enters with a woman in short shorts and frosted blond hair. She sees you first, puts a hand on his arm. "Henry?"

"Oh. Ah, hi, sweetheart, Bernadette."

"Hi," you and Bernadette croak in unison.

Bernadette looks green.

"I thought . . . Weren't you two going to stay at Bernadette's?"

You say, "Um . . ."

"It was late," Bernadette says. "And we . . . were worried about you."

Dad introduces you to his woman-friend, but you forget her name immediately. Everyone tries to play nice, but you reek of booze and Dad just spent the night in jail. Nice family.

"So, you posted bail?" you ask her.

"Yes."

"Thanks. You must be a good friend."

She shifts her weight from one foot to the other. "Well, we, um, work together."

Screwing, in other words. "Ah," you say.

"Henry, I should go, and let you . . ."

"Sure," he says, "sure."

She goes. He closes the door behind her.

"Well," Dad says, "excuse me, I gotta visit the little boy's room."

It's only when you hear the bathroom door close behind him that you remember.

"Oh no. Oh shit."

Bernadette groans.

You wait, hear the toilet flushing, and then he's back, standing in front of you.

You force yourself to meet his eyes.

"What's that?" he says, and waves a hand toward the hallway.

"Nothing," you say.

"Nothing?"

"Just . . . a joke."

"A joke."

"I was just being stupid, Dad. We had a couple of drinks and . . ."

You see his chin quivering and his shoulders slumping. You stop talking. You feel Bernadette beside you, breathing fast.

"Well," he says. "You're just like your mother, aren't you?"

You blink and swallow. "I'm sorry, I didn't mean it."

"Too late," he says. "Too late."

He takes two steps, sinks into a chair.

This is the worst moment ever. Your dad, no matter what, the dad you love, the dad you need, the dad you would never want to hurt . . . wounded, diminished, brought low when he is already down.

Hurt by you.

Weeping, stabbed, shot down by you, kicked by you, sobbing, shaking, heart broken by you.

Please, please, make it not so.

But it is so.

You piece of shit.

"Daddy . . ." You reach out to touch his shoulder.

He flinches.

Chapter Eleven

I've often wondered what happened to Faith English after she left our high school in disgrace, but my wondering never included the desire to have coffee with her.

Bernadette and I are catching up with Faith as though the three of us were great friends back then.

What I remember is Bernadette's broken heart, the worst fight we ever had, guilt over Faith's meltdown—bad times.

Of course, she still looks perfect, her yellow hair stick-straight, brown eyes big and long-lashed, and her clothing—lilac cashmere turtleneck, black pants, leather boots—conservative but stylish.

"So, nonprofit, that's admirable," Bernadette says to Faith. "You like it?"

Faith nods. "We never have enough funding, of course, but the people I work with are fab. How's your family?"

Bernadette blushes. "Fine. Good."

"Your brothers still like to wrestle with you?"

"Oh, I kicked Martin's butt for good years ago, and Paul is way too dignified to wrestle these days. I can't believe you remember that."

"Well," Faith looks down and then up again. "You used to have bruises."

Okay, wow, suddenly I may as well not be here.

I excuse myself and go to the washroom, where I hide out for a couple of minutes. Crazy protesters, riot police, and now Faith English. This day is seriously killing me.

"Bee, I need to get home," I tell her when I return to the table.

She blinks at me like she's forgotten who I am. "Oh! Yeah, sorry."

Out on the sidewalk we both shake hands with Faith.

"It was great to see you both," she says. "Really, really great."

"Mm," I say.

"Absolutely," Bernadette says.

"Yeah," Faith says, not leaving. "You said you live on Euclid?"

Bernadette beams. "303A," she says.

"Great, great. Well, maybe I'll . . . see you in the neighborhood."

"Maybe. Bye, Faith," Bernadette says, and we walk away.

Half a block up, Bernadette says, "Do you think she'll call?"

"You gave her your number?"

"Nope."

"You think she'll actually remember your address?"

"Faith has an excellent memory for numbers."

"Bee, I don't think . . . I'm not sure this would be . . . positive for you."

Bernadette chuckles at my concern, and we keep walking.

I'm feeling unwell. My stomach is queasy, my temples are throbbing, and I feel, that is, my body is convinced, that something bad is about to happen. I hear thudding in my ears, inside my head. I look around. Some vengeful ex could leap out of an alleyway and stab Bernadette, a rabid dog or raccoon might attack us. We are in front of Sappho when I suddenly can't walk any farther. I'm having a heart attack, a stroke. I need to sit down, but there are no benches and too many germs on the ground. Lead, dirt . . . I will never leave my house again.

Hugo will think I've stood him up tomorrow night and give up on me. People will realize my paintings are shit and stop buying them. Sal will cut me off and I will lose the house, have to be forcibly removed, evicted, and I will live in the park until Bernadette finds me and by then I'll be terminally ill. Tuberculosis, malnutrition—

"Mara!"

I blink twice and find Bernadette standing in front of me with her hands on my shoulders. Right. I am on Church Street on a chilly autumn day. There are tears in my eyes and I'm shaking.

"Mara?"

"Hi," I say. "Ah, what's up?"

"What's up? What's up! What the hell is going on? We were having a conversation and suddenly you were gone. You just stopped in the middle of the sidewalk."

"I'm fine, it's okay. I got, ah, tired."

"And it made you cry?" She puts an arm around my waist and starts walking us forward again.

"I guess I'm just a bit overwhelmed."

"But you're all right?"

"I'm fine, good as ever," I say.

She sighs with relief. "Okay," she says, and squeezes me close to her. "Let's get you home then."

"Thanks."

"I'm sorry, I forget you're so sensitive sometimes."

"It's okay, I'm fine."

"Listen, dude," she says. "You fucking scared me."

"Please don't call me *dude*," I say. "Because that scares *me*."

Normally a day in bed wouldn't be a big deal.

I could hide here until the world seemed safe again. But tonight Hugo is waiting for me and I can't get up, can't do anything. I am overwhelmed, exhausted, neurotic. I hate it, hate myself for it.

And do I have his phone number so I can call and cancel? Do I even know his last name? No, because I am a paranoid, difficult, ridiculous fool.

I sigh. Failure is inevitable. I will lay here staring at the ceiling, shuffle to the bathroom to pee, and watch the minutes and hours go by as my chance at love passes me by. My imagination could spiral into variations of worst-case scenario, but I might already be there.

Good-bye Hugo.

I pull the covers up high so they tuck under my chin. The sheets feel cozy, the comforter soft, but I can't get comfortable and every second that goes by, I feel worse.

He is there by now, waiting at the usual table by the front window. Perhaps he's ordered his Bloody Mary and my soda and is sitting watching the bubbles rise past the ice cubes to the top and then burst into the air. The bubbles will come slower and slower the longer he waits, until finally the carbonation is gone, the drink flat, the evening over.

He is there, he is there. Without me.

Wait a sec . . . He's *there*.

I sit up fast, exposing my upper body to the chilly bedroom air. I don't have his last name or phone number, but HELLO!? Sappho is a business. Businesses have telephones.

I reach my hand out to the bedside table and grab the receiver.

Don't think too much, Mara, don't think about it, just . . .

I dial 411.

I don't even have to leave my precious bed.

Crazy adrenaline rocks through me as I dial Sappho, count the rings till they pick up, and beg the bartender to find the only man in the bar and ask him to come to the phone.

"It's a matter of life and death," I tell her.

She puts the phone down and I wait. And then, some shouts among the roar of the bar, a clunking sound in my ear, and there he is.

"MARA?" he shouts.

"Yes! Hi!" I say.

"I CAN'T HEAR YOU, I'M NEXT TO THE SPEAKER."

"YES! YES, HUGO, IT'S ME."

"OH GOOD! I THOUGHT MAYBE . . . WHAT'S UP? WHERE ARE YOU?"

"HOME. I, UM, I'M NOT FEELING WELL."

"HANG ON, THIS IS BRUTAL. IF I GIVE YOU MY CELL NUMBER WILL YOU CALL ME BACK IN TWO MINUTES SO I CAN GO OUTSIDE?"

"YES."

"YOU HAVE A PEN?"

"YES."

He hollers the number out and I write it on the back of my electric bill envelope.

"OKAY," I say, "I'LL CALL YOU BACK. BYE."

"WAIT!" he says.

"WHAT?"

"YOU PROMISE YOU'RE GOING TO CALL?"

"YES."

"CUZ OTHERWISE I'M GOING TO HANG MYSELF."

I laugh, but he has reason to think I might chicken out.

"YOU GIVE ME YOUR NUMBER TOO!" he says.

"OKAY."

I could give him the Pizza Pizza number, but I don't.

We hang up and I start counting. The phone rings before I reach sixty.

"Have some faith!" I say when I pick up.

"Is this the elusive woman I'm supposedly not dating?" he says.

"Yes."

"Is she 'not there'?"

"Very funny."

"Hi."

"Hi."

"So what's up?" he says.

"I'm sort of sick," I say. "I've been in bed since yesterday."

"You contagious?"

"Um . . ."

Do I tell him? Maybe I should try to explain.

Sure. *Oh, Hugo, by the way, sometimes I can't walk down the street without losing my mind and occasionally I'm so overwhelmed I can't get out of bed in the morning and speaking of beds, after I saw you the other night, even though I really like you, I went and had sex with my jerk of a lover who's suddenly acting like he gives a shit about me, which is another problem . . .* Yeah, that'll work.

"No," I say, "not contagious."

"Is it a migraine or something?"

"Kind of. More like a stress headache."

That's close to honest, right?

"That sucks," he says.

"Yeah."

"Sounds like you need some TLC."

"You think?"

"I think. How about I come over?" he suggests.

"Over?" I say, like a total dolt. "Here?"

At this he bursts into a full-bellied laugh.

"Well, yeah, there."

"Oh. Um."

"What's your address?"

"No, no. I haven't . . . You can't . . ."

"I'll bring diet soda," he says.

"That's . . ."

"And hot food."

My stomach, back from the dead, it seems, gives a long, low rumble. I give in and tell him my address.

Holy shit.

Who needs caffeine? Who needs therapy? Just invite a man over to your house when you have fur on your teeth and you're sitting in the dark in ugly, unwashed pajamas.

I'm up!

I shower, towel my hair, throw on clothes, and nearly brush my teeth with face cream.

My house smells stale, like a sick person.

Windows open, candles lit . . .

But now it looks like I'm staging a seduction. Which I'm certainly not ready to do, given the state of my inner landscape. Plus Hugo and I haven't even kissed or gone on an official date and I intend to do something about Erik before things get any messier. Like stop fucking him, for example.

Candles out, fan the air, holy shit!

Ding dong.

I'm not ready for this.

Maybe I could make a break for the back door. What was I thinking? What happened to being cautious? Taking it slowly?

Oh, no, not me! Days of resistance and then in one weak moment I'm having him to my house. I may as well whip my clothes off and answer the door naked and tell him I want to bear his children.

Who said anything about children?

Ahh! Ahh! Aaahhhhh!

Ding dong.

Move your loser feet toward that door, you pathetic wretch. There's a nice man out there. He has food.

Right, left, right, left. Fingers to bolts. Hand to door-knob. Turn, pull.

"I'm not ready to have children," I blurt out before he has a chance to open his mouth.

"How about gnocchi?" he says.

"What?"

"Are you ready to have gnocchi? Arrabbiata sauce."

"Oh." I step out of the doorframe and let him into the foyer.

"Not sure what else you had in mind," he says and gives me a wicked grin.

I take the bags of food from him and walk to the kitchen.

"Just ignore me," I say. "I'm a freak."

"How're you feeling?"

"Better."

"Good," he says, and follows me. "Do I get a tour?"

I think about the state of my bedroom.

"Not today," I say. "Help me unpack the food and we'll eat in the front room."

He stands next to me at the countertop and we divvy up the feast. My stomach growls and we both laugh.

Eating is awkward at first. I forgot to turn music on, so the only sounds are those of chewing and swallowing. But the food smells amazing and I haven't eaten since yesterday, so I tell myself to get over it.

I stuff myself and warmth spreads over my entire body. Ahh.

Once we've finished eating, we put our plates aside and lean on opposite arms of the couch with our feet up, facing in.

"So," I say, "you heard about my family, what about yours?"

"I have a pretty good family," he says, and shifts deeper into the couch. "I've got a brother and a sister—I think I've mentioned that."

"Yeah. You said your brother's very . . . competitive."

"Exactly. Not a bad guy, though. Just needs to make everything about status. I have no patience for that shit. My sister's cool though. We've always been close."

"And your mom and dad? They're together?"

He nods.

"Are they happy?"

"I think so. They fight sometimes but they also make each other laugh. My mom likes to take the piss out of my dad and he never seems to mind. And they have a lot of friends over, you know, dinner parties and stuff."

"Wow. Your life sounds so normal."

He winces.

"No, that's good. That's nice," I assure him. "And you know, it sounds very . . . populated. Compared to being an only child, I guess."

"I've heard only children often have intense relationships with their parents," he says. "Good or bad."

"Huh," I say.

"Seems like it might be true for you."

"You could say that. Add a divorce, personality conflicts . . . addictions. Yeah, it gets intense. The alimony and the acrimony!"

He laughs.

"But that's boring," I say. "Let's talk about something else."

"Like what?"

"Umm . . ."

Our feet are touching.

"Isn't this where you ask me to sleep with you?" Hugo says.

I try to laugh but it doesn't quite come out that way—it sounds more like I'm choking.

"No," I say.

"Why not?"

"Because."

"Back to your old communicative self," he says. "Because why?"

"Because now you're in my house."

"Doesn't seem like a deterrent to me," he says.

"And because now I like you."

"You liked me before."

"Maybe."

"So now you like me more?"

"Possibly."

"And this means you stop asking me to have sex with you?" His brow creases. "Want me to search for my inner bastard?"

I laugh. "No."

"What then?"

"You know what I really want?" I say.

"I can't wait to hear," he says.

"Your hair."

"Hunh?"

"Your hair, I want it. I like it."

He laughs and reaches up to tug on a curl.

"Should I be worried?" he asks. "Have you lured me here so you can lull me into a lustful stupor and then scalp me in my sleep?"

"Yep, it's a bit of a fetish."

"I knew there was something strange about you."

"First your hair, then your identity!"

"Woe is me!" he says. "Hey, that rhymed—me, identity—did you notice?"

"Amazing talents you have, Hugo."

"What is it you want to do with my hair, Mara?"

I feel the skin on the back of my neck getting hot again. I look down and shrug.

"Oh, I don't know. I think I'd just like to . . . grab handfuls of it, weave it through my fingers."

"You can," he says, and leans forward, offering his head.

I push myself forward, reach out with one hand and touch.

His hair is soft, the individual curls tight and silky.

Our faces are close and he looks right into my eyes.

"You can use both hands," he says.

"Really."

"Uh, hunh."

I resist the urge to lick my lips, and lift my other hand.

I hold both sides of his head, spread my fingers and thumbs out and explore.

Hugo sighs and shuts his eyes.

His hair is blondish-brown, but to my artist brain it feels . . . blue. Blue like a sky with fluffy white clouds in it.

"Mmm," he says.

"Your scalp is purple and your hair is a lovely blue," I whisper.

"Mmm," he says. "Anything you say."

I massage around the back of his head and to his neck, but our position—cross-legged, facing each other—is getting uncomfortable. I uncross my legs and place them over his, on either side, so I can move closer.

His eyes open, and we are inches apart.

"Hi," he says.

"Hi."

"Is *this* where you ask me to sleep with you?"

"No."

"Damn," he says.

"It might be where I ask you to kiss me though."

"Ah," he says, and pulls me up onto his lap.

"It's possible I could do that," he says.

My hands are still lost in his hair.

I wrap my legs around him and squeeze.

His lips are hot.

Hot and thick and moving against mine.

He kisses me until I am dizzy, until I am past dizzy.

His mouth moves to my throat, his tongue traces my collarbone. I moan and drag him back up to my lips.

I am beyond dizzy, I am falling.

Oh, boy, I should not be kissing this man. I should not be sharing breath with him or feeling his heartbeat. I should not be pulling him closer and letting myself feel that crazy stupid thing people call love.

I should not be falling in love,
because love will pull me under.

Chapter Twelve

I am with Lucas. His hair is pale and his eyes blank, the way they always are when he works.

I pose on the bed of our Belmont Street apartment. I am naked, arms crossed, legs crossed, eyes open.

Under his hands, a lump of clay begins to resemble me. It is me, but not me. A separate me, distinct for her elegance, her mystery, her beauty.

His thumb circles to create the contour of an ankle, then a knee, thighs . . .

I shudder with want, and then with envy for the beautiful, half-formed other.

He slices away to reveal a jagged hip bone, then the small of her back, the hint of vertebrae. I breathe faster. He looks, sees it, but his hands stay on her. Perhaps she is better. Yes. She is what he needs, what he thought I was.

But maybe here, maybe this time I can want him enough to make him stay.

Yes.

She begins to breathe and then to press against the callused warmth of his hands.

My skin is burning. I whisper his name. "Please."

"Promise?" he says.

I swallow. "Please?"

He abandons her, steps toward me, reaches out.

I lock my eyes to his. I must, I must, or he will disappear.

He places a fingertip on my elbow, and behind him I see her. The limbs soften, her face dissolves, crumbles.

He needs me, he has come.

But the clay behind him is shapeless, is cold, and so am I.

Even in dreams, I fail.

Chapter Thirteen

Aaron Deeter is having the party of the year.

No parents, an indoor pool and sauna, and a DJ! It will go all night and the entire school, minus losers, will be there.

"I'll die if we can't go," Bernadette says. "Martin can get us some weed, but we need to tell our mothers that we're staying at each other's house."

"Isn't that kind of an old trick?"

"We'll have to risk it. Too bad it's not your dad's weekend."

"Because he has zero moral authority and doesn't care what happens to me?"

"Not true, Mar, not true," she says. "Well, maybe the moral authority part. Hey, even Faith English is going, and she has the strictest parents in the world."

"How?"

"She said she's going to a study-focus slumber party."

"What, did she spawn from morons?"

Bernadette sniffs. "That's not the nicest thing you've ever said."

"What crawled up your ass?"

"Never mind. Nothing."

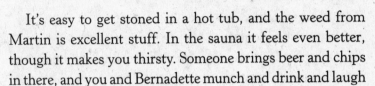

It's easy to get stoned in a hot tub, and the weed from Martin is excellent stuff. In the sauna it feels even better, though it makes you thirsty. Someone brings beer and chips in there, and you and Bernadette munch and drink and laugh until you can barely breathe.

You can feel all the molecules in every part of the air. So cool.

But hot. Too hot to be cool.

"Which is why I'm going to the pool! Ha HA! I rhyme!" you say to Bernadette.

"It's about TIME!" she says, and beams at you.

"You're a genius. You wanna come?"

Some people push the door open and come in. Oh, that cool air is *so* nice.

Bernadette looks at the newcomers and gives you the peace sign. "I'm cooool," she says, and laughs. "I'll come in a, what's it called, a minute. In a minute."

" 'Kay."

So sleepy, but the pool is very nice. Cold and floaty and nobody bothers you. Just floating, laughing . . .

Finally, your feet and hands feel funny, pruny.

Proooonnnneeeeee.

Ha ha.

They're so pruny, you have to show Bee.

Bee is where . . .?

Sauna.

Wait till she sees your feet, your hands . . .

You find the door to the sauna, but it is so heavy. Shoulder against it, and then you are in.

It's hot, hotter than before.

And what is that?

Oh no! Nonononono.

Something is wrong with Bernadette. She's melted, she's red, she has . . . multiplied!

Holy cow!

Bernadette has two heads, four arms intertwined . . . FOUR BOOBS!

No, no, this can't be.

"Mara!" She jumps up.

"Bee! What's wrong, what's wrong! Are you . . . what the—?"

Whoa. Holy shit! The other arms and head and boobs are not hers, they belong to Faith English.

Bernadette is naked, yelling at you. "You're supposed to be in the pool!"

"S-sorry."

You stand blinking at them, trying to clear your head.

"Get out!" Bernadette says. "Can't you see when you're not wanted?"

"But . . ."

"Get out, get out, get the fuck out! You're not wanted!"

Not wanted.

You go. You go and you run, out the doors, into the yard past clusters of people smiling, singing, having fun.

Behind the house is a ravine and you run down into it, away from the yelling, away from all of it.

Bernadette has never spoken to you like that before, never ever. Worse, actually, because you saw it in her eyes. She hates you.

You must have done something.

And now you're alone.

Alone again, probably for good.

Alone in a bathing suit with bare feet in the woods.

With a spinning head.

Well, who cares? You lean on a tree and puke out barbecue potato chips. You stay until everything stops spinning and the ground stops feeling wobbly.

You get cold.

Back at the house you find all your clothes except your socks.

Somebody stole your fucking socks.

Bastards.

"You want a beer?"

It's Aaron Deeter, with his skier tan and rugby shirt.

"Have you seen Bernadette?"

"Think she left. Beer or no?"

"What the hell—why be sober?"

Sensation is starting to return and your feet are freezing.

Aaron hands you a beer.

"Can I borrow a pair of socks? I lost mine."

"Sure," he says. "Come with me."

His bedroom walls are covered with posters of David Wilcox and the Grateful Dead.

"Here." He hands you a pair of gray wool socks with blue stripes and you plop down on the edge of his bed to put them on.

You take long swigs of beer and try not to think of Bernadette screaming that you're not wanted. But you hear her, over and over, and it hurts. It hurts so much you would do anything to get rid of this pain.

Bernadette is gone.

Nobody is left.

Aaron Deeter hovers by the doorway to the hall.

You smile at him. His shoulders are nice and broad. He has clean socks and seems kind of sweet.

"Have you ever done it?" you ask him.

"Done what?"

"It. Sex. Fucking."

His face and neck turn red.

Cute.

"Sure," he says. "Of course."

"I haven't."

He leans on the doorframe.

"Oh," he says.

"So, like, you know what you're doing, right?"

"Uh . . ."

"I mean, d'you sweat and grunt and then come in two seconds?"

"No! Why would you think—?"

"I've just heard that's what usually happens."

"Well, not with me," he insists.

You take a drink.

"Okay then," you say. "You want to?"

"Now?" he says, voice cracking.

"Aaron, you're a teenage guy, you're not supposed to turn down an offer for sex."

"I'm not, I'm not!"

"Good. Just let me finish this beer." You lay back, roll on your side, and tip the bottle up. You put the empty bottle on the floor beside the bed.

"You might want to come in and close the door," you tell Aaron, who's still standing, like a doofus, in the doorway.

"Oh, right. Right." He closes the door, locks it, and comes to sit on the bed.

You're about to lose your virginity to a guy with Spider-Man sheets. It would be funny if everything inside didn't hurt so much.

You hope it hurts when he does it. You hope it hurts and goes on for a long time and keeps hurting until it drives out the pain of no best friend, no one home, no one to count on.

Aaron Deeter takes off his clothes and so do you. Music thumps from the speakers outside.

He sweats and grunts and comes in two seconds.

He rolls off you.

"Sorry," he says.

You barely felt a twinge.

Barely felt anything.

"How soon can you do it again?"

"Again?"

"Yeah, again. You can do it again, can't you?"

"Um . . ."

"Here, let me help."

He will do it again. He will do it until it feels really good or really bad—either will do.

The second and third time last much longer and you start to figure out how to move your hips to get a good, deep rhythm. Between the second and third time he goes to check on the party and brings back tequila shots.

And finally, finally . . . so drunk, so sore, you fall asleep.

You wake around 4 a.m. Your throat is dry, your mouth tastes like ass.

Aaron is gone, presumably partying.

You can't stand the idea of staying here and you can't go to Bernadette's house. Fuck it, you decide, and start the long walk home to Mom's.

You try to be quiet on the way in, turning the lock slowly, walking on tiptoes to the stairs.

But you wipe out and yelp and suddenly the lights come on and Mom is at the top of the staircase with a baseball bat in her hand.

"Don' shoot, it's me," you say, and try to upright yourself.

"Good Lord. What are you doing here?"

"People keep asking me that. 'What are you doing here, get out, get out'," you mutter. "I live here."

Mom puts the bat down.

"Where is Bernadette?" she says.

"Dunno."

"You don't know?"

"She's gone, Mom. She left." You start to cry. "Gone! Gone, gone, gone without me. No more Bernadette. Stolen from me."

You feel Mom's feet thumping down the stairs, and she comes to stand below you.

"Mara!" she snaps.

"Mm?" Sniff, sniff.

"Do I need to call Bernadette's parents? Or the police?"

"No."

"Is she in trouble, or did you just have a fight?"

"No trouble," you mutter. "She's probably at home."

"Is she drunk too?"

Uh oh. "Drunk?"

Mom folds her arms under her chest and shakes her head.

"I wasn't born yesterday, young lady. Don't think you can bullshit me."

You hang your head, which feels like the inside of a bongo drum. Another whimper escapes.

"Oh, go to bed," Mom says. "You're disgusting."

Chapter Fourteen

8 a.m.: I stare into space.

9 a.m.: brush in hand. I'm supposed to be working, but instead I'm brooding. I'm thinking about Hugo—his voice, his mouth—and then Lucas, alive in my dreams last night.

And my call display shows three calls from Erik, but there are no messages. Erik doesn't call. Ever. I'm trying not to think about him and now this.

And what have I got to show for my efforts this morning? A blob.

A distinctly non-geometric, un-Zen-like chartreuse blob on a background of smaller red blobs.

Christmas Travesty, I should call it, or *Christmas Blob. Snotty Nose Blown onto Canvas* is another option.

Pathetic.

Not only that, but I slept in this morning, and no amount of coffee is going to restore me to productivity today.

Basically, love is bad for art. And lust too, unless it's contained.

I am jerked out of my morass of self-pity by a sharp tapping sound on my back door. I look out the window and see a stocky middle-aged man in a dark suit standing in my backyard.

Sal—my unlikely patron and friend.

I turn the painting around and open the door.

"Thanks for scaring the crap out of me," I say.

"Aw, it's good for ya," he says. "Besides, it didn't look like you were doing much."

I feel my face flush.

"Hey, kidding," he says, then pulls me in for the European two-cheek kiss and simultaneously pinches my butt.

I pinch him back.

"Yow!" he says.

"Hi, Sal."

"Hey, babe."

No one but Sal has ever called me babe, but somehow coming from him, it works. Sal is a New World man, a second-generation Canadian, a self-made man with expensive shoes, an SUV, and the vocal delivery of a construction worker.

"So, babe, I got your message," he says. "Whadya got for me?"

My five recent pieces are stacked on the back wall, but I'd rather he didn't see today's work.

"Let's go to the kitchen," I say.

Once inside, I offer Sal a drink from the bottle of grappa I keep especially for him, but he declines.

"Too early," he says. He settles into a chair with his feet planted wide and slaps his hands on his thighs. "Ya got coffee?"

"Sure," I say, and try to hide a smile.

"What?"

"Nothing."

"Don't give me that shit, what's funny?"

"You really know how to take up a chair, Sal."

"You expect me to cross my legs like some kind of fairy?"

"Hey, I'm fond of fairies—both kinds," I say, and take the espresso from the freezer.

"I know, I know. Thing is, my boys need space, they need room to breathe."

I glance at his crotch. "Thanks for the visual."

"Oh, if it's visual you want, I can do better."

"Don't even think about it, Sal."

He grins up at me with a hand on his belt buckle.

"Ya sure?"

"Quite," I say, and start the espresso machine.

"Door's always open."

"Don't you mean the fly?"

Sal guffaws and slaps his hands on his thighs again.

I shake my head.

"It's good to see you, Sal."

"You too."

I hand him the coffee and sit down at the table. He studies my face.

"You okay? You look a little . . . off."

"I'm fine, Sal. I'm good."

"Tired?"

"A little."

"Okay," he says, "but I don't like to see you . . . you know."

"I know."

He means he doesn't like to see me falling apart.

I wasn't at my best when Sal and I met. Lucas was gone and I was jobless, drunk nightly, unable to paint. Bernadette was worried crazy. My parents, of course, were happy in their lifetime presumption that I was fine. I wasn't.

I went to work as the nighttime security guard at a chichi Queen's Quay condo building where I had lots of time to ponder the screwed-up state of my life and sip from a flask I kept tucked under the desk. Sal was a slightly annoying resident who came in late and liked to lean on my desk and talk about his girlfriends, his stocks, and the bars he'd been to that night. His visits alleviated the tedium of my job, though, and I started looking forward to seeing him.

One night someone called in a noise complaint and I found myself in the foyer of Sal's stunning penthouse. He invited me to join the party, but I refused.

A week later, he asked me to come up for a drink after my shift.

I probably should have said no, but two things compromised my common sense: first, I liked him; second, in the brief time I'd spent in his foyer, I'd seen his walls. And his walls were covered, bursting, with unusual and fabulous paintings. The man had incredible taste, or a decorator with incredible taste. Either way, he had a Collection, and I had to get another look at it.

Turned out it was his taste. His taste, his collection.

"You're thinkin' I'm an unlikely collector," he said when I asked him how he got interested in art.

I was tipsy and therefore blunt. "It doesn't exactly fit with your image."

He leaned back in his leather chair, loosened his tie and smiled.

"My first wife, the best one, somehow she loved me even though she said I acted like a thug. A rich thug, I told her." He cleared his throat. "Anyways . . . she was artsy-fartsy. She'd drag my ass to museums and galleries and shit. I was bored but I felt so lucky to have her, I'd do anything. Then I got into it. We bought some stuff and I thought, shit, this is a big investment, I better learn somethin'. Plus I didn't like my lady knowing more than me, ya know? So I did some research, went to the library, talked to some people, got into it."

"Wow."

"So now she's gone, but I got the passion."

"And the collection."

"Yeah. That too."

"What happened to her?"

He sighed, then leaned forward and refilled my glass. "Ask me somethin' else, babe, I don't like that question."

That I could understand.

"Or maybe I can give you the full tour? I can tell you're dyin' to look around."

"That'd be great."

The pieces on his walls made me ache, made me feel high, crazy, reckless.

And Sal started to stand closer to me, to touch my shoulder or my waist as he guided me from one work of art to the next. Standing next to him, his breath tickled my neck.

Do you fuck a man for the sake of his art collection?

Of course not.

Do you fuck him for his excellent taste?

Probably not.

Do you fuck him for the artistic soul beneath the macho facade? Because you're drunk and lonely and have nothing better to do?

Possibly.

Do you keep fucking him because you like him, even though he's fat and bald and has at least three other girlfriends not to mention an ex-wife and a daughter your own age?

Yep.

For a while you do. And for a while you're almost happy, if the absence of total misery and a good fuck to look forward to equal happiness, which sometimes they do.

Then Sal, while helping me move to a new apartment, found out that I painted.

"Whoa, babe," he said. "What're you doin' with all this? You do this?"

"I used to."

"Used to, bullshit! What's the matter with you?"

"Sal, I can't. I can't talk about it. Can you tape this box?"

"We're not done talkin' about this."

"Okay. Another day though, okay?"

A couple of months later, Sal was still bugging me.

"What are you working on? Why aren't you painting? What the fuck you doin' workin' security? You gonna let it go to waste, babe, or are you gonna put your balls on the line?" Etcetera.

I ducked and dithered and stonewalled until I was exhausted.

One day, I lay on his satin-covered bed in a post-coital, alcoholic stupor, and he started in again.

"You're a fuckin' mess, aren'tcha?" he said.

"Hunh?"

"About the art. You used to look at it like you wanted to eat it or something, but now . . ."

"What?"

"Now you don't," he said.

"So? I'm used to it. I've seen it. I'd rather look at you."

"Bullshit," he said, and got up from the bed and started pacing naked around the room. "You're avoiding it. That Kostabi in the hallway? The one you used to stand in front of all the time? Just today I saw you look away from it, like it might burn you."

I was silent.

"You think I don't know?" he said. "I may seem like a meathead to you—"

"No."

"Or maybe I don't seem . . . enlightened, or whatever that shit is women want these days, but I'm not stupid, and I know an artist when I see one. I know when a person's wasting their life too."

"Can I have a drink?" I said.

"And that's another thing."

"What?"

"You know."

I looked away. "Sal, I'm fine."

"Don't bullshit a bullshitter, babe. It pisses me off."

I looked back at him. He stood at the foot of the bed, eyes glaring, penis dangling, hands on hips, looking like a bulldog.

"So what would it take to get you outta this sorry state?"

"I don't want out of it. I'm fine."

"Right. Listen, much as I think you're a great piece of ass, I don't think the drinking and the fucking are gonna do it for you long term."

I shrugged.

"Fine, your funeral, babe," he said, and walked out of the bedroom and shut the door.

Great piece of ass. Humph.

I found him an hour later staring out the window at his million-dollar view of downtown. I reached out to touch his arm.

"Sal . . ."

"I got an idea," he said. "I'm gonna get you fired."

"What?"

"From downstairs."

"Very funny."

"I'm serious."

I rolled my eyes. "Great idea."

"And I wanna buy all your stuff."

"What!"

"Some of it's shit, but some of it isn't. I can do something with it."

"Like what?"

"Like what? Like sell it, whaddya think like what?"

"Oh. Well . . ."

"Wait, I'm not done," he continued. "And don't say no right away."

"Okay."

"I'm gonna buy your stuff, and be your, whaddya call it? Patron. I'll be your patron and like, pay you to paint. But you gotta be disciplined, do it every day."

"And?"

"And you gotta stop drinking—it's shit for you, babe, and it's gonna get worse."

"Maybe. What else?"

"Not much—just I own what you produce."

"What if I don't produce anything?"

"No paintings, no money."

"What if you don't like any of it?"

"Tough shit for me then, but I doubt it'll happen, babe."

I moved to sit on the couch.

"Sal," I said, "I don't know if I can. I . . . it's painful to paint the kind of stuff I was doing early on, it puts me in a bad place."

"Hey, start simple, you know? Abstract. I like that rectangular stuff, for example. Could you do more of that?"

I considered. "Maybe, but . . ."

"Come on, whaddya say?"

Of course I said no.

Of course he refused my refusal and insisted I think about it. Then he had a contract drawn up and couriered it to me with a big check for my completed works to show his good faith—a check big enough for a down payment, if only for a tiny bungalow in the east end.

Coincidentally, I got fired because Mrs. Teimen on the fifth floor said she smelled alcohol on my breath and told the management she thought I was "fraternizing" with one of the residents. All true, unfortunately.

I took the contract to my mom's lawyer, who suggested a few changes, including a renewal clause that would allow us to reevaluate annually.

It was time to get my shit together.

Sal's smile practically cracked his face open when I presented him with the modified contract. We signed it, got it witnessed, and went to dinner to celebrate.

"I promise you, no more drinking after tonight," I told him. "You're right about that."

"Good girl," he said, and ordered a bottle of Dom.

We screwed like it was our final night on earth, until at last I slumped over him and buried my face in his neck.

"So, babe . . . That's it, hunh?" he said. "For the fucking, I mean."

His voice was hoarse and his eyes knowing.

I ducked my head, swallowed. "Probably. Yeah. Don't you think?"

"I figured that'd be the deal when you said yes."

"Well, you know, otherwise it's a little . . ."

"I know, babe, I know."

"Okay."

"This wasn't gonna be forever anyway."

"No." I smiled at him and then lay my head on his chest.

"I'll miss ya. I kinda love ya."

My throat tightened.

"Me too," I said.

"And you're a great fuck. Don't ever let anyone tell ya different."

Such a charmer, that Sal.

And he basically saved my life, so I try not to disappoint him.

He likes the five new pieces, pats me on the back.

I help him carry them to the trunk of his SUV.

"These'll do good," he says, and then kisses my cheeks again, gets into the vehicle, and drives away.

Chapter Fifteen

You should be grounded.

If you were grounded, there would be something to think about besides Bernadette not talking to you for a week. It feels like a year.

And what kind of mother ignores the fact that her daughter comes home drunk, stoned and deflowered (not that she knows that part), and wipes out on the stairs in the wee hours of the morning?

"Am I not in trouble or something?" you finally ask.

Mom's eyebrows lift and she gazes at you over the "Number One Mom" coffee mug you gave her last year. "Is there a number two?" she'd asked, and you'd both laughed.

"Trouble? What for?" she asks.

"For last weekend. I figured I'd be grounded."

"No," she says and goes back to the work she's doing at the breakfast table.

"But I was drunk."

"Uh huh." She doesn't even look up.

"And stoned."

"Uh huh."

"Well . . ." You stare at her, willing her to look up, to respond in some way.

Nothing. Damn her!

"Well, if you did ground me, I guess it would be hard to enforce."

"Why's that?" she says, and scribbles.

"You'd have to actually *be home*, you know, to ground me. You'd have to actually give a—" You feel your chin start to tremble and press your lips together.

"Sorry? I didn't hear that last part," Mom says in a hushed, flat voice.

You know better than to push when you hear that tone, but tears are leaking out of your eyes, running down your cheeks. And she's actually paying attention.

"You'd have to give a shit," you say.

There is a short, dark pause before she stands up out of her chair. It falls over and crashes onto the floor.

"You self-centered little bitch," she says in a whisper that sounds like a howl.

She grabs your arm and yanks you from your chair.

"Upstairs," she says, and pulls you along behind her, jerking at your arm.

In your bedroom, she pushes you against the door and glares up at you, face red, eyes fierce. All at once she jerks away like your skin has burned her and you slump against the door, knees weak.

She grabs your suitcase and starts shoving your belongings into it, ranting all the while.

"You want me to join the fucking PTA? You want to make me responsible if you fuck up your life? Who pays for the damned house? Who works overtime and gets treated like shit all day long and has to fight for everything she gets? Who pays for the dentist and the doctor and your books and your clothes and your food? Who does fucking EVERYTHING for you so you don't have to live in a slum with your useless, loser, asshole of a fucking father!"

"Mom—"

"Don't you tell me what I give a shit about, don't you fucking dare. You know nothing. You don't think I had dreams? You don't think I wanted a better life than this?"

"But—"

She slams the suitcase shut, picks it up, and hauls it downstairs. You follow with shaking, rubbery legs, and a roaring panic building in your heart.

At the front door, she confirms your worst fear.

"Get out," she says.

"Mom, no!"

"Go live with your father, see how you like that."

You're crumbling from the inside. You sob her name again, but her eyes are cold.

"Come back when you're grateful," she says, then pushes you out the door and locks it behind you.

Sal is gone and I'm back to thinking about Hugo and the fact that I might be falling in love.

I really should have known better. I should have tied myself to the sink, run away to Tibet, cut off my ear rather than let myself fall in stupid, dangerous, duplicitous love.

But what did I think would happen?

I figured I could control the progression, that's what. I thought I'd step cautiously toward love, walk around it a few times, maybe poke it with a stick before I got too close.

I am a fool.

And now I'm all fluttery, wanting to paint hearts, flowers—even birds, for God's sake!

But there'll be none of that.

Perhaps today, I'll take a crack at something different. Somehow, I can't bear the thought of another circle, square, or triangle. Perhaps I will take the old route, the deeper, darker path . . .

I stare at the green blob from this morning and take a deep breath. It's been a long time.

I turn off the music and shut my eyes. I feel odd, almost trancelike, as I prepare.

Brush to paint, paint to canvas. I expand the blob. It creeps outward in snakelike tendrils, threads. Then the threads wrap around objects. They squeeze, pull, trap each object and then move inexorably out.

And then the canvas is full, but the blob is hungry—it needs more.

Second canvas, sits left of the first. Objects get larger and some are people. Stick figures tangle with the threads, fight, are sliced down, squeezed, squashed. Remains fall and gather in piles. They are shards of bravery, hope, the stuff of loss, heaps of loss, failure, grief.

It's no longer me painting. My fingers, the brush, nothing seems my own. I simply watch the canvas fill up and provide another when the last is full. Fingers to brush, brush to paint, paint to hungry, hope-eating blob. The brush becomes inadequate, and fingertips take its place.

The sun sets and I turn lights on. When my eyes and arms get heavy, I eat crackers and wash them down with juice.

Paint. Only paint. No love, no lover, no friends, no family, nothing. I puke paint, hurl despair, betrayal, and darkness out, and let it eat everything in sight. It takes everything I touch, even me. I start to run out of paint, but it is not done.

Not done, must finish.

Six canvases and the night is quiet and dark.

I find scissors and poke holes in the canvas—gaping mouths with sharp edges; paths to nowhere. Poke, poke, rip, cut.

And then every canvas I have is full, but I can feel, I *know*, it is still not enough.

I open glue, mix globs of it with the remaining paint.

What now?

All my life and the whole world outside this place, thrown out of me and onto the canvas.

What more does it need? What is left?

I wait for an answer.

And wait . . .

And then . . .

Me.

It needs more of me, me thrown on, me ripped out.

Of course.

Hands to scissors, scissors to hair, one clump. Clump to glue, and I place it, strand by strand, onto the canvas. It winds and clumps, and when I need more, I reach up to my head and take it. Cut, glue, brush on, press on, throw on, hang on.

The sun comes up and whatever has been fueling me begins to flicker and then goes out. I stand looking at the monstrous work I've created and feel nothing.

I am empty, sans paint, sans glue, sans hair, etcetera.

Chapter Sixteen

So if your mom kicks you out and you lose your best friend and you have to live with your dad in his tiny apartment . . . suck it up.

The morning you arrive with your huge suitcase, Dad tries the heart-to-heart, but it's not helpful to have him rant about what a bitch Mom is and then punch the wall beside the fridge, get hammered that night, and refuse to go to work the next day.

Certain kinds of support are worse than none at all.

Dad says you can skip school Monday and stay home with him, which gets you out the door and onto the subway lickety-split.

Aaron Deeter is waiting at your locker.

"I heard about your friend," he says. "She do it to you too?"

"Huh?"

"Oh, uh, never mind, I figured you knew," he says. "Anyway, I was wondering, you wanna go out this weekend?"

"Wait a sec, what about Bernadette? What do you mean?"

His face cracks into a grin and he leans in close.

"Lesbo," he says. "We're talking full-on dyke-a-rama. Everyone's saying that's why you're not talking to her, that she tried grabbing your tits or something."

"No, she didn't. Jesus!" You feel like your head's going to explode.

"So, what about this weekend?" he says. "We on?"

"No."

"Oh. You busy?"

"No."

His eyebrows lift and he hold his hands up. "So-rry. That time of the month?"

You had sex with this idiot. Good God.

"Get lost, Aaron."

He shakes his head and walks away.

At lunch you take your tray of goopy macaroni and sit at an empty table. Before you take your first bite, you notice Bernadette a few tables away. Something is happening. Faith English and her clique of preppy friends, Shelby, Ginny and Rebecca, stand over Bernadette.

"Everybody knows what you did," Shelby says.

Bernadette's hand has stopped, halfway to her mouth, with a carrot stick in it. She looks from Faith to Shelby and back.

"Yeah," Ginny says. "Faith told us all about you hitting on her."

"She was *disgusted*," Shelby says. "Weren't you, Faith?"

Shelby stares at Faith until she nods.

"I saw her running out of the sauna right after. She had to go and puke, she was so revolted," Shelby continues.

Bernadette's cheeks are red, and you're afraid she might cry. You get up, move closer. Bernadette and her attackers notice you at the same time.

"Leave her alone," you say.

"Why don't you tell us, Mara," Shelby says.

"Tell you what?"

"Everybody knows you saw. You saw her grabbing Faith's tits and trying to dive for her beaver!"

"It wasn't like that," you say.

"Mara, shut up," Bernadette says.

"But Bee, that's not how it ha—"

"SHUT UP," she says again, emphasizing the "t" and the "p."

Suddenly you realize. Oh, fuck.

"I mean, it didn't happen," you say. "Nothing happened."

"Right," Shelby says, and smirks. "Keep talking, rugmunchers."

"This is bullshit," Bernadette says, and stands up. "It's all bullshit."

"Exactly," you say.

"*Please* shut up, Mara. You're not helping," she says, then picks up her knapsack and leaves the lunchroom. People snicker and call her names as she passes. She stands up straight and doesn't look back.

———

She doesn't come to school for a week.

A few people, fueled by Aaron Deeter, call you dyke and lesbo. You stare them down and say nothing. A few times you pick up the phone to call Bernadette, but after the way you screwed things up, why should she trust you? You search for a way to make it right, something you can offer for the return of her friendship.

One day, during calculus, you follow Faith into the bathroom. You get into the stall next to her, stand up on the toilet seat, and lean over the wall.

"Hi, Faith."

She screams.

"Shh," you say, and put a finger to your lips.

"What are you doing?" she says.

"I saw you," you say.

"Saw me what?" She looks down at her bare upper thighs.

"I saw you. You were even on top."

"You have no idea what you're talking about."

"I saw you kissing her back, touching her. You looked the opposite of disgusted to me."

Her blond hair is not so pretty from this angle. With Guess jeans around her ankles, pink Calvins inside the jeans, and perfect nails—everything about her seems perfect except that she's a liar and a fake and she's ruining Bernadette's life.

"What the hell do you want?" she asks.

"Tell the truth. If Bernadette's a lesbian, then so are you."

"SHHH! Shut up! I'm not."

"There's no one here, and I can see the door," you say.

"I'm not," Faith whispers. "I'm not like that. She might be, but I'm not."

"Then you need to take it back."

"Can I please have some privacy?"

"Say you were lying. No one needs to know what part you were lying about."

She tries to laugh, but it comes out like a sob. You'd feel sorry for her, but your pity is spoken for.

"Or you could say it was a joke," you say.

"Who'd believe that?"

"I don't know. Don't care, either. But it's going to be a long year for you if you don't fix this. My life isn't so great right now, and I have lots of time to hound you. And I could tell everyone what I saw."

"They won't believe you. I'm more popular."

"Then you have more to lose."

She stares up at you with tears in her eyes.

"Please," she finally says, "you don't understand."

"I don't need to."

Now she starts sobbing for real.

"If my parents find out . . . People will forget, but my parents . . . Please don't tell."

"Sorry. No deal."

You leave her weeping and go back to class.

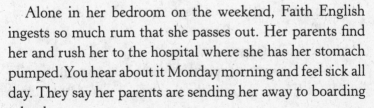

Alone in her bedroom on the weekend, Faith English ingests so much rum that she passes out. Her parents find her and rush her to the hospital where she has her stomach pumped. You hear about it Monday morning and feel sick all day. They say her parents are sending her away to boarding school.

You're early for school Tuesday, and therefore see a pinched, dark-haired woman emptying Faith's locker. Unable to stop yourself, you approach.

"Are you Faith's mom?" you ask.

She turns with narrow, glaring eyes.

"Sorry, I . . ." My God, she looks like she wants to kill someone. "I just wanted to know . . . is Faith all right?"

"Are you a friend?" she asks.

"Sort of."

"Your name?"

"Um, Mara. Mara Foster."

She gives you a long, measuring look and suddenly you feel overly conscious of the pink streak in your hair and the deliberate rips in the knees of your Levi's.

"I wonder," she says, "do the parents of this school have any idea what kind of evil their children are getting up to?"

Evil?

"Um . . ."

"Do your parents know?"

Shit. She knows about Bernadette. She knows about you threatening Faith. She's going to kill you, brand you, chase you with a hot poker!

"The Lord will punish," she says. "The Lord will punish you."

She certainly knows something.

"Look to your salvation, the fires of hell are nigh."

Whoa. If her eyes were the fires of hell, you'd be burning right now.

"Cigarettes! Whoring and drinking! Satan's music!" she says, and then points at Faith's Bon Jovi poster. "Now I know. Faith was an innocent before she came to this school, and she will be an innocent again."

Yikes.

"Listen," you say, "I don't think Faith was, ahem, whoring or smoking or—"

Her arm whips out and she points a finger at you.

"Jezebel! Stay away from my daughter."

"Um . . ."

She moves closer and stares fiercely up into your eyes. The smell of mothballs and stale sweat nearly overcomes you. "Stay away. You and all of your friends—tell them to stay away from her."

You blink.

She turns back to the locker, rips down the poster. Pulling out two chemistry books from the shelf, she jams them into her purse.

You should be running, but you just stand staring.

Mrs. English slams the locker door. The sound jolts you. You are backing away when her hand reaches out like a claw and clamps on to your arm.

"I want my daughter back," she croaks, and tears come to her eyes. "Give me my daughter back."

Holy shit. You pull your arm away and take another step back.

"Give me my daughter back!" she repeats, louder this time.

Oh my God, oh my God.

You keep moving, but she follows you.

"GIVE ME MY DAUGHTER BACK!"

You bump into someone behind you and then pivot and run as fast as you can, out of the school, into the yard and all the way to the bus station.

You can't stop seeing her, those eyes ripping into you with their pain, her voice on the verge of lunacy. Too late, your heart is filled with horror for Faith, who must be living in her own kind of hell.

Chapter Seventeen

The sun is beating down on my face. The sheets are sticking to me, I have to pee and my stomach is growling.

What day is it?

I shuffle to my desk and check my computer for the date. I've been sleeping for over twenty-four hours. Again.

I scream when I see myself in the bathroom mirror.

My hair is gone.

Worse than gone—I look like a drunken elf has ridden a lawnmower all over my head. Who did this to me!

Oh. Wait . . .

It all comes back—the blob, the paint, the scissors, the glue.

I groan.

Whatever I did back there in the studio, it's guaranteed to be frightening. I don't even want to see it.

Tomorrow. I'll deal with it tomorrow. Maybe.

In the kitchen, my message light is flashing and I play two messages from Bernadette, one from Dad, and then (thump, thump) one from Hugo.

"Hi, Mara. Thanks for, uh, having me over and . . . all of it. Now that we've got each other's digits, maybe we could make a real plan? Tomorrow night? Call me."

Oh boy.

I eat some leftover gnocchi and then, avoiding one problem with another, call Dad.

"Hola!" he says.

"Hey, Dad."

"Buenos días," he says, mangling the accent on even this simple Spanish.

"Aren't you jolly."

"Yes I am!" he says. "Shauna and I are moving to Mexico."

Uh oh.

"Really."

"Sí. We're buying a house in Puerto Vallarta."

Purchase of property anywhere, much less in Mexico, is both unlikely and unwise when you're my dad.

"Really," I say.

"So we're learning Spanish," he says.

Yep. I hear "Yellowbird" in the background and I'm sure "Guantanamera" isn't far behind.

"And we're doing the cha-cha," Dad says. "Or is it the merengue?"

This is going to be good.

"So why don't you bring your boyfriend over later. We're having—"

"Let me guess. Margaritas?"

"Banana daiquiris, actually," he says.

"Well, I don't have a boyfriend."

"Sure you do."

"Not for a few years."

"Well, get one, sweetie! Get one and bring him over. We're having a party! Invite Bernadette and her latest chippy if you want."

"Chippy?"

"Chicky, chippy, whatever. Call her."

Double groan.

"Shauna would love to see you, too, honey."

"I'll see," I say, and get off the phone before I have to hear any more.

I fret and pace. I do laundry, clean the kitchen, wash the front hall, check e-mail, read the news.

Lunatic art in the studio.

No hair.

Bring your boyfriend.

Frightening.

I eat chips until my taste buds are burning, then give in and call Bernadette.

"You have to come to Dad's with me tonight."

"Hello to you too," she says. "Where've you been?"

"Uh . . ." I glance toward the back of the house and the studio, which I've been avoiding. "I'll tell you later. Dad's learning the cha-cha and moving to Mexico."

"Uh oh."

"They're having a fiesta tonight, and I think I need to check on him."

"No kidding. Sounds fun though."

"Yeah, right."

"Well, it sounds like a better idea than . . . what was the last one?"

"Coed strip clubs," I say, and wince.

"Right," Bernadette says, "Mexico sounds innocent in comparison to that. I'm in."

"Thanks. Can you come over here first?"

"What time?"

"Now?"

"Now?" she repeats.

"Now-ish?"

"Some of us work," she says.

"Some of us make excuses to leave early whenever it suits us."

"Well . . ." she considers, "it's three now . . ."

"You can bring a chippy," I say.

"A what?"

"Dad's word, he said you could bring a 'chippy'."

Bernadette snorts. "Cute."

"And I might invite a boy," I say.

"A boy?"

"A man . . . guy . . . person . . ."

"A man-guy-person?"

I clear my throat. "A date."

"What!?"

Ha, that's got her.

"What date? What guy? Start talking!"

"And I might need some help with my hair."

"Okay, what is going on?"

"I'll tell you when you get here," I say.

"Give me an hour."

While I wait, I listen to Hugo's message a few times and memorize all his phone numbers.

I walk to the studio door, but can't bring myself to go in.

Great use of Sal's money, Mara. Great way to use up a month's worth of supplies.

Oh, yes, no doubt the avant-garde of Toronto'll be peeing their pants to see my split ends displayed on canvas.

I roll my eyes and shake my head.

Forget it for now, just forget it.

"You're kidding me," Bernadette says when she sees my hair. "Did someone attack your head?"

"Gremlins?"

She marches past me and into the kitchen.

"Scissors," she says.

"Can we do that later?"

"Okay," she says, and frowns at me. "So, the man-guy-person . . . Is he the reason you cut your hair?"

"Not directly."

"Who is he?"

I duck my head and mumble, "Hugo. The guy from Sappho."

"Holy shit! I need a drink." She goes to the cupboard and takes out Sal's grappa.

"Hey, it's not such a big deal."

"Okay, the world is shifting on its axis here. You've massacred your hair and you're suddenly interested in a guy. It's a big deal." She takes a swig directly from the bottle and nearly chokes. "Jeez, this stuff is strong!"

"Sorry, I should have warned you."

She waves a dismissive hand. "Never mind. Hair, Hugo. Dish."

I still don't know how to explain the hair, so I tell her about Hugo. She grills me for details until she has the whole story, minus my troubles leaving the house and the painting marathon.

"So you like him."

"Yeah."

"And you want to invite him to your dad's?"

I nod.

"Hmm," she says.

"What?"

She gets up and starts looking for food in the fridge.

"Are you sure you're not trying to scare him off?" she asks, and wrinkles her nose at the contents of my crisper. "You eat like a rabbit."

"He doesn't scare that easily."

"So I'm right!" she says.

"No, not anymore. I was, but I'm past it."

"Right," she says. "You've never officially been on a date, and the first time you plan one, you're inviting me along—with or without 'chippy'—and taking him to meet your Dad, who's—"

"Nuts," I supply.

"Slightly unstable," she says. "Let's be nice."

"Okay."

"Not to mention you've cut your hair so you look like a prisoner of war. And you're telling me you're not trying to run him off?"

"Well, when you put it that way . . ."

"Exactly. So, if he doesn't run screaming?"

I look her in the eye. "Then I'm in trouble."

"You're in trouble already."

She has a point.

"So, when's he coming over? We've got to fix your hair."

"Oh, I haven't, um, called him back yet."

Bernadette buries her face in her hands and moans.

"I know, I know. I memorized his number though."

She rolls her eyes. "That's very helpful, Mar, good job."

She picks up the cordless and passes it to me.

Oh yikes.

I take a deep breath and dial his home number.

He answers on the first ring.

"Hi," I say.

Bernadette gives me the thumbs up.

"Mara? Hi!" he says. "You called!"

"Yeah."

"How are you?" he asks.

"Umm . . . fine. Good."

"Good."

"Listen," I say, "I'm not great with telephones."

"Somehow I'm not surprised," he says, and laughs. "What's up?"

"Ahem. Are you busy tonight?"

"As a matter of fact, I'm not. Why?"

"Uh, my dad is having a party, and I wondered if you wanted to come. With me."

"Sure."

"Oh, and Bernadette too," I add.

"Your friend from the bar?"

"Yeah, she's coming too."

"Perfect," Hugo says.

"Great. See you later then."

"Okay."

"Okay bye," I say, and press the end button.

Whew. Wow.

I did it. I rock!

So why is Bernadette laughing and pointing at me?

"What?"

"You didn't . . ." She cackles and slaps her thighs.

"What! I didn't what?"

"You just . . ." she tries, and then shakes her head, unable to speak. She points at the phone.

It rings!

I frown at her and pick it up.

"Hello?"

"Mara? Hugo."

I turn back to Bernadette and make shushing motions.

"Yes?" I say.

"What's that noise?" he says.

"Oh, that's Bernadette. She, uh, has a condition," I say.

"Ah. Is it a laughing condition?" he asks.

"Yes, she's been possessed by a hyena," I say. "What's up?"

"I was so excited you called, I didn't realize until I hung up that—"

"You can't make it."

"No. I mean, yes, I can make it."

"Oh. You don't want to."

"No! I want to," he says. "Jeez."

"Oh. Okay, good."

Bernadette has stopped giggling so she can eavesdrop.

"So what is it then?" I ask.

She sidles up and puts her ear near the receiver.

"I just need to know where and when."

"Huh? Oh. OH!"

Bernadette covers her mouth and bolts into the dining room.

I am pathetic.

"So if you really want me to come," Hugo says, "you'll have to give me the details."

"I'm so sorry," I say.

"It's okay," he says. "Do you want me to come to your place?"

"Sure."

"Good," he says.

"Oh, and do you like Mexican food?" I add. "Because I think that's going to be the theme."

"Mexican's great."

"Okay, I'll see you," I say. "Bye."

"Wait!" he says. "What—"

"Time! Shit! I'm sorry," I say.

I double check that he has all the info he needs and we say our good-byes.

Bernadette peeks her head back around the corner, a huge grin on her face.

"So?" she says.

"So?"

"So you have a DATE!!!!!" she shouts and then starts jumping up and down.

I do.

Oh, my God, yes I do.

I feel a bit queasy.

"Oh, and I invited Faith," Bernadette says.

"Faith?"

As if Hugo wasn't enough. I'm going to throw up for sure.

Chapter Eighteen

You go straight from school to Bernadette's.

What you're going to say, how you're going to say it are still a mystery, but whatever it takes, you will get your friend back.

Please, please.

Bernadette's mom answers the door and gives you a warm smile.

"Hello, dear," she says.

You stammer your request to see Bernadette and wonder if Mrs. Delavier knows anything is wrong.

"Come in, come in," she says. "We've missed you."

"Me too."

"Perhaps your visit will have a beneficial effect," she says.

"Sorry?"

"On Bernadette's health." She gives you a long look.

You put your shoes by the antique umbrella stand.

"I hope so," you say.

God, it's hard to speak when you're trying not to cry.

"I think she was sleeping, let me check," Mrs. Delavier says, and then slips up the staircase and out of sight.

Alone in the entryway, you look around in an effort to distract yourself. Bernadette's house is usually soothing, with its dark, comfortable furniture, the shelves spilling over with books, the baking aromas, and the scattered evidence of the Delavier family hobbies.

It used to feel like home, and you hope it will again.

But that depends on Bernadette, and on your ability to bridge the gap that has opened up between you.

And then you see her on the landing above you, looking sleepy and forlorn in her faded Frankie Says Relax T-shirt and a pair of boxers. Her usually spiky reddish-brown hair is flat and limp and she has circles under her eyes.

"Hey," she says.

"Hi."

"What's up?" She shifts from one foot to the other.

"Um . . ."

She leans on the railing. "You look like shit," she says.

"I feel like shit. Are you . . . Are you okay?"

"Fine."

"Good." You nod and then twist your hands together.

"You can come up, Mara. It's not . . . I'm not contagious."

"Of course not. I never thought . . ." You bite your bottom lip and feel your chin starting to quiver.

"Sure," she says.

"Listen, can I . . . can we—"

"Okay."

"Talk?"

"Okay," she says again. "Come on."

She heads up the second set of stairs and you follow her to her bedroom.

She closes the door behind you. Her hand is shaking. She sits on the bed—the usual place for your conversations—then changes her mind and goes to sit at her desk. She waves you to the window seat and you sit.

"Could I talk first?"

"Go ahead," she says.

"Okay." You take a deep breath. "I've been thinking that you hate me. I figured you did. But then, maybe you don't, and I have to take the chance."

Silence. She nods.

"I was thinking, maybe you're just scared. Maybe you're afraid that I would judge, or disapprove or something."

More silence.

"I don't though. Whatever you want to do, want to be—I have no problem. The thing is, that night, I was so out of it, I don't really know what I did or said wrong. Whatever it was, I'm sorry. And I'm sorry about making things worse in the lunchroom."

"You were trying to help that day," she says. "Don't worry about it."

"At the party though, I must have said something . . . but honestly, I don't remember."

"No, you didn't say anything," Bernadette says. "It was the look on your face that said something. No matter what you say now, I saw how you felt on your face."

"But—"

"You're disgusted by it. Like everyone else."

"No, I'm not! I wasn't."

"You were totally disgusted," she insists. "Freaked out."

You think back to the moment when you walked in on them and suddenly realize.

"Bee, no! Remember how stoned we were?"

"Yeah?"

"Well, when I came in, I thought you had two heads! So I was freaked out, but not because . . . I figured either I was having a bad trip or something terrible had happened to you."

Bernadette's mouth twitches. "Seriously?"

"Seriously! And no matter what, you're my best friend. I don't care who you want to fool around with, or fall in love with, or anything."

She looks down at her lap.

"And I miss you," you say. "I hate it."

Bernadette looks up, tears in her eyes and a happy grin on her face. "I missed you too," she says.

You hurl yourselves into a long, teary, laughing hug.

"Thank God, thank God," you say.

"I know," she says. "I'm so glad you came. And I'm so sorry too."

Cookies and chips are liberated from the kitchen and you sit cross-legged on Bernadette's bed and eat them.

"So," you say, "you like girls, hunh?"

"I wish I didn't," she says, "but yeah."

"I don't know much about this, but do you like guys too? Or just girls—oops, I should probably say women."

"No boys, no men. Can't seem to do it."

"Wow."

"Yeah."

"That must be scary," you say.

She nods.

"Have you . . . How did you find out?"

She shrugs.

"I just know."

"Okay," you say, and nod your head quickly, wanting to reassure her. "That's okay, right?"

"I guess. Oh, Mar, I was so afraid for you to find out."

"Did you think I wouldn't want to be your friend anymore?"

"I didn't know."

"Not the case."

"I know that now."

"So . . . what was the deal with Faith? What happened?"

Bernadette swallows, turns pink, and puts her cookie down.

"I had a crush on her for a long time, and I thought maybe . . . but it's hard to know, right? Anyway, we had a project together in History and after that we started talking on the phone almost every night. But at school we barely talked. It was awkward."

"Probably because you liked each other."

"I think so. So nothing was ever said, exactly, just hinted. And then we were alone in the sauna and . . . well, you saw what happened."

You nod.

"It was totally mutual," she says. "But later, on the phone, she said it was just because she was drunk, that she didn't know what she was doing."

"Bullshit."

Bernadette shrugs. "I guess I'll never know."

"You heard she's gone?"

"Yeah."

"Bee, there's something else," you say, and then you tell her about the bathroom incident. To your surprise, she's not angry.

"Thanks for sticking up for me," she says. And then, "So . . . did she say anything else? About me?"

You shake your head. "Were you . . . are you in love, Bee?"

By the look of longing on her face you know she is. Oh, boy. Oh girl, actually.

Even though you have her back, you're going to lose her—to Faith, or some other girl. Because a girl can share secrets and go to movies and be your friend. A girl could be your best friend *and* your lover. What would you need a best friend for?

What will Bernadette need you for?

Nothing.

You feel like you've been whacked in the gut. Bernadette might need you now, but someday she's going to find someone and that person will replace you.

Please make it not true.

You would do anything to make it not true.

How do you fight though? You don't want another best friend, you want the one you have. You want Bernadette, who makes you laugh and protects you and understands everything. How can you keep your place at her side?

"Bee . . . ?" you say.

"Yeah?" She's more relaxed now, eating chips, licking the flavor off both sides before putting them in her mouth.

You take a deep breath.

"If you . . . If you need . . . If you like women . . ."

"Yeah?"

"Um . . ."

"Spit it out, Mara," she says. "No more secrets, right?"

You swallow.

"Okay. I was just thinking that I could be . . . I mean, would you want me to be . . ."

"Huh?" she frowns.

"You know."

"You've lost me."

"Well, if Faith doesn't . . . If she doesn't want to be with you, I . . . I could."

She blinks twice. "What?"

"I could be with you, if that's what you need."

"Mara . . ."

"Wait, just listen. I'm already your best friend, right? We already know everything about each other . . . mostly. So you could trust me, and I'm sure it wouldn't be that hard— we've seen each other naked and stuff. So we could be together and things could stay the same . . . pretty much. We would just be a little bit . . . closer."

"Are you saying . . . ?"

"I could be your girlfriend."

Bernadette looks at you like you're speaking Russian. "My girlfriend."

"Yeah, I could . . ."

"I heard you, you don't have to say it again!"

"Well?"

"No! Oh, my God! What the hell? You're my . . . and you want to be my—"

"Girlfriend," you say, feeling bolder now. "Why not?"

Bernadette jumps up from the bed and starts pacing.

You stand too. "Why not?" you ask again.

She stops a few paces away and stares at you. She looks mad. Suddenly she walks forward, grabs you by the shoulders and kisses you. Your mouths mash together and your teeth knock. After the first second of shock, you try to kiss her back, but it's over and she's stepping away.

"So?" she says.

"Uh . . ."

"Feel anything?"

"Um, it was a little fast. Maybe we should try it again?"

"You didn't feel anything," Bernadette states.

"Well . . . no."

"Neither did I."

"No?"

"Nothing whatsoever."

"Oh."

"I'm not attracted to you. No offense."

"Okay."

"And you've never been attracted to me either," Bernadette continues. "Right?"

"No, but—"

"Or any other woman. Right?"

"Well, no."

"So you, my friend, are straight." She laughs. "I swear, you look disappointed!"

"I am."

She lifts her eyebrows, studies you. "What's the deal, Bones?"

You sink down onto the edge of the bed.

"I feel like I'm always losing people. My mom, my dad— they're not gone, but they are. You know?"

She comes to sit beside you, takes your hand.

"I get it. You're not going to lose me though. I only want one best friend, and you don't need to sleep with me to keep the position."

"Okay."

"Not that I don't appreciate your being willing to sacrifice your sexuality," she says.

You laugh.

"I love you, Bee," you say, a huge grin on your face.

"I love you back," she says.

"Good."

"Please don't ever hit on me again though, okay? It gives me the heebie-jeebies."

Chapter Nineteen

"Not Faith English again!"

Bernadette's eyes are full of mischief.

"Yep. She remembered my address and looked me up, just like I hoped. We've been talking."

"But what happened to Janet?" I sputter.

"Who?"

"No, wait, I mean the other one, the new one."

"Oh, Darya?" Bernadette says.

"Yeah."

"Too many issues."

"Faith English is the *definition* of too many issues!"

Bernadette's eyes dart away. "That was years ago," she says.

"Humph," I say. "We'll see."

"Come on," she says, and grabs the scissors. "Let's do something about that hair."

Hugo arrives an hour later. He looks awfully cute in a sombrero.

"Hi," I say. "You're very prompt."

"Hello. Where's your hair?" he says.

"I, uh, sacrificed it."

"I see," he says.

"You hate it."

"No, no! It's chic. And cute. You look very . . . pixie-ish."

Pixie-ish is better than prisoner-of-war, and cute is an adjective rarely associated with me. Chic, I can take or leave.

"Thanks," I say. "Come in."

"So I'm meeting your best friend *and* your family," he says. "Is this a date yet?"

"Yes," Bernadette pipes up from the other room before I have a chance to say maybe or no.

"Thanks Bee," I toss over my shoulder before turning back to Hugo. "No comment."

"Just using me as arm-candy then," Hugo says with a nod that almost dislodges his enormous hat.

"Sure," I say.

"And my hot lips," he says.

Bernadette, on her way down the hallway, gives a great whoop of laughter and I stand there feeling my cheeks get hot.

"You didn't tell me he was funny," she says, and then whoops again as he leans over and gives me a big, loud, messy smooch.

Faith meets us on Jarvis Street, across from my father's building. She looks anxious and I wonder if it's about Bernadette or the neighborhood, which used to be one of the worst in the city.

I hadn't bargained on sharing the paradox that is my father with anyone besides Hugo and Bernadette tonight, but she's here and there's nothing I can do about it.

Hellos and introductions are made and we head inside.

The elevator has got to be fifty years old and looks from the outside like a broom closet. The hallway is a vision of brown and beige made dull by years of traffic, kitchen grease, and cigarette smoke. It's easy to envision the decades worth of Toronto's down-but-not-quite-out trudging along, wearing the garish red carpet down to thread at the center.

It's lucky I'm not trying to make a good impression.

I glance over at Hugo and raise my eyebrows.

"Lotta history in this building," he says.

"Yep."

"I like it."

Bernadette gives me a wink. She likes him.

I press the button and we wait. With much whining and clunking, the elevator arrives. I open the outer door, pull the grate open, and Hugo, Bernadette and Faith step in ahead of me. I squeeze in, leaving room for Hugo's hat. I shut the gate, and send out a prayer to the elevator gods that we don't get stuck between floors today.

More whirs and clunks and we begin to ascend.

Faith looks at the ceiling and flinches at every thunk and hiss. I'm tempted to tell her about the time I spent an hour stuck between floors with my (drunk) father, but I don't.

"Don't worry," I tell her. "We'll make it out alive."

"Oh, I'm not worried," she says, and lifts her chin.

Sure.

"It's never plummeted to the basement or anything," I add. "And if it did, we're only going to the eighth floor, so we'd probably be fine."

"Right," she says. Is it me, or does she look a tad green?

"Mara," Bernadette says.

Faith has never brought out the best in me.

I shut up, and we make it to the eighth floor alive. The elevator does stop a foot too low and we have to step up to get out. This hallway smells like cooked cabbage and incense. I wrinkle my nose and wish that Dad would move.

"By the way, don't give my father any money," I say as we walk toward his door.

"Why would I?" Faith asks.

"He's going to ask for money?" Hugo says.

"Not exactly."

"Put it this way," Bernadette says, "by the end of the night you could own a time-share in Cancun or Florida."

"Or Siberia," I add.

"Maybe I want a time-share in Cancun," Hugo says.

"Not with my dad you don't."

"And don't play poker with him either," Bernadette says.

"Or blackjack—"

"Or Trivial Pursuit—"

"Or bridge—"

"Monopoly—"

"Risk—"

"Okay, I got it. No investing, no cards, no games," Hugo says.

"Exactly," I say.

"Anything else?" he says.

"Sink or swim?" Bernadette says, and then knocks on the door.

"Okay, thanks." Hugo takes a deep breath.

Faith stands close to Bernadette. Strains of "La Bamba" come through the door. I take pity on Hugo and put a hand on his arm.

"Don't worry," I say, "he's really quite pleasant."

"Good."

"At least he was earlier."

Finally we try the door, find it unlocked, and let ourselves in.

The party is happening. It's more than a get-together, and the theme is more than Mexican, or even Spanish. In among people dressed as bullfighters, flamenco dancers, and a couple of Zorros are women in grass skirts, three belly dancers, and . . . oh dear . . . a mime.

Unfortunately, the guy in the Miami Vice getup is Dad. Yep, it's Dad and it's a damned shame he's doing disco moves to "La Bamba."

The shabbiness of the apartment is disguised by a thick layer of ersatz Mexican and not-so-Mexican decorations, including streamers, a huge crepe palm tree and posters of beaches. Beer bottles are being served with umbrellas in them and there's a table piled with coconuts, pineapples, salsa and corn chips.

"Don't eat the corn chips," I say in a low voice to Bernadette, Faith and Hugo.

"Why not?" Hugo asks.

"Dad bought six cases of them on sale at Honest Ed's," I say, "five years ago."

Bernadette winces. Faith shudders.

"He was going to resell them, but he lost his enthusiasm."

Dad catches sight of us and boogies over.

"Sweetheart!" he says, and kisses my cheek.

"Hi, Dad."

"Hola! Arriba! Cómo estás?" he says.

"I'm fine, good."

I introduce Hugo and Dad takes his hand and pumps his arm before giving Bernadette a hug.

"Still playing for the losing team?" he asks her, and then chortles at his own joke. I look down at the parquet floor. Bernadette laughs and punches Dad on the arm.

"My team's doing just fine," she says, and then introduces him to Faith.

"You too?" he asks.

Bernadette shoots a panicked look at me.

"Me too what?" Faith asks.

"Never mind, Faith," I say. "Just an old . . . football joke, right, Dad?" I grab his arm and squeeze.

"Oh," Faith says. "No, I get it. I wouldn't say our team is losing, would you, Bernadette?"

"Ah, no," Bee says, and then swallows. "No, our team is . . . better than ever."

Faith ducks her head and Bernadette blushes. The sparks are flying, God help us all.

"Well, well . . . excellent!" Dad says. "Come in then. Drink! Dance! Cha-cha-cha!"

Bernadette and Faith wander off to get beer/umbrella mixes while Hugo follows me into the kitchen and watches me forage in the fridge for something nonalcoholic.

"Listen," I say, "I'm sure you want a beer, so go ahead and get one."

"You sure? I'll come right back."

"Go," I say, and then poke my head back into the fridge.

Miraculously, I find a bottle of juice. I crack it open, shut the fridge, turn around and come face to face with Dad's girlfriend, Shauna.

"Oh! Hey," I say.

"Hello there, my dear," she says.

She pulls me toward her and I narrowly miss her customary kiss on the mouth before I'm crushed in a hug. "Lovely to see you."

"Mmhm," I mumble, and disentangle myself. "You too."

As always, she looks good, but with a haziness in her wide blue eyes that makes people mistake her for ditzy, drunk, or both. Though her attachment to my dad might suggest otherwise, she is neither.

"Your haircut is tres chic!" she chirps, changing the subject.

I'm starting to think that the uglier a haircut is, the more chic people find it.

"Thank you," I say.

"Have you seen your father yet?"

"Yeah, on the way in."

Shauna does a quick swivel, checking over her shoulder and making her shiny brown curls bounce around her shoulders. "I think this time he's really better," she says. "He's been good for weeks now, and the counselor says—" She breaks off as Dad enters the kitchen.

"How do you like your old man's moves?" he asks.

"Interesting," I say. "That's . . . what, Mexican? South American?"

"It's a fusion."

"Ah ha," I say. "Now I see."

When Hugo returns I'm so grateful I want to leap into his arms. Two cocktail umbrellas are lodged in his hair and I raise my eyebrows. He gives me a sheepish grin and points to the mime.

Introductions are made and Shauna gives me very unsubtle, meaningful looks of approval and inquiry. As if I'd tell her anything.

"So we're moving to Puerto Vallarta!" Dad says.

"Yeah, you mentioned that," I say.

"What are you moving for?" Hugo asks.

I'm afraid to hear the answer.

"To begin a new life!" Dad says.

Right. New life #584.

"New life, hunh?" I say. "Does the new life have a job attached to it?"

"Let's be positive, dear," Shauna says.

"Actually," Dad says, puffing out his chest, "I've been offered a job at a posh resort."

"Sounds nice," Hugo says. "What's the position?"

"Customer relations," Dad says.

"Bartending?" I ask, accustomed to my father's euphemisms.

Hugo looks from me to Dad and raises his eyebrows. He probably thinks I'm being a bitch, but I have ample reason to worry about Dad working in a bar. I have ample reason to worry about Dad, period.

"Well, sweetheart, you'll be happy to hear that I'll be *managing* the bar," he says.

Ah ha.

"And I'm going with him," Shauna says. "While your father's working, I'm finally going to finish my novel."

"She can write it on the beach!" Dad says.

"Ah," I say.

Shauna has been working on this "novel" for the past five years. "Be happy for us!" Dad says. "It's going to be great."

I hate when this happens. Hugo puts a hand on my shoulder and squeezes.

"Of course," I say. "Excuse me, I need to get something to eat."

Hugo catches up with me at the food table and stops me as I'm about to eat one of the corn chips.

"Shit! Gross!" I say, dropping the chip onto the table. "How could I forget? Typical."

Hugo puts a hand on my arm.

"Sorry," I say. "And thanks."

"You're welcome. I actually tasted one earlier," he says.

"On purpose?"

He grins. "Yeah, just to see."

"And?"

He shakes his head and grimaces.

"Not good," he says. "Possibly life threatening."

I feel a smile cracking my lips.

"So you owe me big time," he says, then takes my hand and leads me over to Faith and Bernadette.

We mingle, chat, pick at the food.

Faith dazzles us all with her merengue.

Dad corners Hugo while I'm getting the life story of the belly dancer, and I hope Hugo remembers our warnings.

We're getting ready to leave when Dad puts an arm around my shoulder and takes me aside.

"Thanks for coming, sweetheart," he says.

"No problem, Dad."

"Can you keep a secret?"

"What is it?"

"Listen," he says, and puts both hands on my shoulders. "I need you to be happy for me, kiddo."

"Sure, Dad."

"I need your support. I haven't told anyone else, but this job . . . well this job is just a stepping stone to what I'm really planning to do."

Uh oh.

"Which is?"

"I'm going to build an importing business. A huge business! We'll have offices in Mexico and Canada—I'll be a jet-setter! You see, I met this guy . . ."

And it goes on. He talks right in my face, breathing sour tequila breath and staring at me with eyes that hardly blink.

"Dad," I say, finally managing to break in, "have you talked to Dr. Tower about this? Have you . . . are you taking your pills?"

He takes two deep breaths, in, out, in, out.

"Have some faith," he says when the breathing exercise is done. "For once could you have some faith!"

"I do, but—"

"I thought you'd be excited," he says. "You of all people know the potential I have, the people skills and the business savvy! I've just never had the opportunity. And I've been sabotaged in the past. But this . . . this is going to be GREAT. It's going to be HUGE!"

"Okay, Dad, that's good but—"

"I thought you'd be proud," he says. Eyes wide and forehead crumpled, he looks like he's five and someone stole his lollipop.

I put my arms around him and pull him into a hug so I don't have to smell the alcohol on his breath, or look at him while I lie.

"I am proud of you, Dad."

"Really?"

"Of course."

"Oh good," he says and sighs happily into my shoulder. "I knew you would be."

I squeeze my eyes shut and hold him close.

"Don't forget," he says, "it's a secret."

"I know, I know."

I look around the room on my way out. The party is still going, but it doesn't seem festive to me. None of these people, with the possible exception of Shauna, are true friends of my dad. They're people he's met in bars and then charmed and bullshitted. They think he's on the brink of something big and that he'll be bringing them along.

They won't be here tomorrow, next week or whenever it is that he admits to himself that his latest dream has no substance and that he's out of control. Again. They won't be here, except those who show up looking for their "seed money." And I will stand at the door and repel them one way or another, because the money will be gone.

Even Shauna leaves him when it gets bad. She reasons, lectures, cries, then gives the ultimatum . . . and walks out.

She calls it tough love.

I call it abandonment.

I will be here.

I will be here and I will pour tequila down the sink and drag Dad back to treatment and shove pills down his throat and listen to the sad, sad story of his life, and feel mine drain out.

Again.

⸺

Out on the sidewalk, Bernadette and Faith hold hands. Jarvis Street is famous for prostitutes after dark, so it shouldn't be a surprise when some idiot pulls up and asks them how much it would cost him to join in.

Bernadette looks ready to surge forward and pummel him, and Hugo steps toward the car too, but Faith and I both say, "No, thank you" at the same time and pull our angry dates backward.

"Fucking freaks!" the guy hollers and roars away.

"Limp-dick, pea-brain misogynist!" Bernadette shouts.

"Bee," I say, and grab her by the shoulder. "Let's go."

We make our way to Hugo's car and I sigh with relief as he shuts the passenger door.

We drop the still-fuming Bernadette and Faith off at Seven West, a three-story all-night bar and occasional lesbian haunt, where they will likely be necking in an attic corner until the wee hours.

Once we're alone, driving back to my house, Hugo says, "This is supposed to be a secret, but your dad says he's going into importing."

I don't know whether to laugh or cry. I look at Hugo, who reaches out to squeeze my hand, eyes twinkling. I choose to laugh because, really, things could be a lot worse.

In the car, outside my house, he says, "So really, was this a date?"

"Maybe." I smile and duck my head. "I mean, sure. Okay."

"Wow, so certain," he says. "Next thing you know I'm going to be your boyfriend."

"Ha!" I say. It comes out more like a bark than a laugh.

Hugo raises his eyebrows.

"I mean, now that you've experienced my dad's corn chips and seen that he's the next Don Johnson I know I'm looking like a great catch but . . . you know, don't be too hasty."

He laughs and brushes his lips across mine.

"You're funny when you're scared," he says.

"You think?"

He smiles, kisses me again, and I put the "boyfriend" issue out of my head.

Alone inside, I find Erik's number on the call display. Again, no message. An ache pulses in my gut, followed by a cold thread of worry. I pick up the phone.

"Mara," he says.

"Erik. You all right?"

A pause.

"Yeah. Why?"

"Oh, nothing," I say. "You busy?"

"Very."

Which means he isn't.

"I'll see you soon, then."

"I'll get rid of the strippers and the crack-heads."

"Funny."

Of course, he is alone when I arrive. My throat feels tight and I wonder how I'll manage to get out of here with my clothes still on, because that's what I have to do. Regardless of my official "status" with Hugo, this isn't fair to him. And after what happened last time with Erik, I know it's not fair to him either.

Stalling for time, I walk to the window and look out at the fire escape.

It would be easier if he could just go back to being an asshole.

"You said something to me the other day," I say after a long pause.

"Yeah?"

"Yeah." I turn around and lean on the windowsill. " 'Not running fast enough, are you?' "

"I remember." He is in the middle of the room, hands in his pockets, and I can't help thinking how beautiful he is, thinking that I will always want him. How is that possible when I'm falling for someone else?

"So . . . are you?" I ask.

"Running fast enough?"

I nod.

He looks down, rocks back on his heels. "Sometimes."

"How?" This isn't what I meant to ask, isn't what I came to talk about, but I can't seem to help myself.

"I smoke a lot of pot. I keep busy," he says and then moves toward me.

"That's it?" My voice comes out squeaky. He's close and the smell of him hijacks my hormones.

"No," he says, even closer. "There's this too." His mouth collides with mine and before I know it I'm kissing him back, my arms are around his neck and my brain is making a run for Mexico. I try to form the thought, the word: Hugo. I try, but my hands are dragging Erik closer and his are on my bare skin.

"Wait," I finally manage to gasp. "Stop."

He pulls away, but his hands don't stop.

"What?" he says, and his fingers brush my over my breasts.

"I . . . I wanted to talk. I just wanted to talk."

"Talk then," he says.

He knows exactly how to touch me. Now he does it slowly, watches my face and waits.

"You called me," I say.

"So?"

"I was worried."

"How sweet. I'm fine. Is that all?" He has my bra unhooked and I'm about to lose my shirt.

"Yes."

Hugo.

"I mean, no. We have to . . . we can't . . . this isn't good."

"Really?" His mouth on mine again, my fingers pressing into his back . . .

But it is good. It's always good.

Hugo.

Not my boyfriend yet . . .

Shit.

"Wait, no. Erik. We have to stop this." I slide away, stand and try to catch my breath. "You know that, don't you?"

"You want to stop," he says. "As in, stop? Totally stop?"

I nod.

He shakes his head, not believing me.

"We have to," I say. "It's not good for either of us."

"Fine, we'll stop. We'll just . . . stop." He shrugs and looks away. "Doesn't matter to me."

"Liar."

His eyes whip back to mine. "Oh, I'm not the liar," he says. "And I'm not the one who keeps coming back, either. But hey, you want it done, it's done."

"Please," I say. "Don't . . . I didn't want it to be like this. I want . . ."

"What?" he snaps. "You want to have a nice good-bye? You want to be friends?"

"No, but—"

"Fuck you. Just go."

"No."

"What? Oh, now you're going to stand there and cry?"

I put my hand to my mouth, but I can't stop.

"Jesus Christ, I'm not up for this," he says. "Go. Go live your fucked up life and I'll live mine. It's not like I need my cock in your mouth to get through the day."

"You're such an asshole."

"Isn't that the point?"

"No, it's not the fucking point!" I surprise myself by shouting. "The point is that we can't just keep doing this. There's no future here, Erik."

"I know! I fucking know that. You want to go try and be happy or some bullshit, go ahead. Good luck. I really don't care."

"Yes you do," I say, and wipe tears off my face with the back of my hand. "And so do I."

"Go." He strides to the door and flings it open.

"Erik, please." I walk over to him.

"Don't fucking touch me," he says, as I get closer.

I reach a hand toward his face and he seizes it. I reach the other hand up and he does the same thing.

"I. Said. Don't."

Being the twisted slut I am, this turns me on. He grips my wrists and tries to stare me down but behind the anger I see ferocious pain and need—a match to my own.

"I'm going," I say, but my breath is short and my body is leaning into his.

"I know you are," he says. "But we're not done."

In my mind, he grabs me, kicks the door shut and we are clawing our clothes off, then naked and fucking on the floor. Tears stream down our faces but we ignore them and crash together until we feel we will both rip open. We shift, roll, slow down, move deeper, our lips so close we breathe the same breath. Our hands, our tongues, our eyes, do everything one last time and then one more time, just to be sure.

In my mind I dress slowly and leave us both peaceful and complete.

In reality we have not moved and I'd like to leave with some semblance of a clear conscience even though I'm on fire. Even if it means I leave this unfinished.

"I'm sorry," I say.

I pull my arms from his and drag myself into the hallway and down the stairs.

Chapter Twenty

Living at Dad's sucks in terms of getting to school. It takes two subways and a bus to get up to North York. Dad's cool about it if you want to skip some days. He never liked school either.

And ever since the Faith/Bernadette scandal, you don't trust anyone—they're all snobs and bitches underneath, even though everyone has pretended to forget. You and Bernadette grit your teeth and wait for summer.

Since she kicked you out, Mom calls to fight about money with Dad, but doesn't ever ask to speak to you.

Screw her. You can wait her out.

"Mar," Bernadette says one day when you're having a butt behind the bleachers, "you can't keep cutting class. I know this place sucks, and not to sound like a nerd, but grades are important."

You sigh, take a long drag.

"Besides, if you flunk out, your mom'll win."

"You think?"

"You want to show her you don't need her?"

You narrow your eyes. "Yeah, of course."

Bernadette looks at you with her bright, wise eyes. "Then succeed. Figure out what you want to do and fucking rock at it."

You feel a burn, a surge of energy. She's right.

"And if it's too hard commuting, you can always crash at my house. You know my mom loves you."

You finish the year with a 90% average. Ha.

Summer arrives and so does Bernadette's driver's license and a blue Miata.

"Waaaaahoooo!" Bernadette hollers as you head downtown with The Cure blasting and the windows down.

Music on Queen Street, vintage jeans from Kensington Market, Chinese restaurants where they don't ask for ID . . . Sandalwood incense, vegetarian food, Doc Martens . . .

Art . . . Paintings, drawings, sculptures in galleries large and small! Suddenly you know. You ache from your toes to your solar plexus to make things—to paint, to capture *something*, to yank it from inside and put it onto paper, onto canvas, anywhere!

This is it.

Bernadette picks you up at Dad's one day, her eyes leaping with excitement and talking fast.

"Mar, you won't believe it. I can't believe I didn't know. Fucking suburbs, we're so sheltered there . . . ."

"Huh?"

"There's a neighborhood! Right around the corner from here, a *gay* neighborhood! They call it the village. How'd we miss it all this time?"

"Cuz we're antisocial losers?"

"Exactly! But no more. We have to go, we have to go to-day! How do I look? There are bars and coffee shops and . . . and . . . others!"

"Other what?"

"Other gay people! We might be able to go dancing, maybe they won't care that we're sixteen. Can we go? I know we're supposed to go to the gallery, but . . . please? We can walk from here! Oh, my God, I'm so nervous, I'm going to have a heart attack!"

And so begins your lifelong traipsing up and down Church Street by the side of Bernadette.

Bernadette learns to flirt. You don't. Instead, you bargain for time: girl bars for her at night, galleries and art stores for you during the day.

At the Chamber Gallery one day, you stand in front of a painting for so long that Bernadette gets bored and begs to meet up with you later.

"Sure, go," you say, barely turning your head. "I'll see you later."

It's not her fault she doesn't feel the longing, the tug, the absolute YES that ricochets through you when you see something so wild and beautiful.

You will never be this good, but now you have to spend your life trying.

And so you stand and stare . . . and stare . . . and try to take it in.

You nearly jump out of your skin when someone speaks right behind you.

"Sorry to scare you," he says. "You've been standing there so long, I just wondered, what do you see?"

You search for the words. "Fire? Fire inside her and . . . something bad, something, I don't know, rotten?"

"How do you see that? Where?"

You haven't even turned around, but you can tell this guy isn't one of those looking-for-art-to-match-the-couch people.

"Her limbs . . . the angle, the way they fall. And her eyes— one of them is wider than the other. Some of her edges are sharp and others are kind of dissolving." You point. "See?"

"Mmmhm."

You turn to look at him. It's the man from the desk who never talks to anyone that comes in. His face is compelling— eyes wide and dark, etched with mournful lines, chiseled cheekbones and a nose that's been broken. He looks like a tree in November, leafless, naked, battered by the wind.

You look back at the painting, with his face now in your mind.

Ah ha.

"She's dying," you say. "Is that what you meant? When you did this?"

"Um . . ."

"You are Caleb White, aren't you?"

He smiles for the first time. "How old are you?" he says.

"Sixteen."

"You see a lot for sixteen."

"Thank you."

He nods.

"No one ever looks at anything for so long."

"I do," you say, and then take a deep breath. "Could you teach me?"

"What?"

"To paint like that."

"Oh. I don't think so."

"Why not?"

"I don't teach," he says.

"Please?" you say. "Where do you work? Maybe I could just observe."

"What, you think I'm fucking Picasso?"

"I'm sure I could learn a lot if you'd just let me watch."

Something flickers in his eyes and then one side of his mouth twists up into a smile.

"You want to watch, huh?"

"That's right," you say, and return his look without blinking.

You know what he's thinking, but if that's what he wants, you don't care.

Sex is nothing.

You would give more than your body to paint like Caleb White.

———

He's surprised when you show up the next morning.

He doesn't know you yet.

He offers coffee and then, fumbling, a soda. Alone with you in his apartment, he's suddenly awkward, bustling, nervous. Not such a big bad wolf.

"Oh please," you say. "Coffee. I take it black."

"It's a bad habit," he says. "I wouldn't want to corrupt you."

"Don't flatter yourself. I'm corrupted already."

He laughs, lets his eyes stray down your torso for a moment, then shakes himself and walks away down a long, creaky hallway.

"Studio's back here," he says.

Curtains made of sheets hang beside the windows and stacks of canvases lean against the walls. There is only one chair and he gestures toward it.

"Sit."

"Don't you . . ."

"I stand."

"Oh. Okay."

Note: stands while painting.

"Why do you stand?"

"Didn't say I'd give a running commentary."

"Sorry."

You try to make yourself comfortable in the spindly, paint-flecked wooden chair, and realize he's placed you where you can't see the canvas.

Damn.

You don't want him to change his mind so you watch his hands, his eyes, the movement of his arm as he dips the brush and then strokes paint onto the canvas. You listen, too, hearing the rasp of the bristles, the even, deep sound of his breathing. He ignores you, and you stay still, hoping to be inconspicuous.

For three hours you sit and he paints. Neither of you speaks.

Does he think he'll drive you off by boring you to death? If so, it isn't working.

You synchronize your breathing to his and try to guess what he's painting until he turns the easel toward the wall and tells you it's time to go.

"Okay," you say, and let him see you to the door.

For a week you go every morning.

Caleb says virtually nothing.

"Mara," Bernadette says on Friday afternoon, as you browse the bead section at Courage My Love, "this is dangerous, don't you think?"

"I gave you his address and everything," you say. "But trust me, it's fine. He has zero interest in me."

(Which is actually getting annoying, to be honest.)

"Still . . . I support you and everything, but I worry."

"I worry about you fooling around in alleyways with strange women too." You point to a huge glass bead. "What about this one?"

"Oooh," she says. "You think that'll look good with my eyes?"

"Absolutely. I'll buy some leather string and make it for you tonight."

"Cool. About this Caleb guy though . . ."

"Listen, artists have always had apprentices, and many great artists started out as apprentices too. That's what I'm doing, apprenticing. It's totally normal."

She sighs and shakes her head.

"So you paint?" Caleb asks you one morning in the second week of your apprenticeship.

"Yeah."

"What?" He's talking without looking up from his work, but at least he's talking.

"Just . . . so far whatever they ask us to in Art—a bit of everything. Mostly I like painting and drawing."

"You any good?"

You consider this question for a long time.

"Compared to the other people in my class I am, but it's only high school. So no, not really. Not yet."

He looks at you for a moment.

"Hm," he says.

You're dying for him to take a look at your work, but you're afraid to ask and afraid of what he might say. He's blunt and it could hurt.

"I've been imagining what you're painting as you go, since you won't let me see it," you say. "And then later when I get home at night I paint what I've been imagining."

He laughs. "Come look then."

You uncurl from your chair and walk over. This deviation from the set routine feels odd, but it's progress. He steps back as you move in front of the easel and look.

It's different from his previous work. From what you've seen, he usually does portraits.

This is a lake . . . just a lake.

A half-frozen lake in silvers and grays, surrounded by pine trees and the shells of falling-down houses. The longer you look at it, the further you're drawn in. It's not *just* a lake, it's a bleak, beautiful, haunting lake.

"How do you do that without having it in front of you? How do you get all those details?" you ask.

He taps his temple and then his heart. "Got it here," he says. "What do you think of it?"

You turn toward him, finding him unnervingly close and somehow taller. Except to pass you a coffee in the morning, he has not come within three feet of you.

"Nice," you say, "not bad."

And then walk away and back to your chair.

"What were you imagining?" he asks, eyes narrow.

"Something else," you say.

"What do you want from me, Sixteen?"

"I told you already, I want to paint like you."

He steps out from behind the easel.

"Not possible," he says.

"Apprentices did it with the Old Masters. People do it."

He shakes his head and rubs his hands on his jeans, still looking at you.

"Bring something," he says. "Bring something tomorrow."

You duck your head to hide your smile.

You're not smiling when you arrive the next day with two scrapbooks and a large canvas—you're sweating and nervous as hell.

Caleb opens the door, glances down and then lets you inside. You lean your stuff on the wall by the door and perch on a stool while he makes the coffee.

Oh God, you might throw up. If Caleb says you have no talent, you'll have no purpose in life.

He hands you your coffee, and you see him notice your hand shaking. He smiles.

"Okay," he says, "let's see."

He walks over, picks up one of the sketchbooks and starts flipping through. It takes about five seconds. He puts it down and picks up the other. You try to breathe quietly. Five seconds and then he is pulling the garbage bags off your canvas, propping it back against the wall and stepping back to look.

He grunts and then runs a hand through his shaggy black hair. He shakes his head.

"You want to learn to paint like me?"

"Yes."

"You can't."

Oh fuck. Oh no.

"There are things you can learn, but you gotta paint like yourself. This is okay," he points to the canvas, "but it's imitation. Imitation is crap, it's bullshit. Your sketches aren't bad though."

"Do you think I have . . ." you swallow, "talent?"

He hooks thumbs in his belt loops and shakes his head.

"Lots of people have talent," he says. "You have to work."

It's not exactly the highest praise, but you feel a vast relief.

"Come on," he says, "let's get to work."

Chapter Twenty-one

Saying good-bye to Erik leaves me fragile and I stay home for the rest of the weekend, but Monday morning arrives with new canvases from Loomis and I figure if I can deal with Erik, I should be ready to face the studio and whatever is behind the door.

Time to be brave.

It takes me until Tuesday.

6 a.m.: hand to doorknob, turn, push, enter studio.

Yep, it's wild.

And scary.

Even at the height of my "extravagant" phase, I never painted anything this reckless or chaotic. It's an outrageous mess of color and texture, mostly abstract, but with jarring little pockets of realism. The strands and clumps of hair are truly disturbing and the whole thing feels overly personal.

Lucas would have liked it, but it makes me wince.

I roll my shoulders and get to work, moving all six pieces to lean on the far wall, facing backward. I can't look at them and maintain any kind of focus.

I trudge to my front hall, carry my new supplies back to the studio, mix colors, and sit down to work.

What'll it be?

I get a vision of bubbles—big, soapy bubbles, like the kind the kids across the road played with when I was six. Bubbles are circles and circles are symmetrical and I will put the whole hair-painting event behind me.

Blues and whites then, and maybe some silver . . . I begin.

I surface at 4 p.m. and realize I haven't eaten, haven't even touched the coffee that's sitting, now cold, to my right. I've also barely covered a corner of the canvas, and at this rate it'll be spring before I do. Nevertheless, I stop for the day and go inside to check my messages and e-mails.

Hugo has e-mailed. "Our first date?" is the subject line and the text says:

"I love 'not dating' you. When can we 'not date' again? Can we also 'not kiss' again in the front seat of my car? And maybe 'not' do a few other things? Seriously, can't meet tonight, but can I 'not' make you dinner and 'not' introduce you to Pollock this weekend? Maybe Friday?

Yours truly,

Not me."

I reply:

"Let's definitely not."

And smile for at least ten minutes before worry sets in.

Introducing me to his dog—that's serious. Making dinner is serious.

And we'll be alone again, alone in his apartment. My erogenous zones hum at the thought, but of course it's not that simple.

Logically, there could be someone normal out there who will stick by me no matter how screwed up I may be sometimes, and people get more than one chance at love, and we are not doomed to repeat our mistakes, or the mistakes of our parents, or to linger forever in a half-life filled with guilt and grief and fear.

We are not.

I am not.

I don't have to be.

Alone in my bedroom, I purse my lips and let out a long breath.

All of this is true. So what do I do about the fact that I'm walking around convinced that the sky is going to fall? Is it shrink time again?

No.

No, I can deal with this myself, heal myself, take action.

Because if I want a life, if I want Hugo (and I DO!) it's time to get my shit together.

So what's the plan?

For starters . . . I will go out alone.

Every day I'll go somewhere new. When the fears crash down on me, I will breathe deeply and—I wrack my brain for advice from Dr. Phil, Oprah, anybody!—I'll breathe deeply and wait. I'll just stop and wait. Or take a book and stop and read.

I'll tell Bernadette the full extent of my leaving-the-house problem.

I'll be honest with Hugo . . . mostly.

I'll stay away from Erik.

I'll . . .

I bite my lip and shut my eyes. I can do this. I will let go of Lucas. Somehow.

Deep breath.

Ten counts in, ten counts out. Repeat.

Five in, ten out. Repeat.

6 p.m.: microwave frozen dinner and eat.

7 p.m.: leave message for Bernadette.

7:01: pick up phone to call Hugo, then put it down. Needy. Too needy.

7:04: check e-mail again.

7:05: sit on floor in front of closet.

7:10: still sitting.

7:11: listen to traffic.

7:12: reach hand toward box filled with letters and photos.

7:13: chicken out, close closet door, walk away.

7:15: put on shoes and coat.

7:16: walk out front door.

Nothing like fearing something inside to get me outside.

I walk up to the Danforth and turn left. Looking down, afraid of faces, I see my feet. My feet and the sidewalk and the occasional dog, which makes me think of Hugo, which makes me want to turn around and go home to see if he's e-mailed back. Or walk all the way to his place and strip his clothes off and strip my clothes off and run my hands over his shoulders and belly and legs, and let him tickle my skin with his curls and nibble my shoulder and grip my hips and take me to his bedroom and do slippery hot things to me all night long.

But I would have to cross the Bloor viaduct and there are hundreds of people who have jumped from it, smashed their heads open like pumpkins on the highway below. There was that guy who threw his four-year-old over and then jumped after her.

Horrible.

There could be someone there now, ready to jump, even though they put that wall of cable up to try to stop the suicides. Could I talk them down? Or would I make things worse and then have to watch them fall and then maybe lose my balance, one hand trying to hold on, losing my grip, hanging, sliding, flying, falling . . .

Stop!

Stop it right now, Mara.

I try inhaling, exhaling.

Thinking. What was it I was going to do?

Read a book? Forgot to bring one. Breathe. Yes. Look around. Right. Okay. No heads smashed on concrete. Only cafés and furniture stores, people hustling about.

I am not on the Bloor viaduct watching anyone plunge to their death. I am not plunging to my own death. I'm panting and sweating, but I am free and safe for the moment. I can go to the bookstore, buy myself dinner, rent a movie, draw murals on the sidewalk, skip . . .

Oh, sure, skipping is a great option. Lots of people *skip* on the streets of Toronto.

Ha. There, I've made myself laugh.

Whew.

Now what?

I promised myself an hour outside the house, but what do people do?

People shop. Walk their dogs. Have dinner. Take yoga classes and boxing classes and spinning classes. They sit on patios, even in the brisk fall weather, and play chess. Talk on cell phones, jog, read the paper, drink coffee, drink martinis, drink green tea, wheatgrass, soy milk, rice milk, almond milk. They smoke outside. Go to movies. Get involved, get stressed. They stand on corners and talk to each other, or talk to themselves, or talk to people who don't want to talk to them.

"Spare change, miss?"

They beg for money from strangers.

"No, sorry," I say to the woman huddling by a planter box filled with purple and white icicle pansies. I step past her, but I look at her. I don't avert my eyes because I read somewhere that the worst thing for homeless people (aside from being homeless) is that they begin to feel invisible. So I look and try to smile.

"Have a nice day, cunt," she says.

"Thanks, you too," I say out of reflex, and keep walking.

Holy shit.

It's not funny, but I want to laugh.

I could laugh and cry too.

Jeez, I need to go home and stay there.

I need to do *something*.

I duck into a store and buy every newspaper they have— one of each. I add four candy bars and an art magazine and put it all on debit. I take out some cash and plan to give it to the hostile woman outside, but when I get back out on the street she's gone.

I look at my watch.

I've been out for twenty minutes.

Three weeks.

You've memorized his face and body, learned his gestures, looked at his work. You've brought your own paints and canvas and work as he works, but he makes no comment, shares no wisdom. You silently will him to give you more.

He doesn't.

It might take something different.

One morning you stare at his back as he makes coffee. His shoulders are wide, almost like he's wearing football pads, and he holds the right one higher than the left. He has nice proportions, a good body, if a little skinny in places and a little soft in others.

"Caleb?"

"Yo," he says without turning around.

"You have a girlfriend?"

Now he turns. His eyes meet yours for a moment before he looks away.

"No," he says.

"Boyfriend?"

At this he gives a short, sharp laugh. "No."

You lean forward with your elbow on the counter and your chin in your hand. His back is to you again. You watch his body for clues. He takes an apple from a bowl and begins to slice it.

"You know, I'm legal," you say as the knife slides toward the core of the apple and then straight through without pausing.

He turns the apple so it rests on its flat, cut side and gets ready to slice again.

"Legal for what?"

"You know."

He puts the knife down and you see the muscles of his shoulders tensing.

"No, I don't know."

"Figure it out," you say.

You slide off your stool and walk up beside him. You pour yourself a mug of the fresh coffee, then reach out and take some of the apple from the cutting board.

"Thanks," you say, and turn and walk down the hall to the studio. You can barely breathe and you feel like you're going to pee your pants, but you take a careful bite of your apple, chew, swallow, put your coffee down and then begin to work.

All morning, you can't look at him. You feel him trying not to look at you. You paint nothing but lines—squiggly, curly, tangling lines.

As you're leaving for the day he says, "I won't be here tomorrow."

"Why not?"

"Uh, I have a . . . I have something . . . I won't be here," he says.

You feel your cheeks burning and you look down at your hands so you don't have to meet his eyes.

"Okay," you say.

You fucked up, you really fucked up. He got your message and he doesn't want you and now it's all awkward.

And what about the day after tomorrow? Next week? Better not to ask.

You give him what you hope is a normal smile. You wave, turn, and walk toward the stairs. His door should be shutting behind you, but you haven't heard it. You look over your shoulder. He's still there, watching you.

"What?" you say.

He shakes his head. "You'd better go."

Bernadette's at camp and you have no one to tell, no one to help you interpret Caleb's words or the look in his eyes when he told you to go. All the way back to your dad's you play the scene over in your mind. What next?

Next turns out to be Dad on the sidewalk in front of his building with all of your collective belongings.

"Dad?" you call out, and run toward him. "What happened?"

He looks up at you from his perch on the edge of an old, hardcover black suitcase.

"Moving," he says.

"Hunh?"

"S'all right, we're moving."

"What happened?"

He looks away and hangs his head.

"S'not my fault. Th'fucker."

"What fucker?" you ask.

"THE FUCKER WHO EVICTED US!" he jerks up onto his feet and shouts, suddenly crystal clear in his diction. "THAT FUCKING FUCKER, CHUCK!"

~~~~~

Dad's latest girlfriend invites you to crash at her place with Dad.

She believes the story about Chuck cashing his rent checks and then denying Dad paid.

The women Dad dates are all idiots, but you thank her nonetheless. She is, after all, saving your father from home-lessness and offering to do the same for you.

But you can't quite see yourself crashing on her futon for the rest of the summer.

"I think I'll stay with Bernadette for a few days," you say. He doesn't know she's at camp.

He looks relieved and watches you pack a small knapsack.

The rest of Bernadette's family is in Prague and the house is locked and the alarm system is armed. You stash your stuff under the wicker furniture on the back porch, get on the bus, and head back downtown.

On the dark street below Caleb's front window, you stand for a long time before getting the courage to go up and knock on his door.

He might find you intriguing and perhaps even attractive, but he's not your lover and not your friend and may not even like you. Most likely he thinks you're a precocious teenager with a bit of talent and nothing to do all summer. At best, you're a charity case.

But pain drives you and need drives you and you have no place to stay tonight.

So you knock.

He takes a long time to get to the door.

While you wait, you drag your thoughts away from your father, sitting pathetic and drunk on the sidewalk in the middle of the afternoon. You try not to think of Mom's house, cold and unwelcoming, and Mom, apparently unconcerned since she shoved you onto the front doorstep weeks ago. Certain memories, certain thoughts, are holes . . . Holes ripped in you, through which precious things escape and leave you wanting, needing, gaping open. Laughter and belonging and comfort gush out, leaving their tracks but not their substance. And you are left empty, a skeleton, a shell with wind rushing through you and a sensation of sinking, barely existing . . . a few bones, no blood.

And then he opens the door.

You want to say, "Help. Help me, I can't feel my body." But you just look at him.

He looks back at you, shoves his hands into his pockets.

"I don't work at night," he says.

"I know."

"No lessons either," he says.

"You sure?"

He turns and walks inside, leaving the doorway clear for you to enter. You come in and shut the door, then follow him to the kitchen.

He gets himself a drink but doesn't offer you one. It doesn't stop you from getting a glass from the cupboard and pouring one for yourself. He leans against the counter on one hip and watches you as you take a sip.

When he looks at you, your body is there again. It's good. It would be even better if he touched you.

"Have sex with me?" you ask.

"I'm thirty-four."

"So?"

He puts his glass down on the counter and you hear the clink of glass against ceramic. You put your glass down too. In two steps he's in front of you with his hands on your hips and pulling your pelvis toward his.

He's only a couple inches taller, but he still looks down into your eyes. He glares. Ha. He doesn't want to want you, but he does.

"I'm not your boyfriend." His breath is hot on your face.

"I know."

"And I don't love you," he adds. His dick, through his jeans, is hard up against your stomach.

"You don't have to."

You put your hand on him and squeeze.

He shuts his eyes and says, "Damn."

He pushes you up against the kitchen counter and peels off your shirt and then your bra. He rakes his hands up and down your body, brings his teeth to your shoulder, and rubs the sharp stubble of his chin on your breasts.

You unzip his jeans and he pushes you to your knees in front of him. You like the pain in your kneecaps, the ache in your jaw—they mean you are alive.

Soon the cold of the kitchen floor is on your back. Caleb pulls your shorts off, looks at your naked body, then steps back and walks to the bathroom. Something of you slides away.

But he comes back, and with a condom. He puts it on and you pull him in, pull him deep, and wrap your arms and legs around him, so he won't be able to leave you again.

You move together, and you keep your eyes locked on his and your attention on the feel of his hands on your hips and the friction between your legs.

With every in and out, the cold, the sadness, and the ripping, aching, screaming fears that live with you ride on your shoulders. But you drive them back. You drive them back and Caleb drives them back.

You rage together and defy yourself to feel anything, to think of anything, besides this.

"Where are your parents?" Caleb asks later. "I mean, will anyone be looking for you?"

"No one's looking for me," you say.

"Why not?"

You run your hand up the inside of his leg. "Are you almost finished with that drink?" you ask. "I'd like to see your bed."

You lay sleepless and listen to the sounds of the city. You have been on Caleb's bed, watching him, wanting to wake him and make him fuck you again, but he already complained after the second time that he was an old man, not a sixteen-year-old.

It's hard not to think about how alone you are.

You slip out of bed, grab a T-shirt and tiptoe to the kitchen.

By the light coming from the window, you look into cupboards until you find a glass and something to drink. You pour an ounce of something, sip, and enjoy the burn as it slips down your esophagus.

You see the phone and find yourself staring at it. After another shot of the burning liquid, you pick up the receiver and dial. Mom picks up after six rings.

"All right, asshole, now you're starting to piss me off," she says.

You were going to hang up after you heard her voice, but now you don't.

"It's four o'clock in the goddamn morning, what the hell do you want?" she says.

You grip the phone, lick your lips.

"What, are you going to start breathing heavy now?" she says.

She's scared and now you are too.

"Mom? It's okay," you whisper. "It's okay, it's just me."

"Mara?"

"I dialed your number by accident. Sorry I scared you. Are you okay?"

"I'm fine, some asshole's been crank calling, that's all. Who were you calling in the middle of the night?"

"No one. Bernadette."

"Everything okay?"

"Fine. Perfect."

"You're at your father's?"

You look down at your naked legs. "Sure, of course."

And then there is The Long Pause. The long, awkward pause in which the unsaid everything rears up and then is shoved aside, ignored.

"Your room is a mess," Mom says after the pause.

"Really?"

"Next time you're here we should do a big cleaning."

"Um . . . sure."

"And you're probably due for some new clothes. We'll go shopping."

So it's safe. Safe for now, at least. Mended, supposedly mended, by omission, by a careful gliding over.

You shiver with need yet hold on to fury and the desire to punish her by staying away, now that she wants you back. You'll go, but not tonight. Because now you have something of your own to keep you alive and wanting.

Two somethings, actually—art and Caleb.

It's odd to wake up in bed with a man, and the morning light makes the lines on Caleb's face look jagged and deep. He suddenly looks pale, skinny, and old.

And the sheets aren't clean.

A feeling of nausea, a pit of self-disgust, forms deep in your belly and it gets hard to breathe. You ache to be in your bedroom at Mom's, under your own clean sheets, blankets and duvet—safe from the things you are discovering about yourself and the world.

And you can go back. After your conversation with Mom, you know you can go back.

You sit up, trying not to move the covers.

You will go. Right now.

You will go to her and she'll smile her soft smile and hug you, tell you how she's missed you and how she wishes you'd never fought. She will protect you because she is your mother and she loves you and surely she will see that you need her and she will fix everything.

You will wear your flannel jammies and sleep in your own bed and you will not invite strange, tortured artists into that bed even if you are tempted to, because Mom would kill you if you did. And therefore you will never wake up feeling this way again.

You just have to get out of this bed.

And find your clothes.

You edge toward the side of the bed, keeping your eyes away from Caleb.

As your foot touches the floor, a warm fingertip touches your back, then slides down your spine. You freeze.

"Where're you going?" Caleb asks, his voice thick and low with sleep.

The mattress shifts and his arms come around you. He draws your body back to his.

"I . . ."

He moves you back down, so your head is on the pillow again, and pulls his body onto yours. He is hard. Pushing. Grabbing at you.

"Oh," you say.

You want to push him away, roll out from under him, but you don't—you asked for this, you brought it on. You lie still at first then you begin to move your hips with his. You let his legs slide between yours.

And then he stops. He rolls to the side and braces himself on one elbow and looks at you.

"Ah," he says finally.

"What?"

"Not such a big girl today."

You look away.

"Let's try something else," he says.

You don't want to try anything. You want to go home, you want your mother, you hate this man, you hate yourself for being with him.

You say, "Okay."

He puts his hand on your stomach. You shiver. He moves it to your hipbone and rests it there. He watches you and you look back at him. Your skin, under his palm, begins to warm.

You close your eyes.

He moves his hand over your torso, palm down, staying in place until your skin warms and then moving again.

You might not hate this. In fact you might . . .

He straddles you, placing the weight of his hips on yours. His fingertips stroke your neck, the hollow of your throat, the path between your breasts. He watches, listens to your breath, sees you flinch and shiver and then relax.

You find yourself moaning. No one has touched you like this, looked at you like this. Heat moves deeper, from your skin down into your belly and thighs.

He turns you onto your stomach.

Lips to the back of your neck, the crook of your elbow, the inside of your wrist. He touches your palms, your fingers, nibbles on the pad of your thumb. He lies on your back, slides his hands under you and rubs your breasts.

Oh, wow.

You can hardly breathe.

Now you know what it is to really want . . .

You move against him, you have to have him.

He holds you still and says, "Not yet."

It gets worse when he squeezes your nipples and growls in your ear.

"You didn't want me last night," he whispers.

"Yes, I did."

"Not really," he says, then trails his tongue down your spine and sucks on the skin at the small of your back. "Admit it."

"I didn't know," you gasp, looking down at the pillow. "I . . . thought I did."

"You didn't want me a few minutes ago either, but you were willing to do it."

"Yes, but now I . . ."

"I want you to want me," he says, and slides his fingers between your legs.

Holy-mother-of-everything . . . You're going to fucking die if he doesn't . . .

You want to roll over to your back, make him finally do it, but he holds you in place with his body while his fingers torture you.

Nothing will ever fill you up, nothing will ever, ever feel this good and this bad at the same time.

"Do you want me now?" he asks.

He pushes into you with, it feels like, his whole hand.

"Yes!" You shove back against him.

"Good," he says, and then all the warmth of him is gone.

And you are lying, face down, panting, squirming and waiting.

You hear him behind you, his breathing coming in short, sharp gasps, and then the floor creaks under his feet.

"Time to paint," he says.

You roll over and stare at him.

He can't intend to leave you like this.

He can't expect you to work like this.

He grins and walks out of the bedroom.

The bathroom door closes and locks.

The bastard.

Chapter Twenty-two

I continue with my project—every day after painting I venture outside and try to act and feel like a normal person.

I progress to buying newspapers and reading them *in coffee shops*. (Woohoo!)

I've always avoided the birth announcements and obituaries, but now I read them obsessively—I will accept the cycle of life, the inevitability of death, I will become Zen.

And it makes for interesting date conversation.

"If you could write your own obituary, what would you say?" I ask Hugo on Friday night.

We are at his place, which turns out to be the second floor of a beautifully preserved Victorian house in Cabbagetown. On the way there, I stood on the middle of a subway grate and counted to five hundred. Three trains passed and the hot dog vendor started hitting on me, and by that time I was hardly dizzy at all.

My legs are still shaking, but I am at Hugo's, alive and sitting with cranberry juice in my hand and I will be fine.

I am fine already. Really.

"If I could write my own obituary . . . Hmm . . ." he says, and leans sideways on the red suede couch to face me.

"People get some weird stuff written about them," I say. "The only way to prevent that is to write your own."

"I don't think I'd want to write mine," he says. "I'd rather believe someone who loved me would do it, and write nice things of their own accord. I'd be happy with the standard 'beloved of so-and-so' and a few details about my life. Nothing fancy."

He gets up and walks across the tiny living area to the kitchen, motioning me to stay where I am. Little Pollock, who has been eyeing me with suspicion since I walked in, gets up from his spot under the coffee table, takes a couple of waddles toward me and woofs.

"Hello," I say. He wags his tail and goes back to his post.

"He woofed and wagged," I say to Hugo. "Does that mean he likes me?"

"Of course he likes you," he says, opening the oven and checking on whatever he's got cooking inside. "He's just shy."

"Okay."

"So, have you written one yet?"

"An obituary? No, but I've been thinking about it. Mostly though, I've been thinking about what I wouldn't want it to say."

"For example?" he asks and comes back to join me on the couch.

"Lived a lonely life, failed to fulfill her potential . . . That kind of thing."

"I don't think that's what anyone would write about you," he says.

"You know what would be interesting? To have both. I'd love to see the difference between what people would write about themselves versus what others would write about them."

"It'd be a great reality show," Hugo says with a nod.

"Or a play, a movie," I say. "I think it's fascinating, trying to find the truth behind what people say, behind their perceptions of themselves and others."

Hugo gets up again to check on dinner. He's nervous. How cute.

"Here's mine if my dad wrote it," he says. " 'Hugo Warren, beloved son of Bob and Vera Warren. Not a bad hockey player, good with numbers, shoulda been a real doctor.' "

"A real doctor?"

Hugo smiles with one side of his mouth and says, "He had a brain surgeon fantasy for me."

"Ah ha."

"And he's allergic to almost everything, so he's not an animal lover."

"You know, it's odd . . ." I say.

"What?"

"That's the first time I've heard your last name."

He laughs. "That's true."

Pollock trots over to Hugo and fixes his gaze on the kitchen countertop.

"No chance, buddy," Hugo says, but Pollock sits up straighter and gives a little whine. "I swear, I never feed him from here."

"Wroof."

"Buddy, you're making me look bad."

I get up and walk over. "How's the, um, separation anxiety?"

Hugo sighs and shakes his head.

"I'm working on a complicated system of bribery," he confesses. "He'll stay calm as long as I give him something decadent to eat while I'm gone."

"Ah ha."

"The only trouble is it has to be difficult enough to eat that it lasts, but not so difficult that he gives up, and there has to be lots of it."

"Gotcha."

"So basically he's going to get really fat," Hugo says ruefully. "I'm going to look like an incompetent vet."

He goes to the fridge and pulls out a bowl.

"Ever tried bacon-wrapped peanut butter served in crevice-of-petrified-cow-bone?"

"Hunh?"

He grins and waggles his eyebrows. "It's my specialty."

I never considered the possibility of Hugo being that adventurous a cook . . . or of my having to partake.

I gesture toward the bowl, clear my throat and say, "I'm sure it'll be . . . tasty."

Is it too late to pretend I'm vegetarian? Yes. With all the other things that could go wrong, I'm not going to screw up this relationship by being a culinary coward.

"It sounds like a . . . creative infusion of flavor," I add. "I can't wait!"

Hugo gives me a weird look.

Then he bursts out laughing. He holds the bowl up and inside it I see a salad.

"What's so funny?"

"Sorry," he chokes out, "I didn't mean . . . I meant . . . for the dog . . ."

For the dog?

Oh . . .

OH!

Death by embarrassment isn't one of my usual fears, but it's suddenly become a possibility. Either that or I could laugh. If I'm going to die, I might as well do it laughing, right?

I start chuckling and then Pollock starts howling and soon we're laughing so hard we have tears streaming down our faces.

Over dinner, which turns out to be a delicious homemade macaroni casserole and the aforementioned salad, Hugo and I make up funny obituaries for each other and revisit the petrified bone joke quite a few times. Over dessert we talk about dreams.

"Until you asked me just now, I didn't think I had dreams anymore," I say.

"You find them dangerous?"

"I guess so. But I still have them."

He takes my hands and his eyes make me hope for tomorrow.

"Mara Lindsey Foster," Hugo says, "one hundred and twenty years, fully lived. Courageous taster of dog food, activist, groundbreaking artist, wise soul, loyal friend . . . brave and beloved of Hugo."

Beloved of Hugo . . . The word *love* is in there, and by the look in his eyes, he meant it.

Oh boy. Oh God.

Whoosh goes the air in my lungs.

Everything in me wants to rush up and out, to leap from me to him and chain us together forever, heart and soul and body.

"You've only known me a few weeks," I say.

"Which is nothing compared to how long I'm going to know you," he says.

This should lead to caresses and kisses and a long, slow night of love.

I burst into tears, which could still lead to a long slow night of love . . .

Except the kisses don't stop the tears and soon I have a snotty nose and have to pee and lock myself in the bathroom for fifteen minutes while the dog yips and scratches at the door and Hugo's neighbor bangs on the wall because of the racket.

I look at my blotchy face in the mirror. Way to go.

"I'm giving you an assignment," Caleb says.

Until this morning, those words would have thrilled you, but now all you want is to drag him back to the bedroom.

"Assignment?"

He points to the exposed brick wall of the studio.

"Draw that."

"The wall?"

He gives a quick nod and turns to his work.

"You seriously want me to—"

"Don't bug me when I'm working, Sixteen," he says. "You want lessons? Give me a great wall."

Fine. He's probably fucking with you, but you'll draw the damned wall—no doubt the sadistic bastard'll count the bricks.

You begin with the center row.

Bricks. And all you want is to be back in bed with Caleb's hand up your—

Whew! Brick wall, brick wall.

It's a long morning.

In the afternoon, you remember that you are essentially homeless.

"I have to go," you tell Caleb, who still hasn't come near you. "Can I . . . ?"

"I'll be here later," he says.

"Okay, bye."

Nothing. Maybe a hint of a smile at the door. Men suck.

You go to check on Dad, but his girlfriend meets you outside to tell you he's been lying about going to work—he was fired three months ago—and doesn't seem able to get off the couch. She begs you to help him find a therapist and a job, in that order, and you wonder how, as a sixteen-year-old, you are supposed to do either of these things.

You get back on the subway and find yourself heading north.

Outside Mom's house, you stand staring.

The leaves of the maple tree make skittering shadows across the siding. The house looks funny, smaller. You are not the same person, not the same girl who lived here. You are less and more, sadder, wiser . . . darker. Will Mom even know you, when you see her again? She'll probably assume she knows you and never notice for a second that she doesn't. That will be the saddest of all.

So . . . even if you can go back, you can't go back.

There is no safe place.

Somehow you will have to cope with that.

You sit in a doughnut shop for the rest of the afternoon looking at the want ads. Dad probably just needs motivation, a little help. You circle the jobs he might like, and might be able to get. All he has ever done is work in restaurants, so the options are limited. And depressing, since you know how he comes home with smoky, greasy-smelling clothes and sore knees and stories of bad tips, bad people. The last couple of months those stories must have been recycled, made up.

You wonder where he spent his evenings to get that exact same smell every night.

<hr />

Caleb does it again—makes you want him so much you think you'll die, and then stops. He smiles when you reach for him and try to pull him into you, but he steps away and offers you a nightcap instead.

You're going to need a few nightcaps if this keeps up.

He walks around his apartment naked even though there are no curtains on the windows and most of the lights are on. You can't stop looking at him and you can't believe you ever wanted to get away from him. Now you crave him, need him, are desperate for him . . . and he knows it.

You start to talk to him about Dad, and he listens closely. But you see something like pity in his eyes and you don't want that.

"Actually, it's no big deal," you say, cutting the story short with a shrug. "I can go to my mom's. Besides, I'm thinking of getting my own place."

"Really?" he says. "Where?"

He doesn't believe you.

You take another sip of Scotch.

"Downtown somewhere," you say, feeling the burn spread in your chest. "Why won't you have sex with me?"

"You changing the subject?"

"Yep. Why won't you?"

"I did. That first night, if I recall."

"You know what I mean."

He drinks.

"You can stay with me for a while," he says. "If that's what you need."

"Hunh?"

"And I'm wondering if that's why you fucked me last night."

"You think I'd fuck you for a place to stay?"

"It's okay," he says. "That kind of stuff . . . parents . . . it can fuck you up."

"That's not why I wanted to—"

"Fine. Regardless, you can stay here. But maybe we should keep it platonic," he says. "Just in case."

"This is a strange conversation," you say, and start to laugh. "Especially since you're sitting there naked."

"True." And he laughs too and you see him getting hard and you take too big a sip of the Scotch and nearly choke and then cough and then you both laugh more as he whacks you on the back.

You drag him down on the couch.

"I don't want to be platonic," you say.

"I don't want you to think you have to—oh!"

You close your lips around him and then you swirl your tongue and he groans and says he's changed his mind.

The couch is old, with patches of the red velvet rubbed off and springs that poke into you if you lie the wrong way. Caleb doesn't care, even though he must have a spring jabbing at his lower back right now. He pulls your hair away from your face and tells you to slow down. He says girls like you didn't exist when he was your age, and he wishes they had. You wonder if "girls like you" means sluts, but it doesn't matter. You take him deep in your throat until he's about to lose control and then stop and stand up. You're tempted to leave him on the couch with his panting and his raging hard-on to get him, but you want him too much.

You rip the condom open yourself, put it on him and then slide yourself down until he is so deep it hurts. You like the hurt, you pull the hurt into you, hold it close, and let it shimmer and ache up and down your spine and into that place where your soul must be.

You let out a long, low whine and he asks if you are okay. You nod and start to move, slowly at first. His hands reach out to stroke you, and in your mind you see him with the brush in his hand—focused, passionate, determined to render his imagination onto canvas.

Now determined to render you helpless.

And you want to be.

He pulls your chest to his, wraps your arms around his neck and says, "Hold on."

With your legs around his waist, he pushes himself up to a sitting position and then gets up off the couch, holding you tightly to him. He walks to the bedroom and lays you down, all the while moving inside you.

You want to, need to move faster, take more, but he puts his weight on you and holds you so you can't. You shut your eyes and hear yourself moaning. For a long time he moves in slow, deep circles. When you go to touch him he takes both your wrists in one of his hands and holds them above your head. He puts his mouth on your breast and sucks hard and a new thread of sore heat licks up under your skin.

When he pulls back and slides his hand down between your thighs, you move against his fingers and lift your hips to bring him back in deep. You will die, you will lose control of . . . everything . . . forever.

Caleb is staring at you, his eyes wide open. His penis, his fingers and the smell of his sweat take you further, far from the self you know, to a place where you could leap off the edge and fall forever and love the falling and not care for a second about who you were or where you'd been.

He wants you to keep working as he strokes the soft skin in the crook of your elbow and breathes hot breath on the back of your neck.

It's probably not the most normal apprenticeship.

Passion and discipline, equally employed, he says, are the keys to being an artist.

He has a funny way of mixing the two.

"You can study whatever you want, but all you have is what's in you. Figure out how to get it from your head into the work," he says.

"But . . ."

"Shut up, Sixteen, I'm working."

You work together in the mornings, silent and focused. But all the while you wait for him, half hoping, half afraid. Sometimes he puts down his brush and comes to look at your work, sometimes he stands close behind you and talks into your ear about the way you're moving your brush, or what you are doing with the light.

And right now, as you try to add detail to your endless charcoal drawing of the wall, Caleb stands behind you and teases you to see if you can keep your hand steady. If you don't, you will be starting over again, which has happened four times already.

You try to breathe evenly as his hands move to your waist and under your T-shirt to your abdomen where his thumbs rub in circles, gradually moving upward. You shake with the effort to keep silent and ignore your body's response as he pulls himself close against your back.

And then he moves and speaks with clarity about the third brick to the left in the top right corner.

You listen and absorb and ache.

And keep working.

And then you hear his knees cracking and feel his mouth on the small of your back.

And still, your arm is lifted to the paper and the pencil is in your hand.

His fingers tickle the soft spot below your ankle and then you feel his tongue behind your knee.

You shut your eyes.

His hands . . . up from your ankles to your knees . . . under your jean shorts to your hips.

"Keep working," he says, and you open your eyes. Your arm has fallen. You lift it.

Third fucking brick to the left, and you're to add texture.

You add texture as your button fly is pulled open.

And your shorts and underwear fall to the floor.

And one foot at a time, Caleb, still on his knees behind you, helps you step out of them.

And then, his lips at your hip, his teeth nibbling the back of your thigh, his hands pulling your legs apart, his voice talking to you about bricks, his tongue hovering at your inner thigh . . .

Your knees buckling, your arms clinging to the easel . . .

Your upper body falls forward, his tongue draws pictures of want and draws you open and moves along you and in you and over you until you beg and rake your fingernails through the canvas and shake and shudder and finally collapse onto your knees and roll onto your back and see him kneeling over you, covered in stars and magic.

Chapter Twenty-three

Hugo taps on the bathroom door.

"Mara?"

"Don't worry," I call through the door, "I haven't drowned in the toilet."

"You okay?"

I snuffle, wipe my eyes and say, "Fine. I'll be fine."

There is a pause and then he speaks again.

"I'm so sorry, but, uh, Pollock needs to do his thing."

"His—oh. Okay."

"I don't want to leave you here though. You think you could come with us? Maybe the fresh air would . . ."

"Turn me into a normal person?" I say.

"Was that a joke you just made?" he asks.

I open the door.

"Maybe."

His eyes meet mine and he looks like he's going to hug me, but I say, "Better not," and wave my handful of tissue at him, "I might start again."

"Okay."

"Walk?"

"Yeah," he says, "just let me get his leash."

Bernadette is back from camp with a shaved head and a tan and everything she wears is cut off and frayed and tie-dyed. She looks awesome.

You wonder if you should shave your head too.

But Caleb loves your hair.

Sometimes he looks at you the way he looks at a finished canvas, his eyes gliding over the edges of you and seeing to the center. The memory of that look makes funny things happen to your breath and it's all you can do not to bolt out of Baskin-Robbins where you're sitting with Bernadette and run all the way to his apartment and stand in front of him and make him look.

"How old is he again?" Bernadette says.

"Thirty-four."

"And you don't think he's taking advantage of you?"

"No."

"But he says he's not your boyfriend? Does he have a girlfriend? He could be married."

"No, Bee, I don't think so."

"But you don't know."

"Well, no, but . . ."

"Don't you think it's weird that he wants to be with a sixteen-year-old?"

"No. Stop it! Can't you be happy for me?"

She glares at you, rubs her scalp.

"Fine." She sighs. "Is the sex good?"

And then she sees the look on your face.

"Ah," she says, "I see."

In the month of August you work in the mornings, spend the afternoons with Bernadette, and go back to Caleb's at night. He doesn't talk much, but he always wants you. Surely that is enough.

Sometimes you find yourself in North York, standing in front of Mom's house again. Maybe she'll come home sick from work and you'll rush to help her inside and sit by her bed smoothing her forehead with a cool, wet washcloth. "I'm lost without you," she'll say. "Please come back."

Or you might get hit by a car, not badly enough to die, but enough that she finds you on the sidewalk with a broken leg or ankle. You'll be bleeding, but it won't actually hurt that much and she will run, panic in her eyes, and gently pick you up and take you to the hospital and call in sick for a week while she helps you get used to the crutches.

But you're a fool for wishing ill on yourself or Mom. Who knows how powerful your mind might be? If God exists, he or she might take your thoughts as prayers and you could get hit by a car and break your arm instead of your leg and not be able to paint and not get into art school because you have no portfolio. Mom could get sick and die and it would be your fault for thinking of it.

From the want ads you've been clipping for him, Dad gets some job interviews. You and Bernadette offer to go with him to give moral support but he sees through you.

"You don't believe I'll go," he accuses.

You say no and Bernadette shakes her head, but Dad sits on what's-her-name's couch and stares at the worn-out slippers on his feet.

"Thanks a lot," he says.

You get a block away, walking in very careful steps with a very stiff back before you burst into tears. Bernadette holds you and lets you soak her shoulder and agrees with you when you blubber that he is SUCH an ASSHOLE.

You stay away for a week, but finally you are too worried.

You find Dad hopping from one foot to another and singing Bee Gees songs. He has a job.

"And not one of those low-life jobs you wanted me to take," he says. "A real job where they need guys like me— with talent, personality, skills!"

He's selling TVs and stereo equipment and he's certain he'll be running the place six months from now. And that's not all . . .

"I went to see Chuck and he hasn't found a renter for the old place. We can move back!"

"Really?" you say.

"Really. And I think the three of us will get along just fine."

Which means the girlfriend is coming too. You might have to learn her name.

"I know you like staying at Bernadette's, honey," Dad says, "but we wouldn't want her parents to start thinking you're a burden."

"Definitely not."

"And we wouldn't want your m—" He stops himself and clears his throat, "We wouldn't want anyone to think your old man can't take care of you, right?"

"Right," you say and try to smile. "When do we move back?"

"September 1st."

Not only are your morning art lessons about to end, but you have less than three weeks left of sleeping in Caleb's bed. And then you go back to being a high school girl.

Ugh.

You will have homework.

And classes.

And people at home who will know if you're not there at night.

How long will he keep wanting you?

———

You never see Caleb in the afternoon, but you assume he spends it working. Today you go back early, hoping to find a safe place, hoping to get reassurance. You let yourself in and call his name.

You've never been here without him.

You wander into the studio and stand in front of the piece he's working on, studying the composition and the way he layers his colors.

Beside his easel is a sketch pad where he puts his initial ideas, and you glance over at it to see how the painting compares to the original sketch.

Holy shit.

What you are looking at is not the cityscape, but a sketch of you on a bed. There are dark figures around you, one of them possibly Caleb, though it's hard to tell because the figures are ghostly and indistinct, while your naked body and face are rendered in detail. You seem a contrast of soft and sharp, made of angles: hip bones, elbows, cheekbones and knees jutting out, fingers like scissors, hair like needles, splayed out on the pillow. And then your eyes, breasts, belly and mouth are pliable, feathery and round. Your flesh is permissive, vulnerable, while the rest of you forbids with knife-like severity.

And who are the figures around you? None of them is touching you, but there is a sexual feel to the sketch, and something scary. What does it mean? What is it he sees?

You lean closer and then step farther back, the way Caleb has taught you, to see if anything hits you differently, or becomes clearer. From farther away the figure becomes less "you" and more "she."

From this perspective what strikes you most is the eyes, which are large and shadowed and fragile. They are eyes that ask questions. On a sketch pad, or an easel, they would look directly at the artist himself.

Caleb is not *in* the drawing, but he is in the drawing. And he sees you surrounded by shadows. He knows every angle and curve of your body, knows your face better than you do.

That night you grip him hard and taste the salt on his skin and will him to hear what your body is saying because you will never, ever have the words. Nobody, surely, has ever felt like this.

Afterward, as the drying sweat cools your bodies, you lie beside him and ask him if there's anything else he wants.

"Meaning?" he says.

"Anything. Anything sexual or . . . anything else? Is there anything that we haven't done that you . . ." You look down at the sheets, feeling suddenly shy. "Just . . . if there's anything you want, something I might not know you want, you can tell me and I'll do it."

Caleb rolls onto his back and stares at the ceiling. Sometimes, even beside you, he is so far away.

"You're a piece of work, Sixteen," he says finally. "What, are you wondering if I want to tie you up and whip you? Bring a friend and double-team you? Have you stick your thumb up my ass or something?"

You can't tell whether he's joking, serious, or pissed off.

"If, uh, if that's what you want," you say.

"It's not," he says, and then he shuts his eyes. "Go to sleep."

"Okay."

You're silent for a minute.

"Caleb?" you whisper.

"Yo."

"Is there . . . could you . . ."

"What?" he asks.

"Do you like me?" you ask.

He lets out a kind of laugh, a breath through his nose. He turns on his side and looks at you.

"Yeah, you could say that," he says.

"No, but . . ."

"Don't worry, Sixteen, liking you is not a problem," he says. "Well, actually it *is* a problem, but not that kind of problem."

"I'll be seventeen soon. In October."

"Happy birthday," he says and kisses you on the cheek. "In advance."

"You can say it to me on the day."

"Sure." He squeezes his eyes shut.

"And then you'll have to call me Seventeen."

He chuckles at this and opens his eyes to look at you again.

"How come you don't have a girlfriend?" you ask.

"Relationships are complicated," he says. "People want too much from each other. You get into a relationship and then someone wants you to change, to become someone else, cut your hair shorter, see different movies, change your views, your routine, your lifestyle. They want you to pursue their dreams instead of your own."

"I wouldn't."

"Wouldn't what?"

"Expect you to change, ask you to give up your dreams."

"Listen, Sixteen—"

"You could call me Mara."

"Sixteen, I'm not . . . we can't . . ."

"Why don't you ever kiss me? You've never kissed me. Don't you think that's weird?"

"I—"

"You're not a bad kisser, are you?" You reach out and put your index finger on his bottom lip and stroke it lightly. "Don't tell me you don't know how."

His breath catches and his eyelids lower. You are on your sides, facing each other, each with your heads cradled on one hand. You can feel the heat coming from his body.

He brings his face close, touches his forehead to yours, and then moves so you are cheek to cheek and you feel his eyelashes flutter against your temple. You want to put an arm around him and pull his body closer, but instead you hold yourself completely still. He slides his cheek along yours until your lips are centimeters apart. You close your eyes and swallow and hope he can't feel how nervous you are, because it's ridiculous, considering the things you have done together, to be so nervous about a kiss.

But you haven't done this.

You haven't had his lips pressing onto yours, or heard the deep, low whimper that comes from the back of his throat when your lips move in response. You haven't had him hold your face in his hands and felt him shudder, and no painful, heated ache has rocketed down from your open lips to your tongue and fired along your nerve endings and made you feel like your body was on fire.

But now you have. And the world is a different place.

Locked together in a tangled embrace, you travel past desire, past time and age and circumstance, past, even, the barriers of body, to a place where you are together, linked in the deepest sense. And for a few timeless moments, you are not alone.

It is grief to come back, though you lie, still warm, in Caleb's arms. He pulls the covers over you and, for once, does not turn away before he drifts into his dreams.

But the day has changed you and you can't sleep.

Finally you slide out of Caleb's grasp and get out of the bed. You pull on a T-shirt and sit on a chair by the window and look out. On Dundas Street a streetcar clicks and whines as it passes by.

You reach your senses out and hold yourself very still. You look up toward the sky and see only dark against the lamplights, and your mind goes to color and the absence of color that makes black, and the vast universe out there in which you are very small. And those thoughts lead you back to Caleb, behind you in the bed, and the smell of you both, musky, dark, and sweet on your hands and in your breath. Caleb, who channels you with his artist's eye and hand. Caleb, who is sexy and brilliant and elusive . . . and yours tonight.

He does not want to be yours, though, and soon you go back to high school and he will remember to think of you as a child and what you both had tonight might slip away.

How will you bear it?

"Please," you whisper to the night. "Please let me have this."

"It's a great school, but don't ask them about me!" Caleb says when you mention the Ontario College of Art. "I taught there for a couple of years."

"It didn't work out?"

He shrugs and grins at you across the table.

"Students complained that I was surly and uncommunicative," he says, "and I didn't do so well with the faculty politics."

You're out for dinner—a date—progress!

Caleb has put on pants and a shirt with buttons instead of his usual jeans and T-shirt and he looks handsome in his brooding, pale-faced way. You are wearing a dress, high heels and lipstick. You sip at your glass of red wine.

You laugh. "Surly, huh? Those students didn't know what they were missing."

"Not everyone has your fine appreciation of character, Sixteen."

Now and then he reaches across to touch your hand, your face, or your knee. For the first time you talk about books, music and movies. Thank goodness Bernadette has been dragging you out to the rep cinemas, because you actually know who Bertolucci is and you've seen *La Dolce Vita* and *La Femme Nikita,* not to mention every film Woody Allen has ever made. Caleb chuckles and shakes his head and says you are a wonder.

He orders you an Irish coffee and then takes both your hands in his and leans over to kiss you. Nothing in your life has ever been this perfect.

He orders dessert and when it comes he takes the spoon and taps the surface until it breaks open and then dips the spoon in and lifts it to your mouth. You close your eyes to taste it, then open them to tell him it's wonderful . . .

and everything in you freezes,

because behind him stands your mother.

Huge love floods you and you want to leap out of your chair and into her arms. What a fool you were to think you could be safe from this love—you never will be. And love is what you see in her eyes too, and a need as huge as your own.

Then her face changes. Out goes the love and in comes the face that could freeze oceans, the voice that is like a whip cracking.

"What is it you think you're doing?" she says.

She is so damned scary like this.

"Hi, Mom."

"Where is your father?"

"At home I think. Mom, uh, this is my . . . this is my friend, Caleb White. Caleb, my mom."

He clears his throat, looks from you to her and back, then reaches out to shake her hand.

"Hello, Mrs. . . . Ms. . . . ahem . . . nice to meet you."

It doesn't go so well.

"She didn't mean it," you tell him later. "And she can't do anything to you. She wouldn't even know how to find us."

"You're under eighteen and you told her my last name," he says.

"Oh. Oops."

He sighs.

"She won't sue you or whatever it was she threatened. And I don't care what she thinks."

"This is going to cause trouble for your dad, too, isn't it?" he says.

You look down. "She'll just call him and scream a little."

"And what about your friend? The one you told him you're staying with?"

You bite your lip. "I'll handle it."

He holds your head to his chest as you fall asleep and makes love to you in the morning.

It's Labor Day weekend and he breaks his studio schedule and takes you out for brunch and to the Ex where he rides the Octopus and the bumper cars and shares cotton candy with you. At night you drink cold beer and he rubs aloe vera on your sunburned shoulders and cheeks.

On the morning of September 5th he gives you a gift—his sketches of you.

When you ask why he's giving them, he says, "Shh." He kisses you and makes love to you and says your name for the first time. He says it over and over.

You wake in the morning and see him dressed and sitting at the foot of the bed. The expression on his face jolts you awake.

You sit up. "What is it?"

"I'm not the guy, Sixteen," he says.

"What guy?"

"The guy who can . . . I can't do this," he says. "We can't do this."

You reach for him, but he moves away.

"Let's be honest," he says. "Long term, this is not going to work."

"Yes it is! It can, I promise you—"

"You can't hide out here forever. You need to finish high school and then study art somewhere and you need to be with people your own age and not be hiding from your family, no matter how fucked up they are."

"No."

"And you'll leave me, Sixteen, someday you'll leave me. I'm not that great a guy and you're practically a kid, and I'm old and cranky and jaded—"

"I'm jaded too!" you insist. "We're the same."

"You'll leave me, or I'll leave you. We'll get bored of the sex and you'll figure out that you should have made up with your mother and finished school. You'll resent me."

You will not cry. You will not cry.

"I can learn everything I need to about art from you. That's the only education I need if I'm going to be an artist. And I won't be . . . we won't be like that because we . . ." You stop as you feel your voice breaking and then continue, even with the tears running down your face. "Caleb, we love each other, you know we do. And she can threaten all she wants—I'll fight. I'm willing to fight. And besides, in a year I'll be eighteen and I can do whatever I want."

He looks down at his lap and you see his Adam's apple bob down and up again.

"Mara," he says, "you're young and you're brave, but you haven't lived as long as I have. You don't know how it feels to be alienated from your family and up against no money and no success while a bunch of talentless fucks are out there selling crap for six thousand bucks a pop. You think you're brave enough, but your heart can break more times than you realize."

"I do know that," you whisper. "I know that already, that's why we understand each other."

"Pack your stuff, Sixteen, and then I'm taking you home to your mother."

"No."

"Let me be clear, I don't want this. I don't know if it's the right thing, or the wrong thing, but I don't want the mess. All I want, and what I *need*, is to work every day without the distraction of you, and the baggage that comes with you. I'm sorry."

"No."

"Better to have it hurt now and get it over."

He leaves you weeping on the bed and goes to pack your stuff. When your artwork, your toothbrush, your spare shorts, T-shirts, sandals and toiletries are collected by the door, he comes back to the bed with last night's clothes and forces you to put them on, while you, snotty and blubbering, nonetheless make a final attempt to seduce him.

He holds you tight and you feel him shaking.

"You don't want this," you say. "You love me and I know it—you don't want to do this. Please."

"Shhh."

The sight of you, crumpled and miserable on her doorstep, brings out Mom's softer side, and she gently helps you inside. She runs you a bath.

"I know it hurts, sweetie, but you'll get over it," she says.

"*You* never did," you say.

"Pardon me?"

"From Dad."

"I certainly did."

"Sure. That's why you still hate his guts. That's why you never dated again."

Her face goes blank and she leaves you in the bathroom.

You feel like dying. You don't even have the heart to hate her for causing you to lose the only man you'll ever love.

Senior year is supposed to be a big deal, but when school starts you can hardly bring yourself to attend.

A week in, you detour on your way home, and knock on Caleb's door.

He opens it and looks at you and you smile, trying to be brave and grown up and not a sniveling idiot like you were when he saw you last.

He has dark circles under his eyes and he hasn't shaved since you left.

"Can we be friends?" you say. "I'd like to be friends."

He shrugs, gestures you inside and shuts the door behind you.

"Can I hug you?" you say. "Friends hug. And you look like you need a hug."

You don't wait for him to respond, but put your arms around him and pull him in.

He says "Mm," and hugs back.

And after a few moments neither of you has let go. He presses himself closer and you think, "Ha."

And very soon you are without your pants and up against the door with his hands up your shirt and the door clattering rhythmically in its jamb.

September to November, you knock on his door in the late afternoons and every time you come together like it will be the last time.

You never stay long. You never ask him to talk.

You offer yourself and take what he gives and then go home.

You spend your nights aching and wake up lonely in your mother's house and go to school and grit your teeth and sneak away with Bernadette at recess and smoke and talk about the bullshit of it all.

Your midterm report card is not great.

Your life is not great.

But all you have to do is get through this year and create a portfolio and get into art school and then you'll be eighteen. And he will still want you and finally let you move in with him and there will be nothing anyone can do or say. It's not the best plan, but it's the best you can come up with. You will wait it out.

Only, one day he is not there.

And when you try your key in the lock, it doesn't work.

And when you call from a pay phone, the number has been disconnected.

You stand across from his building and stare up at his windows but dusk falls and no lights go on.

At home, when you take your books out of your bag, you find an envelope with your name on it. Inside it is a note, a drawing of your face and a photo of Caleb that he used to have on his fridge.

On the back of the photo, it says: *Mara—you said you liked this picture. Keep it. C.*

And the note says:

I've gone away, maybe for good, and a friend is subletting my place, so you won't find me there.

I'm sorry.

Love, if that's what it is, just doesn't conquer all, Sixteen. Lust conquers even less.

Work hard and become brilliant. Try to forget about me. C.W.

Chapter Twenty-four

Hugo pulls my hand into his coat pocket to keep it warm. The side streets of Cabbagetown are quiet and dim, people's tiny yards perfectly manicured even at this time of year.

We stroll toward Riverdale Park and Pollock does his business on the way. Once there, Hugo produces a glow-in-the-dark ball, unleashes Pollock and throws it. He shouts encouragement and the little dog dashes after the ball and then brings it back, tail wagging furiously, and waits for another throw. The game lasts until Pollock flops down a few feet away, his tongue lolling out the side of his mouth.

"Very cute," I say.

"Pollock?" Hugo beams. "Yeah, he's not bad."

"And you," I say. "The two of you together."

He smiles and ducks his head, which is also cute.

"Thanks for giving me time to recover," I say, and he nods like it was no big deal.

We collect Pollock and start walking back toward Hugo's.

"So . . ." he says.

"Yes?"

"Was that, ah, good crying or bad crying?"

I bump his hip with mine and he gives a surprised yelp.

"Good then? Good-ish?" he says, bumping me back.

"Yeah," I say, "good-ish."

"Okay," he says.

"Hugo?"

"Yeah?"

"Can we sit down for a sec?" I gesture toward a bench at the edge of the park and we walk to it and sit. Pollock sniffs at the leaves under the bench, finds a stick, and deposits himself at Hugo's feet to chew on it.

Brave and beloved, he called me. I don't feel so brave, but I have to try.

"What's up?" he asks, still holding my hand inside his pocket.

"Uh, not to lay anything heavy on you but . . . my last boyfriend . . ."

"Yeah?"

"He died."

Hugo gets very still for a moment and then goes, "Whoa."

"Yeah."

"Jesus, Mara!" he says. "Jeez. No wonder. My God."

"Sorry to . . . I know it's . . ." I trail off, not sure what else to say.

"Listen, don't be sorry. I'm glad you told me," he says. "You've got nothing to be sorry about."

I squeeze his hand.

"Ah . . . when did it . . . I mean, you don't have to talk about it but . . ."

"Five years ago. It was . . . there was an accident."

"Wow."

"His name was Lucas."

We sit and watch Orion rising up over the restored hundred-year-old row houses across the street. On the corner is an old-fashioned General Store and I wonder if Hugo and I might come here in the summer and buy ice cream cones, like normal, happy people who are in love. Then I wonder if Lucas can see me, if saying his name out loud brings him closer. I wonder what he would think of me now, sitting with Hugo and trying to envision a future. I wonder whether I will ever breathe air that is clear of his ghost.

"So, your reticence about dating," Hugo says, "your fear of getting involved . . . that's the reason."

"I guess so. But it was a long time ago. I should be over it."

"The soul doesn't experience time the same way the mind does," he says. "Have you had grief counseling or anything?"

"Um, sort of."

"Sort of?"

"I've . . . talked to people." Bernadette, my dad . . .

"And . . .?"

"And talking helps to a point and then it's about . . . time, I guess," I say. "Time and moving forward. And I'm doing that."

"Hm."

"I'll be honest, the counseling route didn't work that well for me. It was pretty short-lived," I admit.

"Well, it's not for everyone," he says.

"No."

Pollock is snuffling at our feet and looking bored, so we get up from the bench and stroll back to Hugo's.

Back inside, Hugo leads me to the couch. He takes my hands and rubs them between his to warm them.

"Thanks," I say.

He gives me a look.

"What?"

"I'm just digesting what you told me. You're a survivor."

I humph and look away.

"You are," he says, and then grins. "You're scrappy."

"Scrappy?"

"Absolutely."

"Well, that's not the most romantic adjective ever," I say.

He waggles his eyebrows at me in response.

I laugh and then reach out, pull one of his curls, and watch it spring back into place when I release it. He blinks in surprise and I do it again.

"I've been wanting to do that," I say.

"My hair is yours to command," he says.

I start laughing. "Careful what you say, I do strange things with hair."

"Really."

"So," I ask, seeing that he's still looking at me as though he really, really likes me. "Was your last girlfriend the most boring woman in the world or something?"

"What!"

"Because I'm trying to figure out why you like me, and all I can figure is that you were bored to tears by someone in the past and are breaking out in the opposite direction."

"I thought you didn't want to do this," he says with a teasing look on his face.

"Do what?"

"I think you called it 'the litany'."

"Oh, um . . ." I say, momentarily stymied.

"Ah ha!" he says, "but now you're curious. You want to know things about me."

"Don't be smug."

"Don't be surly," he shoots back.

"Well, hello!" I say, throwing my arms out, "you must be craving drama or something to still like me. It's like: 'screwed up, anti-social, crazy father, estranged mother, dead boyfriend—total package, wow, she's for me!' So I figure your last relationship must have been a snoozer."

"No," he says. "Not a snoozer, just not the right person."

"So you did have someone serious."

"I had the same girlfriend all the way through university and for a few years after. Things just . . . stopped working. She wanted to travel, I was unhappy working in insurance and wanted to go back to school to become a vet. We both started making plans and they didn't seem to include each other. It was sad, but it was just . . . over."

"And since then?"

"Nobody serious since then," he says. "Nobody that really intrigued me."

"And I intrigue you? Is that it?"

"There's that," he says. "Plus you're tough, smart, beautiful . . ."

"Oh my."

". . . Sexy."

"Ah ha."

"But maybe it's just because you make me laugh."

"Uh hunh."

"Or maybe it's because I like making you laugh," he says, and he reaches over to me and starts tickling me until I shriek for mercy.

Then we neck on the couch for a while, and even though we're both hot and breathing fast, we don't do anything else. I should probably feel fourteen again, except I skipped right past this part when I was fourteen. Now I wish I hadn't.

Chapter Twenty-five

6 a.m.: painting.

The bubble piece is turning out less-than-Zen and not very geometric.

A small departure, I tell myself, and totally within reason. And besides, my mind is riffing on bubbles: Hugo and me in our own cozy, lust-filled bubble, Bernadette and Faith in theirs, my father who has lived in and burst more of them than I care to remember . . .

Shut up and paint, Mara.

I dip my brush into the white then start the next round shape. When I'm done, it looks like a cracked-open egg instead of a bubble.

More departure.

Oh, yes, I am cracking open, maybe cracking up, finding it impossible to live the way I've been living.

I layer more color on, thankful that I'm using acrylics since they dry so fast, and fill in the egg thing, making it brighter and thicker. Creamy white and blue, a hint of metallic gold, it's a strange, shimmery egg, a tactile egg that threatens to seep in between the perfectly rounded bubbles.

What the hell is happening? I don't like asymmetry. I like clean lines, definite shapes. Things that have a beginning, middle and end. I like to have control over my creativity and I don't care if that's contradictory.

I leave the studio early for lunch.

As part of my self-healing act-like-a-normal-person regime, I have decided that today I will *go out* for lunch.

Woohoo, wild stuff.

I have a plan: I will walk along side streets, through the park, and then up to the Danforth again. I will buy a sub sandwich and an iced tea and a cookie. I will eat them in the shop. I will then take the same route home.

Feeling like a better-adjusted, stronger person, I will call the man I have a crush on and talk to him before going back into the studio to work.

People do these things every day, right? I used to do these things every day; at least, I assume I did.

And today I have a secret weapon . . .

I read somewhere that if you wear an elastic band around your wrist and snap it whenever you have a negative thought, you can break the pattern—kind of a low-tech biofeedback thing. It might have been a tool for quitting smoking—I can't remember—but I figure it'll work just as well for me.

So out I go, a thick blue rubber band on my wrist. Crossing the street, I give the band an experimental snap. The sound and the twinge on my wrist are quite satisfying.

I snap twice more and make it to the sub shop alive.

I manage to eat lunch without getting food poisoning, although it could set in later on, and I could be puking my guts out and then dry heaving, rushed to the hospital for dehydration. That is, *if* I could make it to the telephone in my weakened state, and what if I forgot to pay my phone bill! Have I? I make it to the phone but my service is cut off, so I stagger to my computer, send out an SOS, and then lay dying on the floor. Alone and dead. Alone, alone, no one knowing where I am or what has happened. Dying, dying, dead, starting to decompose . . .

Snap! Snap snap!

Ow.

On the way back, I make eye contact with two people, though one of them does say, "What?" Perhaps my gaze is too intense. Perhaps I shouldn't look at strangers. I could look at someone the wrong way and they might decide to shoot me, to beat me up . . .

Snap. As in, snap out of it!

Walking home through the park, I attempt to enjoy the fresh air. I envision myself as outdoorsy: going on camping trips, kayaking, learning to do an Eskimo roll, and sitting around campfires with Hugo and Pollock, and singing songs or roasting marshmallows or whatever it is people do at campfires. I would not be afraid of bears or malaria or getting lost because I would be a new person. A healed, healthy, better person. A person who does not get lost.

My wrist is rather pink by the time I close the front door behind me. But I am better. I must be getting better.

Bernadette drops by after work. She takes five minutes to vent about her boss and then says, "I'm in love with Faith."

I sigh. "That's what I was afraid of."

"I've loved her since high school, Mar, I can't help it."

She flops down on the couch and twirls a strand of hair around her finger.

"You obviously think I'm crazy," she says, and looks hard at me.

I sit down. "She seems nice, I'm just—"

"A mother hen?" Bernadette suggests, then softens the comment with a smile.

"Yeah, maybe."

"Don't worry, I'm a tough girl."

"Okay."

"And I'm happy." She sits up, leans toward me. "So, what about Hugo-boy-man-person? Is it still on?"

I feel my face color.

"Aha!" she says. "Very on!"

"It's going well. But I, uh, can't help thinking about . . . you know."

"Have you told Hugo?"

"Last night. He was sweet."

"That," she says, and taps my knee, "is what I would expect from him. I like him."

"Me too."

"This might be the year," she says.

"Of what?"

"Of us both finding happiness."

I make a humph-like sound.

She laughs at me . . . and hums on her way out.

——————

And then there was Lucas.

Second year, Art History, first row. White-blond hair and the most infectious laugh.

He is beyond beautiful. Everyone wants him—men and women alike.

You take two months edging from the back of the class toward the front, until you are arriving early in order to get a seat right behind him. You see him in Technicolor, in shades of sunlight. You dream of him, look for him in the hallways, then turn your eyes away when your paths cross.

You have no chance. And anyway, it's better to love from a distance.

One day he puts a hand on your arm and stops you as you walk by. "Mara, right?"

Your mouth opens, but no words come out.

"We're in Art History together. I'm Lucas."

Ab-da-da-ga-ga . . .

"It's a nice name," you finally manage to say.

"Thanks. My parents say it means 'light'," he says. "You think it suits you?"

He laughs and his mouth opens to reveal a row of perfect, shining teeth.

"Nobody's ever asked me that," he says. "What do you think?"

"I don't know, maybe you have a twisted soul. Maybe you like to torture gerbils or something." You're such a weirdo, such a dork—can't you come up with anything better to say?

But Lucas shakes his head and chuckles and stares at you.

"That's an interesting possibility," he says. "No gerbils yet, though."

"Good. That's good."

"Anyway, I missed class yesterday . . ."

"I know—it ruined my day."

"What?" He frowns.

Shut up, Mara!

"Nothing. Sorry."

His eyes narrow. "No, I heard you."

"Oh. I was kidding. Just kidding. You were saying?"

"I just wondered if I could borrow your notes."

"Sure."

"Thanks!"

His bright green eyes brim with curiosity and goodwill, and something about him demands to be liked. Something about him feels like everything you've never had and never been and must get close to.

But no one this good looking could possibly be this nice. And there's no way he'll ever be interested in you.

But the exchange of notes turns into coffee on campus and then beer drinking at Sneaky Dee's and a sweet, sloppy kiss outside at the bus stop in front of the graffiti art.

It's a remarkably short journey from his lips on yours to your hands in each other's pants to rolling around naked on your futon and laughing so loud that Bernadette bangs on the wall of your shared apartment.

And love is easy at first, because Lucas is easy to love.

Miraculously, he loves you back.

Though you're not quite sure he would if he really knew you, if he knew the things you've done and the family you have and the sad, dark, panicky places that come out and haunt you at night. He would never understand how being happy makes you sad. How the happier you are the more you know the sky is about to explode into tiny, sparkling shards of glass that will pick up speed as they fall to the earth and slice right through you leaving your skin with little holes in it, leaving your heart bleeding.

These are not things that touch Lucas, not things he would find logical or right or positive, and he is very logical, right and positive. These are things you love about him and that you need from him.

You keep quiet about the you that lies awake at night, twisting the corners of the sheets around your fingers while he sleeps peaceful dreams.

In the daytime, Lucas has big dreams—he wants to sculpt huge pieces, create entire dwellings that are works of art.

"Like Gaudi," he says. "Someday I'm going to make us a Gaudi house. Except the vision will be mine. We'll change the landscape."

You just want to paint and draw, but the idea sounds good, so you go along with it.

And there are nice things that you've never had before, like hugs, kisses on the cheek, ice cream at 3 a.m. And laughter, lots of laughter. It bubbles up and spills over, stains you with regret for what you've missed.

You are young and in love and finding out what it feels like to smile for no reason, and draw pictures of bumble bees with Lucas's laughing face, and make love on sun-filled afternoons, and sleep with your head on his shoulder and strands of your hair falling across his chest.

"I don't know what the big deal is," Lucas says over breakfast at his place. "People go away to school all the time."

"I know. I've just . . . never been without Bernadette. England is far."

"We'll visit her there, maybe travel a bit," he says. "I know you'll miss her, but you have me."

"I know." It's not the same, but he doesn't seem to get that. And you do have him, which means everything.

"Anyway," he says, "now that she'll be moving out, have you thought about where you're going to live in September?"

"No," you say. "Why?"

Lucas grimaces and looks away for a second. "My brother's coming back from military college and my parents are bugging me to let him live here with me."

"You never told me you had a brother."

"Half-brother. It's a long story," he says, and then abruptly segues into his next subject. "You want to move in with me?"

You give your head a shake, not sure you've heard correctly. "Sorry?"

"Move in with me."

"Uh . . ."

"Come on, it'll be great," he says, and reaches across the kitchen table to hold your hand.

"But why?"

"I just told you—"

"Because you don't want to live with your brother?"

"Not just because of that, I didn't mean . . ." He breaks off and takes his hand away. "If you don't want to, that's fine."

"Why?" was clearly not the response he was looking for—he's hurt . . . sulking.

Still, you know too well from Mom and Dad about the fallout when things don't work out, the price of moving too fast.

"Lucas, it's a big deal. It's not something we should do just for convenience."

His face and neck start to get red and he stands up.

Oh shit, oh shit.

"I thought we were going somewhere, I thought we were serious."

"I, ah . . ."

"So what's the deal, Mara? Is it just play for you? Just casual?"

His face is cold, angry. How did he get so angry so fast?

You want to speak but your throat is closing. Your mouth moves, but no sound comes out. This seems to piss him off more. He starts pacing, demanding an answer, but you can't answer. You can't speak at all. In your head, the voices of Mom and Dad are rising up, all the hateful words, all the shouting, the weeping, the screaming.

Mom crumpled on the floor, Dad throwing the pepper mill against the glass cabinet . . .

You grip the edge of the table and try to stop shaking. You must speak, you must do something . . .

Lucas slams a hand on the table.

Mom shouting, I'll fucking kill you, you son of a bitch! Wish I'd never met you, you lying bastard! Dad screaming back, Stupid cunt!

Help, help, help . . .

Liar, you're such a liar. Fucking slut. Loser, lowlife. Hate you. Hate you, wish I'd never set eyes on you. Get the fuck out, get the hell away from me and don't come back. I won't, up yours, you uptight bitch. Uneducated hack, fuck off and die . . .

Lucas is shouting in your face, waving his arms. The earth is sliding out from beneath you.

Then, just like every fight you ever witnessed, every fear you ever held, he leaves. Leaves and slams the door.

And it's over. Love always turns out this way.

In the bathroom, you puke until there is nothing left and your stomach is heaving out bile.

You huddle in front of the toilet and shiver.

Eventually you get up.

You will collect your things and go. One foot in front of the other, just get out, get home, get to Bernadette . . .

In the closet, your backpack is tangled up in a heap of laundry. It's too much, you can't move anymore.

Small. You need to get small. Curl up and hide.

You wiggle yourself into the corner between Lucas's Docs and an old camera case. Safe. Safe and dark. You are small and safe and dark.

Shhh, Mara, shhh, it's okay. It's okay.

You hug your knees and shut your eyes.

Shhh . . .

Shhh . . .

You wake in total darkness, which makes sense, you realize, because you are on the floor of Lucas's closet.

What possessed you to fall asleep here?

It's unfortunate to wake up like this.

But to wake up and find that the daylight is gone and he is gone and something has just landed on your arm and run down it with tiny, scratchy feet is horrifying. You've jerked awake and now there's no sound of movement around you. No sound, but something is there. You sit still, waiting. Soon enough you hear little scratching sounds, near your feet *and* above your head.

Holy shit.

Mice.

If you're lucky.

It could be rats. Or very large insects, perhaps a spider, a tarantula! You have to get out of this closet before one of them jumps on your head or runs up your shorts, but you can't see a fucking thing and what if you step on the one by your feet and it squeals or squishes and crunches and you feel its furry skeleton collapsing under your weight? Or you might just step on its tail and then it could bite you on the ankle and the other one might land on your head and . . .

And what if there are more than two!

You are holding yourself rigid, peering out the sliding doors of the closet into the gloomy grayish light of Lucas's room. For a moment you wish he was here and then your entire body aches. It's over.

Good thing he didn't find you here or he'd think you were a freak on top of thinking you are a . . . cold bitch. Yes, that's what it was.

If you are such a cold bitch, you should be able to move your damned limbs and get out of this closet without having a meltdown over a couple of harmless furry creatures.

For the moment there are no scratching sounds, probably because the little fuckers are watching you. You put your hands on the floor and push yourself up into a crouch. Your back is killing you and your knees feel permanently bent, but you begin to push yourself up.

Almost upright, you take one step forward. Something brushes your bare shoulder and everything inside you leaps up toward the ceiling. You shriek at the top of your lungs, whack your head, shriek again and then twist and hop and squeal your way out of the closet.

Someone else is shouting.

A shadow emerges from the bed . . .

Suddenly, the lights are on and you and Lucas stand, screaming, in the middle of his bedroom.

"What the hell—?"

"OH MY GOD, OH MY GOD, OH MY FUCK-ING GOD—!"

You hop up on the bed and point to the closet.

"Mice! Jumping on me!"

Lucas shuts the closet door and leads you out of the bedroom to the kitchen where you see his hair standing on end and goose bumps on his naked arms and a bewildered look on his face.

"What the hell? I've been looking for you all day," he says. "What the hell were you . . . Am I losing it or did you just run screaming out of my closet at two o'clock in the morning?"

"I'm sorry, I'll go," you say, and try to pull yourself together. "I know what you think of me, you don't have to explain. I'll just . . . get my stuff."

"No, you won't!" he says, and grips your arm. "I'm sorry we fought. I came back to tell you that, but you weren't here, so I went looking for you."

You burst into tears and he wraps his arms around you and then you pull back to look at him. Your tears turn to laughter and it is long minutes before you can explain any of it.

"If you still want to live together," you say, "we can't live here."

"Why not?"

"The mice."

"Mice?"

"In your closet."

"Oh. Right," he says. "Okay. You know, it was just a fight. It doesn't mean I've stopped loving you."

And you kiss him and tell him that fights scare you and when you seem cold it might actually mean that you're frightened because you don't really know how to fight and you've never done this before.

"What do you mean by 'this'?" he asks.

"You know, having a relationship, being together all the time . . . love."

"Ah," he says, "of course."

Chapter Twenty-six

You like your walls bare, but Lucas says it gives him the creeps.

When he moves in, he brings posters and you negotiate. He gets the walls of the living room. Over time, he gets more than that because his projects are everywhere. But everyone knows Lucas is brilliant—he cannot, *should not* be contained.

So, even if it feels crowded, living together is good. Falling asleep and waking up together is good.

And school is good too . . . except sometimes you feel small and dark in relation to the bright star that is Lucas. You begin to wonder if your paintings are too weird, too personal. Maybe to be a *real* artist you need to challenge people's assumptions, make political statements, explore bigger concepts. Or maybe you should be thinking about your future and how you and Lucas will ever make a living when his installations cost thousands of dollars to create. Maybe only one of you can be a real artist and maybe it's not going to be you.

Doubt is bad for art. You know it. You try to push it back, but it eats into your work, into your satisfaction with your work and soon painting starts to feel like a chore.

You speak to no one. It will pass and things will get easier.

You miss Bernadette—the one person who might understand what you're feeling. She has left a void that cannot be filled by Lucas and cannot be filled by letters or the occasional phone call. But you are loved by someone and there is a security in living together—a different kind of comfort.

"As long as you're happy, sweetheart," Dad says when you tell him about your cohabitation.

Mom says, "I brought you up to be smarter than this."

"After we finish school we'll travel the world," Lucas says. "I want to see Paris and Singapore and the Congo. And then we'll get married and have five children and live in a big, rambling old house that smells like candle wax and clay and paint."

"And paint thinner and dust and unwashed dishes," you add, shooting a look toward the sink.

"We'll have a maid," he says.

"With what money?" But you leave off, because there's nothing worse than Lucas when you doubt his dreams.

He teases you about your pragmatism, asks why you care if your art is saleable. He sculpts dead birds or crumpled pop cans, creates installations that fill entire rooms. His work is brilliant, but will anyone want to buy a beautiful sculpture of a dead pigeon?

You could watch him work for hours—a hangover from Caleb, but that no longer hurts.

Sometimes, sitting quietly inside the door to Bernadette's old bedroom as he works, you feel more *with* him than you do at any other time.

Once, you make the mistake of interrupting him. You take off your clothes and press yourself against the back of his flannel shirt. Your fingers go to the buttons of his jeans.

He leaps up, almost knocking you over.

"What the—?"

"I just . . . never mind. Sorry."

"No, no. It's okay, you just scared me."

"Sorry, sorry."

"I'd rather you didn't . . . I need space when I'm working, sweetie, okay?"

You bite your lip and turn your face away so he cannot see your tears.

In bed that night he whispers in your ear, "How about now?"

You shut your eyes and let him have your body.

Afterward, your thighs ache and your skin is raw.

"I love you," he says, and presses his sweaty body to yours.

"Me too," you say, and lie awake listening to him breathe.

Hugo and I are determined not to rush.

We go on another real date—dinner and a movie. We talk, we make out . . . I come to know the feel of his nose against mine and the exact contours of his mouth. I've never known a man's mouth so well—probably because with every man before this, I was too busy getting to know their penis.

I think about Hugo when I should be working, then work when I should be sleeping.

When Erik comes into my thoughts, I remind myself that he is the past and that I've done a good, strong thing. Every day with Hugo is proof.

Work is a problem, because I've lost control of it. Every time I sit down to begin a new rectangle or square, I look up hours later and find something else in front of me. Burst bubbles and cracked-open eggs are the least of it—now I'm channeling the unfinished paintings of a soul in purgatory.

When Sal calls to check on my progress, I stall. I have nothing for him, nothing I'm willing to share, anyway.

When Dad calls from the airport on his way to Puerto Vallarta, I have a bad day worrying and trouble sleeping for days. Mexico is a long way from home, from me, if—let's be real—*when* Dad's drinking gets out of control and he loses his emotional balance again.

"It means I'll be getting a call," I say on the phone to Hugo. "And this time I'll have to go to freaking Mexico to rescue him."

"But you never thought he'd actually make it that far in the first place," Hugo says.

"And your point is?"

"Maybe he'll exceed your expectations, maybe he'll be okay this time," Hugo says.

"I love your optimism, but no parent of mine has ever exceeded my expectations," I say.

"Oh."

"At least not in a good way."

"Got it," he says. "You okay?"

"Just worried."

"Want me to come over?"

"When?"

"Tonight. I'll bring dinner."

"Okay."

We joke about him taking advantage of my vulnerable state of mind and seducing me and we laugh, a little awkwardly, because the time is coming where we're going to have to do it. The whole buildup to sex thing is getting scarier by the day, and now I know why I never waited this long to sleep with someone. The longer you wait, the more intense your feelings and the more it feels like you'll never be ready. And things get weird.

We don't make out all night, even though that's what we've been doing every time we see each other. We don't even kiss.

We barely touch each other. We act like buddies.

He actually makes it to the door and goes to put his coat on before I say, "No."

"No what?"

"No, yes," I say.

"Yes?"

"Yes," I say. "Stay."

"All right."

He puts his coat down, moves toward me, runs his hands down my sides, kisses my cheeks, my forehead, the tip of my nose. He runs his fingertips up to my shoulders and then down the front of my T-shirt where my nipples come alive and ache to be touched.

I shudder at the heat of his palms and the friction of cotton on my skin, moan when my neck is kissed, my earlobe nibbled, my T-shirt lifted. Hands slide up my back, knead my muscles. Lips flutter kisses on my eyelids and his cheek rubs against mine.

I hear my name whispered, hands cover my butt and pull us closer, hip to hip, chest to chest. We rock into each other, sway on our feet as our mouths meet.

"Is it . . ."

"Yes?"

"It's not too soon?" he asks.

Um . . . My fingertips on his chest, my lips on his collarbone where he smells so . . . Sssooo . . . and he tastes . . . so very sweet and salty and . . .

And he is in my bedroom.

Too soon? Too late?

Hot skin, and the sounds . . . the soft whishhhh of clothing falling, sliding down, off our bodies to the floor.

Too soon?

We are bare and hot, entangled.

Not soon enough, not nearly.

We fall into and over and under each other, surrounded, slipping, subsumed with breath and heartbeat and heat that sears and need that howls.

And now it is too late, far too late, for it to be too soon.

Chapter Twenty-seven

So I have a lover.

A boyfriend.

A relationship.

And I come close to happiness, the weirdest, scariest state of all.

I paint in the day and I take my walks and talk to Bernadette and sleep with Hugo and begin to live like a normal person.

Sort of.

Because being happy makes me nervous, and living like a so-called normal person is not the same as being one.

Some nights I wake, drenched in sweat with visions of explosions and crashes and loss rocketing through my head.

"I'm sorry," I tell Hugo, "I have a lot of nightmares."

"Shhhh," Hugo says when it happens. "Shhh, it's not real, Mara, it's not real."

And I shake in his arms. "I saw . . . I was . . . You were . . . And then . . ."

Sometimes, in the depths of his eyes, I see that he finds my dreams as horrifying as I do. But over and over, he says, "It's okay, it's not real."

"But—"

"Look at me, I'm real," he says. "Here, pull my hair."

He offers his hair for pulling and makes monkey faces and cuddles and cajoles me until I can laugh, until I can sleep.

Sometimes if we are together during the day—weekends usually—I have day-dreads. I see him falling off an escalator, kidnapped, drugged, robbed, and left dying in a gutter somewhere. These things flash before my eyes and I banish them as fast as I can—snap! Snap!

Sometimes they won't go.

Perhaps I am too happy. I try not to let the universe know I am happy. If I am too happy, I will lose Hugo.

"You make love as if it's the last time," Hugo says one Sunday afternoon.

I nod.

"Always, every single time," he says, his breath still short and beads of sweat still hovering on his forehead.

"Yes," I say.

"Not that I'm complaining."

"I know."

He pulls me closer and draws his thumb along the line of my hipbone. I shiver and he places his palm on the goose bumps.

"I want to be with you like this forever," he says. "This is how it should be. I never realized it before, never had . . . this."

"That's good," I say.

"I want us to be like this forever."

"Mm," I say, "me too."

I shut my eyes tight. I try to seal in this feeling, to memorize it, to know the path that brought me here so I can always come back.

But that night I can't sleep. I wish he hadn't said anything, because fear and dread move through me like hundreds of tiny, spinning wheels that collide and clang and ricochet off of my stomach and lungs and heart.

Sometimes I get religious when I'm afraid. I start speaking to God like I did when I was a kid. I find myself offering deals, though we all know you cannot bargain with God, whether you believe in her/him or not. If you don't have faith on a normal day, I'm certain that God is unimpressed to have you show up on the doorstep to ask for an advance on your allowance or an extension of your life or whatever it is that has made you feel you are in extremity.

And yet I do it, because I don't know who or what may be out there, and you just never know what might help.

I try not to ask for much.

But I'm in love, and in the best of all possible worlds I would be allowed to have this love. I would be allowed to have this beautiful man who makes my soul feel lighter than I thought possible.

"He makes me laugh," I say.

I am sitting near the windows in my dark studio, clasping my hands and looking up at the sky.

My feet are cold but I do not move to tuck them under me or break my focus to go find a pair of socks. No, I am hard at work with wishing, also known as bargaining, and perhaps the universe will see my cold feet as an offering of some kind.

"Doubt is so easy," I say to the night sky. "Please help me not to doubt so much."

Moments of my parents' relationship flash through my mind.

"Please make him stay." But that seems wrong, coercive. "Please have him *want* to stay. Let me be right, let us be right for each other," I continue. And then, feeling frustrated with trying to find the right words, I close my mouth and try to lay my heart open. Perhaps all I am communing with is myself, but I visualize my awareness expanding outward and simultaneously pull myself open to ask for what I need.

And there, swimming in my ears and eyes, is Erik and beside him, Lucas.

Lucas with the eyes of a child.

Lucas and me and my failures, one leading to the next until finally there was death and no way to call him back, or do it over, or make it right. Not for me. Not with him. Not ever.

And there, in my memory, still alive beneath my skin, is the thing I fear: that somehow, with Hugo, I will lose myself—I will betray myself, and then I will betray us both.

I can't bear it.

Not again.

I make love as if it's the last time . . . because it might be.

"I can't believe she didn't tell me!" Bernadette says, and strides back and forth in my kitchen.

I sit and watch from my seat at the table. I'm feeling rather queasy at the news.

"You're the compulsive newsie—did you know it was her?" Bernadette asks.

"No," I admit. "I never made the connection."

It turns out Faith's mom—the scary evangelist of our youth—is a member of parliament, and a very outspoken one at that. Problem is, she's speaking out against gay marriage and has been from the beginning.

"And she's not one of those 'let them have equal rights but let's not call it marriage' people," Bernadette says. "She's one of the 'homosexuality is evil and gay marriage leads to bigamy, bestiality, and the legalization of incest' people."

"I know," I say, "and look at all those bigamists and sheep-fuckers that have come forward demanding equal status since they passed the legislation."

"Hey, sheep-fuckers are people too."

We laugh.

"Seriously though," Bernadette says, "Minister English is *way* far on the right."

I repress a shudder. "She tries to hide it, but she's still . . ."

"Scary," Bee says.

"Yeah. How'd she end up in politics anyway?"

"I guess Mrs. English got involved with a bunch of causes and then tried to get her husband to run, and he said: no thanks, but you go ahead. Apparently he's sort of . . . bookish. First it was the school board, then city council, and the next thing they knew, she had all this support and was running for parliament."

"Wow. So should I even ask how they feel about Faith's sexuality?"

Bernadette's shoulders droop and she sits across from me. "Faith hasn't, uh . . ."

"Told them?"

Bernadette shakes her head. "She gave me this speech about her private life being private and how there's no need for them to know."

"Uh oh," I say.

"And she . . ." Bernadette breaks off and gets up to pad back and forth on the linoleum again.

"She what?"

"She's gay. Not bi, not confused. But she goes on dates with men."

"What!"

"Her family and people from her church are always trying to set her up, and to keep anyone from suspecting, she goes."

"Bee," I say, and get up from the table to pour her some water, "you've got to dump her."

Bernadette's face crumples. "I love her though."

"But . . ."

"And she loves me, she told me," she says, and starts to cry. I wrap my arms around her and let her snuffle into my shoulder.

I've got a crisis on my hands.

I lead us to the front room, tuck her onto the couch with a fleece throw around her legs and feet, turn on the gas fireplace, and grab a box of tissues.

"I'm so happy with her when we're alone," Bernadette sniffles, "but she's paranoid in public—she won't even hold my hand on Church. She doesn't want to be seen near the village in case someone tells her family, so we spend all our time alone in our apartments. But she's so beautiful and sweet. I just feel, when I'm with her, like I'm . . . like I'm home."

"But Bee, how can you be with someone like that? How can it work?" I ask, trying to keep my voice gentle.

"I don't know. I just don't know. But I have to try. My family was, I mean, it's always hard to come out, but my family was great—pretty easy compared to most people's families."

"Still . . ."

"I'm just saying . . . I never had any real fear that I'd lose them, you know? I was scared, but I knew they'd come around, I knew they'd still love me," Bernadette says. "But Faith . . . for her, if she tells them, or if they find out somehow, it would be major. It would be major for her mom politically if it got out, and on a personal level they would probably disown her or try to lock her up or something."

"I know."

"You know that school they sent her to? In high school?"

"I knew they sent her away somewhere," I say.

"Well . . ." Bernadette sits up and leans forward. "It wasn't just an ordinary boarding school, Mara. It was like some kind of jail. It was one of those private schools in the Caribbean where they punish you with solitary confinement. They used to make her lie facedown on a concrete floor for looking at them the wrong way."

"Whoa."

"Can you imagine! And this was a 'Christian values' school," Bernadette says. "Freaking hypocrites who think they're following the way of God when there's no freaking way God would sanction people being treated that way, or that God would discriminate against people for loving each other," Bee rants. "It's just wrong."

"I know."

"Thinking about her there . . . I could cry for days. It makes me want to hit someone. And then I think, how can she love them? Her family, I mean. How can she stand to be surrounded by such bullshit, and why doesn't she just walk away? She could make a family with me."

"I don't know if you can walk away from family, Bee," I say. "You can try, but they're still there, still part of you."

"I know," she says. "I get it. And I get that she's scared. I don't know what to do."

"It's not much as far as advice goes," I say, "but maybe you just need to give it time."

"Yeah."

"See how it goes."

"I know," she says, and wraps her arms around her knees.

"Distract me," she says. "Tell me about you."

"Okay," I say.

"And let me get drunk and crash on your couch."

"All right," I say. "Let's go get you another drink and then I'll show you something really fucked up."

She gives me a nod and grins.

"Follow me," I say, and head for the kitchen.

Bernadette stands in the center of the studio.

I have pulled the new paintings out of their hiding place in the basement and leaned them up against the walls for her to see.

She looks from one piece to another, and for a long time she doesn't say anything. I'm afraid to look at her face, but I can see she is holding her left hand over her heart and she has been taking huge gulps of grappa, which is not an easy thing to do.

"This is all since you met Hugo?" she asks.

"Yeah."

She reaches out to touch something on one of the first pieces—a painted clump of my hair. She shivers and then steps back.

"Wow," she says. "Is this . . . what technique is this?"

"Puke-of-existential-angst-on-canvas?"

"Funny," she says.

"Seriously, I don't know."

"What about this one?" She walks over to a piece where I have layered the acrylic in huge, thick, circular sweeps and then, before it dried, carved the suggestion of a face into the paint.

"I was awake at night," I say, "and it just . . . there's no plan. It's like I get taken over and then hours later, I emerge, or wake up and . . . and this is what has happened."

Bernadette points at the face. "He was wrong for you."

My breath hitches. "Who?"

She turns to face me and I feel like her eyes might burn right through me.

"You know who," she says. "I've never said it, but he was wrong."

"Bee, don't."

She takes a step toward me. "He was wrong. And if he hadn't died, you would have figured that out. I'm sorry he died, Mara, I'm really, really sorry. And I'm sorry for what it's done to you, but you have to . . . Well, maybe you have to do this." She waves her hand toward the leaning canvases. "Maybe this will finally do it, but more importantly you need to—"

"Please don't start with the 'forgive yourself' bullshit!"

"There's nothing to forgive yourself for. You have to realize that you're allowed to keep on living. And he wasn't some kind of paragon. He wasn't perfect, Mara, and you're not the only reason your relationship was—"

"Stop!"

"About to break up!"

"It wasn't breaking," I say, staring her down. "It was broken. And I broke it."

Chapter Twenty-eight

In less than a month, Dad is back from Mexico and in treatment. I count myself lucky that he got himself home without my having to take the trip down.

Surprisingly, Shauna is still with him. I can tell from her voice that something has changed. She sounds grim but not hysterical the way she usually gets.

I head to the center, and as soon as I see the wedding band on her finger, I know what has changed.

"For better or for worse?" I say to her outside the door to my dad's room.

She nods.

"I would have come. Even if it was just the two of you on the beach." As I say it, I realize I actually mean it. I would have somehow managed to get on an airplane and gone down there to be with him. With them. This love thing is messing with me. Making me all mushy and optimistic.

"That's sweet," she says, "but I wanted to seize the moment."

"Are you sure you know what you're doing?" I say. "What you're getting yourself into?"

"I do," she says.

I take her by the shoulders and hold my face close to hers. Her big eyes blink but otherwise the gaze she returns is steady.

"Don't leave him then," I say, and hope my voice doesn't break.

"I won't."

I believe her. That is, I believe her as much as I ever believe anyone.

It doesn't happen all at once this time, but instead creeps up on me.

I tell myself it's just stress, but if it is stress, it also increases my stress and therefore . . . it does not get better.

With our bodies naked and Hugo's arms around me, suddenly I do not trust his hands.

Small patches of my skin, and then bigger chunks and then huge swaths, defect. They flinch and cry and ache— they flee from touch.

When I tie his hands to the headboard, Hugo thinks I'm being kinky. I hiss at him not to move and I refuse him my most sensitive parts and I shut my eyes and tighten my muscles and grind against him hard and fast.

I ask him not to talk, but what I really need is for him not to say he loves me and not to talk softly and not to invade my sore places with nice words or soft fingers or clean love.

I still come most of the time, which is something.

And Hugo is still amazed at how I always fuck like it's the last time.

He uses the words "make love," but I am not making love anymore. I am fucking. I am begging my body to stay with me at least for that.

I have dreams of Erik. I have dreams of Erik and Lucas and all of us together with paint brushes that we use to erase parts of each other's bodies.

I awake wet and take Hugo's wrists in my hand and hold them over his head and lower myself onto his cock as he struggles to emerge from the fog of sleep. Faces of the men I've fucked leap into my mind, and then superimpose themselves on Hugo's face. Lucas, Erik, Caleb, Sal and a few whose names I never learned look back at me and their eyes are filled with hatred, with want, with need. I take my hands to my eyes in an effort to banish them and Hugo, now freed, brings his hands to my breasts and squeezes.

I nearly scream.

I want to hit him.

It's not really him I'm seeing, it's just . . . hands . . . hands that want me, that want to do things to me and make me feel, and make me surrender and push past who I am and who I need to be and poke and prod and squeeze where I am young and raw and hurt. I cannot be touched. I might lose my mind. I might scream and howl for centuries. I might break into small, bleeding fragments and never be whole again because there is no safe place, no safe place . . .

I don't hit him.

I have felt this before and while most of me is roaring, still another part holds me in an icy grip and says, "Stay. Stay or you will not find love again. Stay because you will be alone. Stay, you fucking loser, because you are a freak and you must hide it and you do not deserve love."

I push everything away, all the voices, all the emotions, all the pain. I push it back, push it down. I put my hands on Hugo's hands and hope he does not know the real reason for my panting. I draw his hands from my breasts and put them on my hips.

"Hold me there," I say, and start moving again. "Hold me there and don't let go."

He does what I ask and I lay myself down so my breasts are on his chest. I wrap my arms tight around him so nothing, no intruding hand or finger or mouth or tongue can get between us. I bury my face in his neck and squeeze my eyes shut. I move my hips in tight circles, hoping he will come fast.

Don't cry, Mara.

Don't you fucking cry.

I lay awake all night, failure in the bed beside me. Failure lies awake too and smirks at me, taunts me. Failure says I am, again and still, less than I need to be. I am wired wrong, broken, unable to control reactions that are, in face of the facts, ridiculous.

Erik would laugh if he saw me now. No, that's not true. He wouldn't be surprised, but he wouldn't be so cruel as to laugh. And I can't help thinking, if he were the one having sex with me, he would know.

In the morning Hugo and I have coffee, then he goes to work and I go to the studio. I mix my colors, sit down, and force myself to trace a circle. Around me are the Uglies, as I've dubbed them, left out from showing Bernadette, and the other new pieces, which are also disturbing and too weird for furniture stores. They reproach me as I begin to fill in the circle with even, controlled strokes.

I must have something for Sal.

I must regain some control, some simplicity.

I paint over last night, erasing it with each stroke of midnight blue. I yawn and sip my coffee and try to stack my insides up, creating order and space.

But every breath reminds me, takes me back to that moment of searing, of inner chaos, of the battle that has raged in me so many times, that I hoped I could escape with Hugo.

I cannot escape.

And that means everything I have been building can tumble down in an instant and my love and my hopes can become bleeding, crumbling dust.

It takes me a while to realize the noise I'm hearing is knocking on my back door.

I look outside.

"Fuck," I say.

It's Sal.

I go to the door, open it, and step forward so I'm leaning on the frame and, hopefully, blocking his view of the studio.

"Yo, babe!" Sal says. "You gonna let me in or what?"

"Hi, Sal. Um . . ."

He grabs me in the two-cheek kiss and then gives me the customary butt slap.

"I haven't heard from you, so I thought I'd better, ya know, come and check you out."

"I'm fine," I say, still attempting to block the door even though it's freezing outside.

"Since when do you leave me in the yard?"

"Oh, well . . . I'm working Sal," I say. "I'm kind of . . . into something."

"You're actin' like you got somebody tied up naked in there."

"Ha ha."

"Hey, don't think I've forgotten what you're like."

"Sal—"

"You're a fuckin' demon, babe. It's been years, but I swear to God, my dick still hurts!"

"There's no one tied up in here, Sal."

"All right, well let me see what you're doin' then, cuz I got five furniture stores busting my balls for more of your stuff."

He pushes past me, and I step aside and follow him in.

I point toward this morning's work, hoping somehow that he won't see what lines the walls.

Fat chance.

He stops mid-stride on his way to the easel and lets out a bark of surprise.

"What the fuck!"

Jesus. He's going to hate them. Or worse, he might like them. There is no way I'm sending them out into the world, it would be like strangers reading my journal, not that I keep one . . .

I can't tell from the look in his eyes if he loves them or hates them. Fuck. I start to babble.

"Oh, Sal, those are nothing. I was, um, playing around. I was blocked. And as you can see they're just experimental, well, shit. I'm going to paint over them and start over because I know none of your customers would . . . Actually I might burn them. As you can see, I'm back at the geometrics. You don't have to worry."

Sal turns to face me and his look shuts me up.

"I've done a lot for you, babe."

"I know."

"And nobody lies to me. It gives me hives."

"I'm . . . I haven't been."

"You been hiding this stuff from me?"

"Um . . ."

"And lyin' about it? Yes or no, babe?"

"No. I mean, yes. I have been hiding it, but . . ."

"YES OR NO?"

"Y-yes." I close my eyes. How could I have forgotten about Sal's temper?

"There's a thing called loyalty, babe," he says, his voice dangerously quiet now.

There'll be no talking to him. That is, if I *could* talk to him, if I didn't feel like I was being strangled.

"So," he says, walking right up to me. "Who'd you make a deal with?"

I try to swallow.

"Who's buying it?"

A bead of sweat runs from my armpit and down my side. He likes them. He thinks they're good. I open my mouth but nothing comes out.

"You told me you couldn't paint like this anymore and I fucking believed you."

All I can do is shake my head.

"You got a deal with somebody," he says, his voice dangerous and low. "You were gonna keep giving me this . . . this geometric shit and let me keep sellin' it to piddly fuckin' furniture stores and all the while you were capable of this?! What the fuck!"

His arms start waving and suddenly he is raging. I'm terrified.

"YOU GOT NOTHIN' TO SAY, IS THAT IT? NOTHIN' AT ALL?"

My legs start to shake. I open my mouth, then shut it.

Apparently not.

"Well, babe, your silence is fuckin' deafening."

He marches toward the door.

"Go get yourself a job, chicky, cuz' there won't be any more deposits from me. We're done."

He slams the door hard enough to make the windows rattle, and then storms to his car and drives away.

I hear the tires squealing and I sink to the floor and bury my face in my hands.

When I can speak again, I call Bernadette at work. She arrives within an hour with ice cream and chocolate syrup.

I am too sick to eat.

I try not to cry as I tell her about Sal.

"It's a disaster," I say in conclusion.

"You probably don't want to hear this, but you're better off without him," she says.

"How can you say that? Without him I have NO MONEY, Bernadette! No money, no livelihood, nothing."

"Yes but—"

"You're suspicious of him—you've always been suspicious of him."

"And my suspicion is now confirmed!" she says. "No matter what his intentions, he has too much power over you. And I don't like that you've felt you had to just . . . crank out the same kind of stuff over and over."

"I thought you liked my 'stuff'."

"I do, but . . . I remember, Mara—I remember the work you were doing before you started dating Lucas."

I flinch.

"You had a chance. But instead you met him and started to close up. And then he went and died and you holed yourself up here with barely enough money to live on and started painting circles and squares like some kind of lobotomized zombie-genius. And now, when you finally start to try something new, you feel the need to hide it from your supposed mentor."

"I didn't hide it because of him," I protest. "I hid it because I didn't like it—it's crap."

"It's not crap, Mara, and I'm sure you know it."

And here, suddenly overwhelmed with everything that's been going wrong, I burst into the tears I've been repressing.

"It is crap!" I sob. "Everything is crap!"

Bernadette grabs me and holds me by the shoulders.

"Shh," she says. "Shh, it'll be okay."

"It won't," I say. "Because it's not just Sal. Everything is going wrong . . . with Hugo too."

"What about Hugo?"

Shame fills me and though Bernadette is my closest and only real friend, the thought of explaining is almost too much. Fighting with the shame, though, is the need to tell someone, to confess it, to get it out.

"I can't . . ." I start. "There's something wrong with me. And I can barely . . . I can barely have sex."

"Okay . . ." she says. "Tell me."

"Last night while we were in bed, I nearly hit him," I confess. "I came really close."

Bernadette frowns.

"I don't get it," she says.

"Neither do I. I start feeling so . . . violated. It starts to hurt, not physically, but psychically, emotionally—although I guess I feel it physically."

"Has he done something to you?!" Bernadette asks. "Has he hurt you, or forced you into something?"

"No, no! No, Bee, that's not what I meant. He's been great, very sweet."

"So . . . is the sex bad? Is he bad in bed?"

"No, up till now it's been amazing—he's good. But all of a sudden it's like my skin, the surface of my skin is one huge bruise, or an open wound and Hugo is, with his hands, poking into the wound, pressing on the bruise. It's my skin, my skin and his hands. He touches me and I want to deck him."

"You're sure he hasn't done anything?"

"It's not him, Bee, it's me."

"How do you know?"

"It's happened before."

Bernadette's eyes widen. "With Lucas?" she says.

"Yes."

"Ah ha . . ."

"Only when there's love, it seems."

"So with Sal, and with . . ." she grimaces, not wanting to say his name.

"Erik," I say for her.

She nods.

"Never happened," I say. "With them, or any of the others, the casual ones, it's always been easy."

Bernadette shuts her eyes and shakes her head.

"Mara, Mara . . ." she says. "Why didn't you tell me?"

Chapter Twenty-nine

"Honey?"

"Hi, Mom," you say. "How's it going?"

As if ringing her doorbell at midnight is a normal occurrence.

"What's wrong?" she says, and pulls her robe tightly around her.

"I need help."

"What is it?" Her eyes are sharp—she quickly notices the taxi waiting on the street. "Who's in the cab?"

"He's sick, Mom. He's really sick."

"Lucas? You'd better take him to emergency."

"No, um . . ."

"You want me to come?"

"No. Mom, it's not Lucas. Lucas is fine, but he's, um, he has to finish his thesis piece or he'll fail the year, so I can't disturb him."

"Then who—?"

"It's Dad. He won't go to the hospital and I can't handle him by myself. He's sick."

Her posture changes—she stiffens, stands up straighter.

"Mom?" you ask when the pause gets too long. "Please, will you help me? Can I bring him in? I don't think he'd hurt anybody but he's . . ."

"Drunk?"

"Well, yes."

"Take him home and chuck him in a cold shower."

"I can't take him to his apartment, Mom. If he causes a disruption he'll get evicted again. And I can't take him home because Lucas . . ." You trail off. "Because there's no room at our place."

She considers it, glancing from you to the car and back.

"No," she says finally. "I said I would never let that man in my house again, and I meant it. I'm sure there's something else you can do with him."

"But Mom . . ."

"I gave years of energy to him, honey, and I'm done. Some people will suck you dry, Mara. Maybe you need to ask yourself if this is doing you any good."

"He's my father."

"Nevertheless."

She's saying no. She's actually fucking refusing.

"What am I supposed to do with him? He's gone crazy, Mom, he's not just drunk."

She looks you straight in the eye and says, "Some people have to hit bottom before they're willing to change, Mara. Maybe you have to let him hit bottom. Stop rescuing him."

You hear shouting behind you and you look back to see Dad lurching out of the taxi.

"Uh oh," you say.

Mom steps back from the doorstep.

"Do you need money for the cab?" she asks.

"No thanks." You lift your chin, fight the tears. "I don't need anything from you."

"I'm sorry," she says, and shuts the door.

By the time you get Dad back into the taxi, the driver insists on taking you to the police station. You beg him not to, but he radios ahead and by the time you get there, two uniformed officers are waiting.

"You promised," Dad says.

"I'm sorry, Dad. I'm so sorry."

He tries to fight, which makes it all worse.

Lucas opens the living room door with a flourish.

"Ta da!" he says. "What do you think?"

You haven't seen the inside of this room for a month—since Lucas began his grand effort to finish his thesis piece on time. It'll be nice to have the room back, to sit on the couch, look out the window . . .

Or not. Because the couch, what was the couch, has been transformed. The entire room has been transformed. The walls and (beautiful hardwood) floors are painted glossy black. The wooden arms of the couch and chairs have been covered in a papier-mâché of dollar bills and newspaper and the cushions have been completely resurfaced with tennis balls, all sitting shoulder to shoulder. There is cardboard duct-taped to the window and the only light comes from a blinking string of blue and red Christmas lights.

You stand very still.

"Check this out," Lucas says, and practically bounces past you into the room. He points to a pair of jeans he has shellacked to the floor. They're yours. Your eyes now follow the path of the jeans and then land on another piece of clothing—a beige bra. Next is a T-shirt, then a sock, and finally, crumpled on the floor in front of the couch, a pair of not-so-new yellow cotton underwear. All of it is shellacked to the floor. All of it is yours.

The couch, all the furniture, everything in the room, is yours—carefully chosen and bought with hard-earned bartending money, with the job you got at nineteen when you realized you had to pay your way through school.

Lucas has a trust fund. Lucas has never had to preserve things like clothes and furniture because he could always replace them. Without working for it. Lucas has never stood for hours in beer-soaked running shoes. Never had his butt pinched while carrying dishes of half-eaten chicken wings, never had smoke blown in his face by creepy, drunk men who he smiled at anyway because he needed the tip. If he had, he might have hesitated to ruin your furniture.

Not a lamp has been left unmolested.

"I'm calling it *Life Inside*," he says.

"Hm."

How about: *I Stole My Girlfriend's Panties and Glued Them to the Living Room Floor*?

"You like it?" he says.

Do you like it?

Um, no. You're fucking furious. And frozen. Because fury comes up against fear and neither wins. You can't say anything because then you will fight and bad things will happen. Nothing good ever happens when people fight, only screaming, words as weapons, points for damage done. It doesn't matter what he's done, you can't fight, you won't. And yet you want to rip him into shreds for this.

Do you like it?

The answer is supposed to be yes.

"Very unique," you say and hold your arms rigid at your sides. You will not fight, you will not fight.

"Cool, huh?"

Breathe. Cool air in, warm air out.

"Cool. Mmhmm. How is the committee going to see it?" you say, but you already know the answer.

"They have to come here!" Lucas says. "The whole faculty can just come here!"

Of course. Who needs privacy?

"So what else? I want your opinion," he says.

"It's . . . shocking." You are under control, you are fine.

He grins. "That's what I was trying for."

"I just hope we don't get evicted."

"Imagine the publicity if we did though," he says.

Your eyes keep going back to your crumpled underwear, on the floor for everyone to see. Your urge to clean it up is going to get you exactly nowhere.

You can only hope he didn't take it from the laundry bin.

"What's wrong?" he says.

"Nothing."

"No, really."

"I, um," carefully, gently. "No big deal, I just wish you'd asked me."

"Oh, you mean about the clothes?"

Duh.

"All of it. I mean, this is my furniture—*was* my furniture."

He gets that look in his eyes, the wide-eyed wounded look.

"I no longer look at things as yours or mine," he says. "We're together."

"Yes, but—"

"I thought you'd understand—this is art. Art is for everyone. Art is to be shared."

"Does my underwear need to be shared though? Do we have to sacrifice my furniture?" You try to say it with a laugh, with a funny shrug and a touch of irony. No fight, nothing serious, just a little cajoling to make the point.

But Lucas looks incredulous, isn't buying it.

"Do you hear yourself?" he says. "*My* this, *my* that—if we're going to talk that way, then what about me? What about my chance to prove myself? We only have a few weeks left and then we're out in the world. I need to have something to show for my schooling—something big. You can replace the furniture, but my reputation? I have to *build* it. Why do you have to ruin this for me?"

"But did you have to—"

He shakes his head.

"I never realized you were such a pedant," he says, and then strides over to the couch and rips a tennis ball off, revealing the glue-encrusted fabric beneath.

"What are you doing?"

"Taking it apart. You win. You can have your couch back. And your damned underwear."

His rips off another one and looks at you. "Happy? Come on. Come and help!"

He reaches for a third.

"Stop!" you say. "Stop it. It's fine."

"Oh no, it's no problem," he says. "I'm sure I can whip up something else by the end of the week."

He'll fail. He's neglected to hand in a lot of projects, done badly in his academic courses, and been warned that his thesis project better be impressive. He'll fail and he'll blame you. He'll leave you.

And you'll prove to yourself, once again, that you are incapable of sustaining a relationship.

Besides, it's not his fault that he hasn't had to work as hard as you have, not his fault he doesn't understand. You are the one who is damaged, who is freakish and possessive and unable to let things go.

"I'm sorry," you say. "Please stop. Leave it."

He pauses, studies your face.

"Really?"

He's not perfect, but he loves you. He loves you and he has stayed with you. No one else has stayed.

"Really. I think it's brilliant. I was just . . . a little surprised, that's all."

His face, his entire demeanor changes and he is once again beautiful, sweet, warm.

He picks you up and twirls you in a circle.

"You are the absolute best," he says, and kisses you. "I don't know how you put up with me."

〰️

After the big showing—the tromping of half the school through your apartment and into your living room—Lucas is ecstatic.

You have dinner at China Lily. His blond hair is shaggy and his dress shirt is wrinkled, but he still looks like an angel to you. A fallen angel perhaps, especially with the bags under his eyes.

Graduation looms, and so does the future.

Your classmates have lofty goals, but you are living with a dreamer, so you've been trying to create art people will actually buy. Otherwise there is far too much waitressing in your future. Some of your professors are disappointed, but it's not like they're going to fail you.

Lucas nudges your knee with his under the table.

"Thank you for your patience," he says.

"With what?"

"My thesis project. I realize now I should have asked you, but I was so inspired, and I wanted to surprise you. I just didn't think. I was a bit obsessed."

"That's okay."

"I get carried away sometimes," he says and then looks down at his hands. "And I know I can be selfish. I'm sorry."

"Oh, Lucas, you're passionate, you're an artist. It's part of what makes you talented."

He grins at the compliment. "It's nice of you to say that, but I want to be nice to live with too. And I'm not the only talent in the household."

It's your turn to grin.

"We have a wild future ahead of us. We should move to Prague," he says. "We can live cheap and travel Europe, sell our work to boutique galleries until the big ones recognize us."

"What about our families?" you ask.

"They'll still be here, sweetie."

"And my Dad?"

"We'll come back every few months to visit."

You sigh. "I worry."

"You worry too much. We're going to make a life together, Mara, I've known it since we met."

You smile and tell yourself how lucky you are to have such a guy, such a talented, beautiful guy who loves you. If he's a bit idealistic, acts like a spoiled child sometimes, well, you're not exactly a prize yourself.

And most of the time you're happy. At least, you think so.

Maybe once you're away from here, out of school, far from your families and your too-small apartment, you might be able to feel your happiness.

Because though Lucas is right beside you, though he is holding your hand and staring into your eyes with love, there is always that part of you he cannot reach, a part of you he does not even know is there.

Someday he will, though. These things take time.

Later, in bed, your skin wants to creep from his.

You begin to have headaches and avoid bedtime.

You wonder why your body has abandoned you.

But perhaps your body thinks you have abandoned it.

Lucas begins to notice. He asks if you still find him sexy and if you still love him. You start giving more blow jobs. You try to keep clothes on during sex so he can't touch you.

"If there's something wrong, you can talk to me about it," he says one day when you won't let him touch your stomach. "I'm your friend too."

"I'm fine," you say. "Just stressed."

He gets a phone call from his mother one Sunday afternoon and afterward loses his customary sunny demeanor. When you ask him about it, he shakes his head and rolls his eyes but doesn't tell you anything.

You wonder if you are frigid.

But if you were frigid, you don't think you'd be fantasizing about the new model in Life Drawing class.

On the day he appears, disrobes, and poses on the podium, you feel hot where you haven't in months. It would be a relief, except it doesn't go away. What is it about him?

It could be his body—he's tall and lean and reminds you of Caleb. His hair is long, loose, and red, and freckles cover his torso and thighs.

It could be the scars on his arm. It could be the way his eyes hit yours and held that first time, and the way he shook his head as if to dismiss a strange thought when he finally looked away.

Day by day, you see more of his eyes.

You know him. You don't *know* him, know him, but you understand something about him—you are the same inside.

Your drawing professor watches over your shoulder as you draw him and she says, "Yes, yes, that's it exactly."

On his last day, you take a long time packing up, and he takes his time getting dressed.

Chapter Thirty

I hang up, put the receiver down and groan.

"What's going on?" Hugo says.

We're chopping vegetables, a novel activity in my kitchen, and Pollock, now a frequent visitor, is standing by waiting for bits of food to drop from the counter.

I try to pin down a baby carrot in order to slice it.

"You really want to know?"

Hugo "accidentally" drops a piece of sun-dried tomato on the floor, and Pollock dives for it.

"I love gossip," he says. "So . . .?"

"Short version," I say, "Bee wants Faith to come out to her parents, which will cause a major hoopla and possible schism in Faith's family. Faith accuses Bernadette of being equally in the closet since the people at Bee's work don't know—"

"It's not quite the same thing," Hugo says.

"I know. So. Things got ugly and Faith has now accused Bee of being a hypocrite not only for the work thing, but also because she is working for a patriarchal, wasteful, consumerist industry whose sole purpose is to make money off of women by making them feel shitty about themselves, while at the same time purporting to be a feminist, environmentalist and gay rights activist."

"Wow," Hugo says. "Hey, do you have oregano?"

"No."

"Basil?"

"Nope."

"Chives?"

"Uh unh. Onion salt?" I suggest.

He looks at me and shakes his head.

"Cheese?" he says, and gives me a hopeful smile.

"Jackpot!" I open the fridge and pass him a block of La Roche blue cheese.

He whistles.

"I may not have herbs, but expensive, stinky cheese is another matter," I say.

"I like stinky cheese," he says, taking a whiff. "So, back to Bernadette being a hypocrite in a patriarchal consumerist industry."

"Well, now she's miserable and thinking about quitting her job."

Hugo turns to me, offers me a hunk of cheese, and pops it in my mouth.

"Yum."

As we work, I keep glancing over at him, like he might not be real. I have to keep checking.

We put our homemade pizza in the oven and turn on the timer. Pollock, presumably exhausted from begging, has passed out sideways on the floor.

"Twenty-five minutes," Hugo says. And then he turns to me. "What are you doing for the next twenty-five minutes?"

He's got that look in his eyes. It's the look all men get in their eyes, especially the ones that like you *and* want to fuck you—warm and fuzzy with a hard-on.

"Not much," I say.

He smiles. Desire doesn't even get a chance before I feel tightness descending on my stomach and fear chasing circles inside me.

What is wrong with me!

Nothing. Nothing whatsoever. I let him pull me toward him. Our lips meet. I kiss back. I *want* to want to. I think, *Hugo, Hugo, it's Hugo.* I try to focus my senses, to smell him, to taste him, to recapture the desire I had for him just a few days ago.

Come back! Come back!

I press myself closer but my body is saying, *I'm not coming with you, you stupid bitch—exit! Exit!*

I break away from the kiss. I hold him tightly and hide my face in the crook of his neck.

"You okay?"

"Yeah, um, can we just . . ."

"Sure," he says.

We stay wrapped around each other and I squeeze him hard.

I could do it. I could make myself do it and I could fake it so he wouldn't know, as I did hundreds of times with Lucas.

But Lucas deserved better and so does Hugo.

Hugo does not deserve to make love to my fake, to my cringing double. And if I do it, someday he will see it's not me making love with him and by that time, as much as I love him, I will also hate him. I will hate him for taking my unwilling body and not seeing, for so long, that part of me that hides, crying, in the corner.

As we stand there, he begins to shift his weight from one foot to the other and soon we are swaying side to side. He has not asked me any questions. He has not tried to resume his seduction. He holds me and we execute a rocking, music-less dance.

I begin to relax and let the heat of his body transfer to mine. I am safe for now.

With every breath comes the knowledge that Hugo is precious to me.

But how can I keep him? How can I make his face the first I see in the morning and the last I see at night? How do I keep him alive and healthy and safe? How do I keep him faithful and sane? How do I keep him in love with me?

Because *this is the love I want*. This is a good love, a love that could be right. And if I accept it, if I give back to him what is in me to give, I will have purchased him with my soul. My soul, that has been broken and cobbled back together, with some of the pieces not quite fitting right. And though I believe in time healing these things, still, I do not love with lightness, and I do not hope with confidence and though what I need is forever unconditional, I do not believe in it. I have no evidence to make me believe in it. Oh, how I wish I did.

Under my face, Hugo's T-shirt is damp with my tears. He is still holding me tight and his hand is rubbing my back in warm, slow circles. I didn't realize I was crying.

"Sorry," I whisper.

"Shh," he says. "It's okay."

"People do this," I say.

"Do what?"

"People manage to do it all the time, right?"

"Um . . ."

"I want to know," I say, "is it safe?"

He keeps rocking.

"Is what safe?"

"Is it . . . would it be safe . . ." My voice is now nearly inaudible, but I continue speaking into his neck. "Will it ever feel safe to love you?"

He stops moving, stops breathing even, just for a moment. Then he continues the rocking, holding my body still closer to his.

"I don't know," he says. "I don't know if love is . . . supposed to feel safe."

"That sucks."

"Maybe. If we're in it though, if we're in love," he continues, "we're equally unsafe. Maybe there's a safety in that."

"Maybe."

He pulls his head back and cradles my face in his hands.

"I'll love you the best I can," he says, and there are tears in his eyes. "That I can promise."

I swallow the lump in my throat and nod.

"Okay. Me too," I say.

He kisses me.

And the lips kissing him back are mine, fully, willingly mine. And a sliver of relief slides in. We move our lips slowly, touching each other with our faces—cheeks, noses, chins, eyelashes. I am finally wanting, and thinking about us naked on the dining room floor when the buzzer goes off on the stove and the dog starts howling.

We laugh and kiss one more time and go to retrieve our dinner.

I have retrieved myself, at least for the moment.

⟋⟍

Life as a so-called normal person includes dinners out and political discussion and double-dating with Bernadette and Faith.

Double-dating with Bernadette and Faith includes witnessing them fight and being asked to take sides in their ongoing personal/political dispute about Faith coming out to her family and Bernadette coming out at work.

We are deep in the west end, in a funky underground restaurant where no one from Faith's family would venture. It's dark and features wild paintings of orgies on the walls and sparkling 50s vinyl benches. Ani DiFranco plays on the sound system and Bernadette's hands and arms move in punctuation to the dialogue.

And then . . .

Then there is Erik. Where he should not be.

Erik, who should exist inside his apartment and nowhere else.

Of course he must go out. He must have a life apart from what I see, but I've never imagined it.

And now here he is, loose on the streets of Toronto, loose in the same bar as me and my new, normal life. Here he is at the next table, staring at me, witnessing me in my escape from who I really am, and from what I, what we, have done together.

Erik, Erik, Erik. Where he should not be.

———

A few words, alone in a classroom . . .

"I'm not free," you say, your first words ever to him as he lets his eyes rest on you, his message clear. "Not really, not for . . . not to . . ."

"Everyone is free," he says.

"Yes, but . . ."

"Don't bore me with boyfriends or guilt or bullshit justifications," he says. "I don't give a rat's ass."

"Okay."

"I've seen you looking at me."

"I'm supposed to look at you," you say, "I've been drawing you."

"You're not drawing me now."

"No," you say, with too much hot, fast liquid pulsing through your veins. "No, I'm not."

The classroom door locks so easily.

And then you feel alive, really alive, for the first time in so long. Your locked-up self slides free and wants to put aside future and love and responsibility. She wants the eyes and hands of a strange man on her, wants to let the clothing fall off of her.

You let her.

And you let Erik into your breath, into your blood and bones, into you. Where he should not be.

My fingertips are cold and I have lost track of the conversation. Faith is looking at me, waiting for a response.

"I'm sorry," I say, blinking. "Excuse me, I have to . . ." I gesture toward the back of the bar and stand up.

"You okay?" Hugo asks.

I give him what I hope is a bright smile. "Perfect," I say, and start walking.

There are stairs, and before I'm down them I hear another pair of feet descending. At the bottom, with my feet safely on the orange-painted concrete, I turn to meet him.

For a moment we stand looking at each other, two or three feet of air and space between us. He seems even bigger, takes up more space than I remember.

I swallow.

"Hello," Erik says.

I cross my arms over my chest and try to slow my breathing.

"Hello," I say.

"It all makes sense now," he says. "But you forgot to mention your new boyfriend. He is new, isn't he?"

"Yes."

He exhales. "Well, that's good. If you're happy . . ."

"So far."

"Good," he says, and looks away.

"Uh, how are you?" I ask.

"Fucking great," he says. "Thanks for asking. You take care."

He moves past me toward the door to the men's room. In the second he is brushing by, the scent of him hits me—sandalwood, Scotch, sex, pot—and my mind is filled with a hundred, thousand, million moments of us naked, burning, hurtling toward each other and colliding with sweet, sickening, bottomless need.

"Erik," I call after him, my voice strangled by memory.

He freezes, his back still to me.

"Don't," he says.

"Don't what?"

He comes back to stand in front of me, too close to be casual, should anyone be looking. I glance up the stairs. His hand reaches up, touches my cheek and I don't stop him, then he closes the distance between us until we are pressed together, hip to hip, chest to chest.

I take a step back and run into the wall.

His hand whips up to grab the back of my head, he yanks me forward and presses his mouth to mine. I sink into the deep, painful pleasure that is Erik.

After a couple of seconds I push him away, but I've let it happen and we both know it.

"Damn it," I say. He laughs as he backs off.

"Bye, Mara."

"Good-bye."

He moves toward the stairs.

"Oh," he says, pausing with a foot on the first step.

"Yes?"

"He doesn't have a brother, does he?" Erik asks.

"What?"

"Your new guy. I hope he doesn't have a—"

"You bastard," I say.

And then he's taking the stairs up, two at a time, and all the strength has gone from my legs and I'm sliding down the wall and sitting, crumpled on the cold, dirty floor.

"I didn't know," I whisper, alone in the hallway. "I didn't know."

Not that that's given me a second of comfort.

Bernadette finds me at the bottom of the stairs and drags me into the women's bathroom.

"Okay, what is it?"

"Erik," I say in a whisper.

"Here?"

I nod.

Bernadette puts her arms around me and hugs me hard.

"Holy shit," she says.

But Bernadette doesn't really know. She knows about Erik, though she's never met him, but she doesn't know I ever went back to him after Lucas died. That part is my own burden, and far too difficult to explain, even to Bernadette.

She makes me splash cold water on my face and put on lipstick. I'm paler than usual and my hair is plastered to my head.

"I look like shit."

"You're fine," she says. "Come on, this doesn't have to be a big deal, right?"

"Right."

"If he's still there, you just ignore him," she says.

"Okay."

"Either way, we'll get the bill and leave."

"All right."

She frowns. "He won't . . . he won't say anything . . . he wouldn't, like, come up to us or anything, would he?"

"I don't think so," I say. "I, um, I already talked to him."

"What?"

I nod. "Just now."

"Down here?" she asks.

"Yeah."

She shakes her head. "Whoa. Can you tell me—never mind, you can tell me about that later. Let's go."

I nod again and let her take me by the hand and lead me upstairs.

"He's gone," I say, as we turn the corner at the top of the stairs and the tables come into view.

"Good," Bernadette says. "Come on."

Chapter Thirty-one

You never thought you'd be a cheater.

"We have to stop," you told Erik the last time. It's been over for weeks now, but you will never be clear of him, of it.

And now you walk along Queen Street with Lucas, popping in and out of the tiny galleries that have been sprouting up there, places you both might get a start showing your work. The neighborhood is edgy, scruffy, and replete with homeless people of the mentally ill variety.

"Art and the mentally unstable," Lucas says. He is holding your hand and smiling at the spring sunshine. "It's an appropriate mix, don't you think?"

You laugh and he leans in to kiss your cheek and you blink at the pain his sweetness causes.

You have to leave him. You don't want to, but you are false. False, false, false—you don't deserve him.

But you keep giving yourself one more week, one more day, another hour before you have to do it. You keep hoping to wake up to it all being okay.

You ought to know, just by looking at your parents, that it will never all be okay. Once you are damaged, once you are compromised, there is no way back to the way you were, no retrieval, no healing, nothing but a struggle to keep going.

But one more day cannot be too much to ask.

Especially a crisp, shiny, fresh spring day where you have love in one hand, a steaming latte in the other, and the dream of a bright future filling your eyes.

But evening comes, and dinner with Lucas's parents comes, and the half-brother Lucas hates comes to dinner.

And he is . . .

he is . . .

ohfuckohfuckohfuck . . .

Erik.

Erik, the first son of Lucas's mother. The one you've heard about, the kid whose father took him from his estranged wife when Erik was four and moved from state to state, eluding the authorities. The one who ran away from his dad, got arrested for breaking into a variety store and spent a year with abusive foster parents before coming to live, at age ten, with his mother, stepfather, and little brother, Lucas. Lucas, whose perfect suburban life he un-doubtedly resented. Lucas, who he bullied and tormented and who therefore has, even at twenty-one, no pity for Erik's hardship and no patience for his repentance.

"Nice to meet you," you say, and shake his hand, which is sweating. Erik's hands don't usually sweat. You try to banish your knowledge of him, pretend to yourself that he is new. Your face is hot. You order a Bloody Mary and drink it too fast.

Lucas and his parents are tense, but it has nothing to do with you. You hope. Somehow you survive the evening.

You survive the walk home with Lucas and his ranting and raging about his parents trying to force him to accept Erik, whom he does not consider a brother, into his life.

Despite your guilt, you can't help feeling impatient with Lucas for his intractability, his judgment, his lack of forgiveness for someone who had a nightmare of a childhood.

"And then," Lucas is saying as he stomps back and forth in front of your bed, "then he had the nerve to show up here six months ago and tell me he wanted to start fresh! To . . . what was it he said . . . to make amends and forge a new relationship, to be real brothers!"

"You never told me," you say.

"This is a guy who made my life hell for years! He's not worth our time, Mara."

"But . . ."

"I told him where he could shove his fucking amends," Lucas continues. "I said to him: you'll never change, you're the same loser you've always been, and you're lucky anyone in our family lets you near us. But I don't have to. I might have to help you get a job, but only because our mother begged me to. I don't have to love you or like you or forgive you."

"You helped him get a job?"

"Yeah, at school. I'm not even sure what he ended up doing."

You retreat inward, fighting horror.

Sex is worse than usual that night, but if you have to grit your teeth and fake orgasm and every touch feels like a violation, it's your own fault.

5:55 a.m.: double espresso.

6 a.m.: painting.

I have five hundred dollars left in my bank account, bills to pay, and no credit cards, lines of credit, or surprise inheritances coming in.

I'm fucked, but I must keep working or I will lose all sense of purpose. As it is, whether Hugo is here or not, I'm not sleeping well.

I feel like I'm painting with my eyes shut these days, because I disappear as I work. I have given up on geometrics and am painting whatever I feel like.

The face of Lucas appears in many places—in the shadow of an abstract door, in waves crashing onto a shore of purple sand—and when I sleep, I dream of him.

I sleep with Hugo, and dream of Lucas.

And in the waking light before dawn, sometimes I still want Erik.

Dad comes home from treatment and we have a talk during which he seems almost normal—balanced, practical, aware of his personal pitfalls. Shauna is never far, and I hope she'll do as she promised and stay with him.

"And how are you?" Dad asks, holding both of my hands in his.

In the four seconds it takes me to breathe in and out, I've dismissed the thought of any answer but, "Fine."

"Good," he says, taking me at my word.

Chapter Thirty-two

Hugo is staring at me.

He's been staring for many long minutes, while the only sound has been of my retching into the bedroom garbage can.

I've done it.

I shoved him so hard he went flying off the bed and landed on the floor, cracking his elbow on the bedside table on his way down. There'll be a bruise.

He had no warning, but I did. I should have known.

My skin, all at once, is like an open wound, my insides a battlefield. There is no thought to trace it to, no moment of warning before it happens, and yet I should have known I would not be able to do this.

No matter that my heart begs, my body will not let me love.

Hugo assures me he's okay. But I know he is reconfiguring me, taking me apart and reassembling me with a new fact, a new facet. What does he see?

If I were a painting me, I'd paint a half-person, a woman chased by monsters. They catch at her legs, tear at her clothing, lurk in alleyways and jump out to grab her as she passes, taking chunks of her and swallowing them whole. She reaches for love, runs toward it, grasps and holds it for a beautiful moment before it turns ugly and drags her down.

But I am prone to the melodramatic in my visions. Hugo probably just sees me as a neurotic, a case of damaged goods.

I find my clothes and put them on.

He does the same.

We make our way by silent consent to the family room, away from the bed and the bedroom and all that is contained there. We sit on opposite ends of the couch.

I swallow. "I'm so sorry."

He stares at me with narrowed eyes and eventually nods.

"Mara," he says. "I don't know what the hell is going on here, but I don't like being thrown out of bed."

"Of course not."

"So. . . ?"

This is it, I tell myself, No more hiding, no more lies, no self-pity.

"I have trouble sometimes," I say. "In bed. Actually I have trouble out of bed too."

"Okay, let's try some specifics," he says.

"There are days when I can't leave the house," I say. "And days when I can't get out of bed, can't function at all, really. Other times I'm fine. Since I met you I've been better—I've been working on it."

"So you're . . . what's it called . . ."

"Agoraphobic? Not exactly."

I try to explain that it's not so simple as a diagnosis, that I don't fit the "profile," that I'm just frightened and lacking in faith, with an overactive and morbid imagination.

"And let me guess," he says. "You've had no professional help for this."

"Well . . ."

"And you didn't tell me because you didn't trust me."

"No, it's not like that, I just . . ."

"Don't trust anyone," he says, finishing my thought. "Except maybe Bernadette."

"You don't understand," I say. "It's myself I don't trust. And did you really want to know about me standing for an hour at a stoplight because I can't make myself cross the street? Did you want to hang out and watch me plaster myself against the wall in the subway station because I'm looking for terrorists and scared that someone is going to push me in front of the train? You think you would have stuck around this long?"

"We'll never know, will we?" he says.

I notice he doesn't say "yes."

"Were you ever going to tell me?"

I look down at my hands, ashamed at the answer.

"I see," he says. "Nice."

I swallow hard. The silence lengthens.

The sex issue is hard to tackle. I try to figure out how to start, but Hugo speaks first.

"What about that," he says and jerks his head toward the bedroom. "What's the deal?"

I bite my lip.

"I've never done that before," I say. "I mean, I've never actually shoved someone like that."

"What an honor," he says with a bitter laugh.

"But I've had trouble before. I turn into this horrible ball of tension and suddenly I feel so exposed, almost . . . almost

violated. It just hits me. I try to get through it and I can usually, you know, push through, so to speak, but it gets to the
point where it all just . . . hurts."

"You've been feeling like this while we were having sex
and you kept going? And didn't tell me?"

I feel my face flush, but I meet his eyes and nod.

He stares at me, eyes wounded and angry, his fists clench-
ing and unclenching.

"Damn it, Mara," he says.

"I'm sorry."

"I am too. This is . . . this is fucked up."

"I guess."

"What kind of an asshole do you think I am? You think I'd
want to make love with someone who feels like I'm raping
her?"

"I didn't say it felt like—"

"*Violated* was the word," he says. "But let's not split hairs."

"It's not you," I say. "I mean, it's not about you, it's me."

"But guess what?" he says, his voice getting louder. "It's
me you're in bed with! Which means there are two of us. But
that seems to have escaped you."

"I just mean that the issue is mine. It's happened before."

"What, with the dead guy?" Hugo asks.

My memory flashes back to Lucas sweating on top of me,
eyes closed and grunting, pushing, pushing, not seeing,
never seeing . . .

I shudder and wrench myself back to the present.

"Yes," I say, "it happened with Lucas."

"Well, it still comes back to trust and the fact that apparently we don't have any."

"I know," I say. "I have some things to sort out."

He is silent.

"Hugo," I try to steel myself, but my voice shakes. "It's probably best if . . ."

He waits, almost glaring at me.

"I'm going to need some time. Time apart, I mean, from us."

"You want to break up."

I gulp.

"I thought you were in love with me. Did I imagine that? And is it too much to ask for you to give me some credit? Of course it is, because you have to do everything alone." He has stood up and is pacing the front room.

"Hugo . . ."

"How much of this has even been real, Mara? I mean, what is there to break up? I thought I loved you too, but apparently I've been in love with an illusion. You lied to me. You let me fuck you and all the while you were hating it. I'm the biggest chump."

I jump up from the couch and grab hold of his arms. "Hugo, no, I—"

"And now you want to end it." He jerks away and goes to the door. "It never even started."

"I only meant I wanted to take a break. Some time."

Hugo yanks his jacket on and shoves his feet into his boots.

"Please," I say.

He takes a long look at me. I look back, my heart in my eyes.

"It wasn't fake," I say. "Please believe me. The most important things were real. *Are* real."

"I wish I could believe that." His hand is on the doorknob. "I gotta go."

When he's gone, I stand with my back to the door, leaning on it for support.

I thought I'd been brave enough, with my cute little self-improvement program, cutting things off with Erik, all of it. I thought I was making progress, becoming whole. So how is it that my love life and my career are in the shit and I feel worse than ever?

Not running fast enough . . .

Erik. The bastard. I see his eyes; laughing, cruel and far too wise.

I never stopped running, I just fooled myself into thinking I had.

So here I am, fucked up as ever and stuck with everything I've been trying to escape. Mom, Dad, Lucas, Erik. I am consumed, haunted by the angry words, by love twisted to hate, by the way people disappoint and betray one another and never recover. I am plagued by my failure, with such cautionary examples, to live better, to *be* better.

Most of all I am tormented that my failure killed Lucas.

The thought, once allowed in, causes stabbing pains in my belly. I lurch forward and stumble to the dark kitchen.

How could I have thought anything like love could coexist with this pain? If running doesn't work, what am I supposed to do? How am I supposed to live with this every single day? The alternative to running is to stand and fight, but how? With what?

Horrible sounds pour from me, worse than sobs, worse than anything. I don't want the memories, but they are inexorable and if the final ones come, I'll die, I know I will.

Help. Oh God, I need help.

I open the cupboard with the grappa and take the bottle down. I know it won't bring Hugo back, or Lucas for that matter, but I need it. I need something right now to fill the holes, to slow the onslaught of memory, to buffer me, to save me from the truth.

I put the mouth of the bottle to my lips, tip my head back and pour the hot, bitter liquid down my throat. It tastes terrible. I cough, sputter and then take another swig.

Fuck it. What's the point of being sober? What's the point of any of it? I am doomed and crippled. I am weak and neurotic and a fucking chicken.

A fucking chicken who can't cross the road.

Ha ha ha.

As I laugh at my sad joke, as tears course down my face and the alcohol starts to hit, I realize even my house is not safe. The safety of the house is an illusion, has always been an illusion because the memories are still coming.

Fine. Fuck the house.

I put the stopper in the grappa and half-run, half-limp out my front door, down the steps and onto the sidewalk. It's December and I'm in my socks with no coat, but who cares? I've lost Hugo. Never had him. Doesn't matter. Memory comes, my throat burns, pain twists in my gut.

I go south to Gerrard Street and the nearest streetcar line. It takes a few minutes and as I walk, people's eyes slide past me—I am someone they wish didn't exist; drunk, crying and half-dressed on the streets of Toronto.

I start to run. I see the face of Lucas, hear his voice and race him, race the memories, all the way to the streetcar, to the tracks, to the middle of the road, with my feet slushy and frozen, my body on fire and the bottle gripped in my hand.

I stand in the center of the tracks and hold my arms out.

"I'm here!" I shout. "Come and get me you fucker!"

I see it coming—the streetcar—its red and white colors bright against the night and the hum and whine of it so distinct.

I stay where I am.

Maybe this is what it is to stop running, to be brave. To stand swaying under the sky and let it come. Let it all come and roll over me and then see if I'm alive when it's over.

Everything starts to slow. The red and white comes closer.

"Where are you Lucas?" I whisper, and then shout, "Come get me! Come and fucking get me!"

I hold myself still and wait for a sign.

I have a choice: to let it hit me . . . or to step in front of it at the last second when the driver can't see, can't slow down . . .

As Lucas did.

I look down at the tracks and there he is, where he has been waiting for me all along, with his eyes open and fixed on me, his skull cracked open and his beautiful body bent in unnatural ways.

And again, there he is moments before, knowing the truth, wrecked, furious, screaming and then, so fast, stepping out in front of it.

And I am shouting, screaming a warning, not fast enough and he's not listening to me anyway . . .

And standing, watching it happen in sickening slow motion.

I have been standing watching this happen for years, every second an effort of denial, a fight against this guilt, this grief.

Part of me will be here forever.

Unless I let it come for me. The street where I stand is dark and the driver might not see me in time . . .

I watch it approach.

I unscrew the cap on the grappa and its smell, pure alcohol, wafts up.

It's still coming. He didn't have time to think like I do. Did he mean to do it? Does it matter? I lift the bottle to my lips, take a burning swig, watch the lights get bigger. Any second now . . .

It comes. It comes and I am not afraid. My body has become part of the night, part of the air. I am standing with Lucas who looks up at me with his childish eyes and dares me.

I return his gaze and then slowly shake my head.

"I'm sorry," I say, and I step off the tracks . . . and walk away.

On the way home, I nearly get hit by a car.

Inside my house, as I'm peeling off my socks, I realize how funny that is and laugh until I'm sick. Then I sit in the dark and finish the entire, disgusting bottle of grappa, talk to God and eventually pass out on the bathroom floor.

What else is there to do?

Chapter Thirty-three

I manage to sidestep the rest of the drinking binge, but take a few days to schlep around in my pajamas and consciously revel in self-pity. I cry and write bad poetry and compose letters I will never send (particularly not to Lucas, ha ha). I order pizzas, eat dry cereal, refuse to shower and send Bernadette for five kinds of ice cream.

We eat straight from the cartons and have a good, long talk about love, life, and the state of my bank account since the defection of Sal. She insists on loaning me five hundred dollars to get me through the month and gives me a lecture on the meaning of "best friend," highlighting issues like honesty, disclosure and trust.

"I would have been there for you," she says.

"You're here now."

She shakes her head and comes back the next morning with a more well-rounded bag of groceries, a pile of self-help books and garbage bags.

"Time's up," she says. "Get in the shower."

I grumble about it, but the truth is, I didn't die and I'm getting antsy. There are things I need to deal with and greasy hair and pajamas won't make them any easier.

By the time I'm dressed, Bernadette has cleaned up the garbage and has coffee on. I pour a cup and start thinking seriously about what I need to do.

———

Saturday evening, Bernadette arrives at my door in full Christmas party regalia, Bernadette-style, which means gold tights, silver lace-up boots, and a gold knit minidress.

"No," I say before she even opens her mouth.

"No what?"

"No to whatever it is you want to drag me to."

"You have to," she says. "I won't lie, you'll hate this, but you have to come." She pulls her boots off, marches down the hallway to my bedroom and opens the closet.

"What is it?"

She rummages through my closet. "Minister English's holiday party," she says, holding her fingers up in quotations at the word holiday. "I'm guessing heavy on Jesus, light on Santa and all other religions. I didn't want to bug you, especially since you're going through . . . what you're going through but . . ."

"But . . . ?"

"But I broke up with Faith over the whole in-the-closet issue." Her eyes well up.

"Oh, Bee . . ."

"Yeah, it sucks. But then she called me this afternoon and begged me to come to her mom's party—said she needed to show me something. I doubt it'll change anything, but I guess I'm a glutton for punishment. Will you come?"

The party is north of Toronto and it turns out to be a long drive. As we head north it begins to snow and the roads get icy. I start to feel anxious but then I imagine the streetcar coming for me and I remember the calm I felt right before I stepped off the tracks. Somehow it makes me feel better. Not perfect, but better.

Mrs. English has taken over the second floor of a charming country inn for her event. We stomp the snow off our boots, check our coats, and head up the ribbon-festooned staircase.

Bernadette's outfit gets quite a few surprised-and-quickly-stifled glances, but she is too busy looking for Faith to notice. I keep a wary eye out for Mrs. English.

Being taller, I spot Faith first.

"There she is," I say, and wave.

She waves back and pushes through the crowd to get to us.

"Thanks for coming," she says and gives each of us a kiss on the cheek.

"So," Bernadette says, "what is it you wanted me to see?"

"Just wait."

We don't have to wait long.

The music is turned down and Mrs. English steps onto a makeshift platform near the fireplace at the far side of the room. She is in a well-tailored burgundy suit and looks much more normal than in my high school memories.

"Good evening, friends!" she says and launches into an account of the year's accomplishments.

Beside me, Bernadette is pursing her lips and retucking her hair behind her ear every few seconds. Faith stands with her hands clasped in front of her and her sheet of blond hair falling across her face.

The next section of the speech encompasses finance, family values and the need to fight corruption and moral disintegration. I fight hard not to glaze over.

I glance at Bernadette and she rolls her eyes.

"On a personal note," Mrs. English continues, "though I will continue to be outspoken in my opposition to issues such as gay marriage and abortion . . ."

Faith and Bernadette both go very still.

"I intend to approach these issues with more . . . love in my heart and with the hope that *prayer* will work to guide those who are on the wrong path . . . back to where they belong. God loves all, and we should attempt to do the same. Bless you in the new year and thank you for coming."

While the crowd claps, the three of us turn to look at each other—that is, Bernadette and Faith stare at each other and I stare at them.

"You . . . did you tell her?" Bernadette asks.

Faith nods. "My whole family."

"Holy shit," I say.

"Oh!" Bernadette says, and her hands fly to her face. "Oh, my God. How did it . . . Are you okay? What happened?"

"It wasn't particularly well received," Faith says. "But, well, as you can see, slightly better than I expected."

"They're praying for you to come back to the light?" I say.

She grimaces. "Something like that. I haven't been locked up or married off though, so that's something." She turns back to Bernadette. "I told them about you. I told them you were the reason, that I was going to lose you and I couldn't . . . that I just couldn't."

Suddenly they're both crying. Bernadette reaches out to take Faith's hands.

This is where I should be discreetly stepping away, but instead I'm playing lookout, which turns out to be a good thing.

"She's coming," I say to them in a low voice.

Bernadette drops Faith's hands.

"Will she . . . does she know it's me?" Bernadette asks in a fast whisper.

"Shh," Faith says. "Hi, Mom. Good speech."

"Thank you, dear." She takes a moment to check out Bernadette and then me.

"Which one?" Mrs. English asks.

Faith blushes.

Bernadette reaches out her hand.

"I'm Bernadette and this is my friend, Mara."

Mrs. English narrows her eyes and takes Bernadette's hand.

"It seems you are a person of influence over my daughter," she says.

"Ah . . ." Bernadette says, and darts a questioning gaze at Faith.

"Mom," Faith says, "you promised."

Mrs. English, still holding Bernadette's hand, steps closer and smiles brightly while saying, "You will find that I, too, am a person of influence. I love my daughter."

"Ahem," Bernadette says. "Well, I look forward to getting to know you and your family better. Faith is a wonderful person. You should be very proud of her."

"Humph," Mrs. English says, and glances at Faith. "I said I'd try and I will." She turns back to Bernadette. "I'll be praying for you both."

And she walks off.

I let out a long whistle of air.

"Nice in-laws," I say to Bernadette.

Faith snorts.

"I wish I'd worn a different outfit," Bernadette says.

"I wish you'd shut up and get us all out of here," Faith says, and bats her eyelashes at Bernadette.

With all the love in the car, I'm surprised we don't levitate back to Toronto.

Chapter Thirty-four

Needless to say, I've never liked Christmas.

Every year I spend Christmas Eve with Bernadette's family and reject all invitations for Christmas Day.

For years I was fought over, pressured, guilted by Dad and Mom, to choose between them. One would think they'd come to some kind of half-day-each agreement, but not my parents—why agree when you have the opportunity to wage war? Once I was old enough to choose, I stopped celebrating altogether.

Usually I just paint.

This year though, I go to my closet, take out the Lucas shoebox and bring it to the living room.

Wishing like crazy for a drink, I open the box.

On top is a Polaroid of us at graduation. Our arms are flung around each other and we're grinning like five-year-olds. So young.

Lucas was fond of taking photos, so there are lots. One by one, I go through them. Interspersed with the pictures are Valentine's Day cards, birthday cards, the occasional love note left on my pillow. My throat aches, but I force myself to read every word, take in every detail. I come across a Christmas poem he wrote me one year. It says:

> Mara, Mara, why so sad
> in the happy season?
> Trees and Santa make you mad
> I don't know the reason.

I say it out loud and laugh.

Once the box has yielded up its painful treasures, the question is what to do with it all? Surely going through it isn't enough—not even close.

The phone rings.

Usually I don't answer the phone on Christmas Day, but today I do. It's Mom. Maybe it's just the state I'm in, but something in her voice touches me, forces me to remember I love her. The next thing I know, I'm suggesting we have lunch tomorrow and we're making plans to meet at a pub up the street from me.

I take Dad and Shauna's call too—it seems that capitulation is the theme of the day. Or one might call it change.

I decide to organize the Lucas stuff. I start chronologically, making a pile for each semester and then create subcategories—photos, letters, notes, cards, etcetera. I will buy a better box, one with little files where all of it can go. Or maybe I'll purge most of it. Some of it. But not yet.

There are tiny sketches too, working drafts, and, finally, three sculptures from Lucas's pre-tennis-ball-and-shellac phase that I've been keeping in a dark corner of the basement.

Anything I like, I put on display in the house. Seeing it every day will be hard to get used to, but I think it would make him happy.

I wander from room to room searching my soul for a way to integrate, to rehabilitate, to find someplace less painful for his memory to exist.

And finally I go to my studio and paint until I cannot keep my eyes open or my fingers moving any longer.

It's been over a year since I've seen Mom, so I hardly notice the food at lunch.

As always, I feel scruffy and freakish in my jeans and cotton sweater next to her in her beige wool suit, silk scarf and precarious-looking leather boots.

Even the day after Christmas, she has her laptop, cell and PDA.

"How are you?" she says.

I fiddle with my napkin. "Good. Really good."

And she smiles and is perhaps proud that I am so together.

She regales me with work stories and at the end of lunch hands me a gift bag.

"Mom . . . you didn't have to."

She pats my arm. "Open it."

I reach into the tissue and pull out a small box. Inside is a miniature artist's palette made of crystal.

I am speechless.

Mom starts to shift in her chair. "If you don't like it, I can exchange it."

"No, it's . . . beautiful."

"Well, I know I don't get the whole art thing, but I thought you might like it."

"I do."

"Merry Christmas, honey."

I try not to cry on the walk home.

After the moderate success of lunch, I decide to be really wild and drop in on Dad and Shauna in the evening.

They invite me to dinner and I accept.

Shauna gives me a pair of turquoise earrings from Mexico and Dad sits calmly on the couch watching *Six Feet Under* on DVD and asking the occasional question.

"So," he says, "what happened to your boyfriend . . . Hugo, wasn't it?"

"We broke up."

"How come?"

I sigh. "It's complicated."

Dad nods. "Relationships aren't easy for you, are they?"

"No, Dad," I say. "They're not."

He reaches out and pats my knee.

"It'll get easier someday," he says, and smiles fondly at Shauna. "I promise."

New Year's Eve, I find myself on Erik's doorstep.

He is alone. There are dark circles under his eyes and his skin is pale—he looks like hell.

"Well, well . . ." he says.

"You were right," I say. "We're not quite done."

He crosses his arms over his chest. "I'm not fucking you tonight, Mara."

"I didn't ask you to."

He raises an eyebrow. "You're here."

I flush and he smirks.

"Shouldn't you be at some swanky party with your boyfriend?"

"You know, that really doesn't suit you, Erik."

"You're right." He sighs. "You'd better come in."

I slip past him and make my way to the couch, where I curl up in the corner. Erik gives me a quizzical look and sits down at the other end.

"Hugo and I broke up," I say. "And I went out and stood in traffic."

Erik frowns. "Seems a little over the top. How long have you known the guy?"

"It wasn't about him," I say. "I stood on the streetcar tracks. I stood there and waited and I almost let one hit me. I considered it."

His eyes widen.

"We have to talk about Lucas," I say.

He shakes his head.

"Erik."

"No." He gets up and paces to the bedroom door and back.

"You know you never answered my question that night," I say.

"What question? It was five fucking years ago."

Lucas is a sound sleeper, and there are things you need to know, things only Erik can tell you. You creep from the bed, grab some clothes, and tiptoe to the living room to put them on.

The streetcar carries you across town to Erik's place where you see red light glowing from the window behind the fire escape. You haven't been here for weeks and planned never to come again. This is the last time and you're here for answers.

Since the excruciating family dinner, you've been trying to reconcile the Erik you've been fucking with the half-brother Lucas despises. Your heart and loyalty must be with Lucas, but the story of Erik's childhood speaks to you. You know now why you were drawn to him. It wasn't only his beauty, wasn't just physical. Like you, he knows the extremity of loss, of being lost. He knows what a scary place the world can be. This knowledge is something Lucas does not have, an awareness he is missing. Lucas believes the world is a good place and that people live happily ever after. You were hoping his belief would infect you, inspire you, and perhaps heal your pathetic, jaded soul.

But instead, something in Erik called and you responded, proving your worst fears about yourself. You are doomed to selfishness, doomed to fail the ones you love, just like your parents. You are a faithless piece of shit who will never deserve to be loved. You have a sick feeling that when you go inside and ask the questions you need to ask, Erik might prove he is just as bad, possibly worse.

You go up the stairs and knock on the door. He opens it a crack and peeks out. Seeing it's you, he opens it wider, lets you in and shuts it quickly.

"Did you know?" you ask, and look for an answer on his face.

He lights a cigarette and gazes at you through narrowed eyes.

"You shouldn't have come," he says.

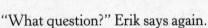

"What question?" Erik says again.

"You remember."

"Not really," he says. "Besides, you were the one cheating on Lucas, not me."

"I know that."

"There's no absolution here, Mara. We have to just live with it."

"I know that too, but someday I'd like to think I might be happy. I'd like to believe that everything I touch isn't going to turn to shit."

"Good luck," he says and shrugs.

"There must be something we can do."

"Besides fucking?" he says.

"Yeah, besides that."

He sneers. "Oh, I get it. You want to talk about feelings and cry and all that shit."

"Well, I want to talk at least."

"Bad news: I don't." But he lowers himself onto a stool and hunches there.

"Tough," I say, and push on. "Let's start with this: why did you have sex with me? In the beginning."

His eyes lift and meet mine. "I thought that was pretty obvious." I can read his wicked thoughts as if they're my own, but I am not to be distracted or deterred.

"Listen." I lean forward. "Let's just get this out of the way, because I've wondered all this time and I need to know."

"Fine. Get to it," he snaps.

"You and Lucas hated each other."

"Check."

"You came back years later and tried to make amends, he rejected you."

"Check."

"He was a spoiled brat who'd had a perfect life compared to yours and he had no empathy, no room in his heart for forgiveness . . ."

"Where're you going with this, Mara?"

"And there he is, all golden and smug with his art and his trust fund and his precious girlfriend . . ."

Erik stands. "I think you'd better shut up."

I stand too. "It wouldn't be that hard, once you get that job at the school, to find out who she was, what class she was in, and then wave your big dick around and fasten your dark-soul eyes on her and somehow know, because you know him, that a part of her must be starving for someone just like you . . ."

"You fucking bitch." He seizes me by the arms.

"I wouldn't judge you, Erik," I say.

"Fuck you."

He pushes me back and my shoulders and head slam against the wall.

I grit my teeth. "I just need to know."

He has me by the shoulders and he's gripping so hard it hurts.

I shove him away, he lands on the floor and I stand over him. "I need to know, Erik. You're not the one who walked out of here and saw him standing there. You didn't hear him calling me a whore and screaming that he was going to kill himself, that we'd be sorry . . ."

My voice cracks as it all comes back: the shock of seeing Lucas in front of Erik's building when I'd left him fast asleep in our bed, his voice when he said he knew what I'd been doing, who lived in the apartment behind me, the tendons on his neck pulsing as he raged, the sick, dizzy feeling in my belly. I was paralyzed, too terrified to speak. I stood shaking my head, gasping for breath, taking the cruel names because, after all, I deserved them. And then the words, those final words: *"I'm going to fucking kill you, I'll kill you both. Better yet, I'll kill myself and then you'll be sorry. Then you'll understand what you've destroyed!"*

Such a manic look in his eyes and underneath, such pain, such bitterness, so much hate coming at you as he starts to back away. You take a step toward him, your eyes begging him to stay, to listen, but he hisses and takes another step.

"You'll be sorry," he says again.

A scream in your head as you see it, and then his name from your lips, ripped from deep inside, a warning that comes a second too late, a second before the sound of flesh and bone colliding with metal, the screeching brakes, his body like a rag doll, twisted and flying . . .

And finally everything goes still and there are only his eyes accusing, his body mangled and dead.

I come back to the present. Erik is staring at me and I must have been speaking, must have been, because he is stricken, frozen in the moment with me.

My face is covered in tears and I am hyperventilating.

"Jesus," Erik finally breathes.

"You can do whatever you want to me," I say in a voice so raw it doesn't even sound like me. "But none of it will ever hurt as much as that hurts. And I deserve it. I deserve worse."

I see tears in Erik's eyes and horror behind them. Erik missed the accusations but he heard the sound, heard my scream, ran outside and saw the same broken body, the same dead eyes that I did. We are reliving it now, but of course neither of us ever really left the scene.

"Like you said," I whisper, "we can never run fast enough."

"No we can't."

I kneel on the floor beside him.

"I'm not trying to shift the blame, Erik. There's no point. I would just like to know if there was even *one* honest thing in the whole mess . . . or if, on top of it all, I was such a fool as to let you play me."

His cheeks are wet with tears and he closes his eyes. "Fuck you for thinking I would," he says.

Something deep inside me loosens, dissolves and floats away, leaving a little more space for breath.

"You didn't know who I was," I say, just to be sure.

He opens his eyes and shakes his head.

"Well, that's something," I say.

Outside, out in the world, the new year arrives.

Chapter Thirty-five

Asleep on Erik's couch, I dream of Lucas.

He floats, like Ophelia, face up in a stream. He is staring at me. Staring at me with eyes that want something.

I try to ask what it is, but my mouth will not open and my body will not move.

Erik wakes me in the early morning and we climb out to the fire escape and shiver as we watch the sun rise.

We both feel awful, but we take a walk because Erik has no food in his fridge.

Last night was the first time I've ever stayed overnight.

We buy coffee and muffins, inhale them in the shop, and talk about Lucas—the small things, the day-to-day memories, who he was to each of us, the bad and the good.

Later, back on the couch, Erik talks about his mother and stepfather and how much they have aged since they lost their son. They have looked to him for answers and he hasn't been able to give them any. They have looked to him to be two good sons and he has failed to be even one.

"You could do better, couldn't you?" I ask. "Now?"

"Maybe."

Tears come and go. Memories come, are spoken aloud, and go.

That night I am still at Erik's, feeling outside of time, somehow unable to leave. I leave a message for Bernadette, letting her know I'm alive.

We lie back on Erik's unmade bed. We've never talked much, he and I, but now, quietly, in fragments, in large chunks, in no particular order, we share our life stories. Sometimes we laugh. Always, we listen.

"What about this guy?" Erik asks. "The boyfriend?"

Hugo's face looms up suddenly in my mind, his eyes gentle and laughing. I'm seized by the urge to leap off the bed and run to find him. I blink and the urge is gone.

"I don't know," I say. "I fell in love and he fell in love . . . but love isn't always strong enough. And I threw him out of bed."

Erik laughs.

"No, not like that. I freaked out in the middle of it and pushed him really hard. Not for fun, but because I didn't want him to touch me. It was building for weeks, this feeling that it hurt to be touched. I tried to fake it and hoped it'd pass, but instead it got worse."

"Wow."

"Yeah. Same thing happened with Lucas."

He closes his eyes for a moment, nods. "Ah."

"'Intimacy problems,' I suppose," I say and wrinkle up my nose. "Seems to happen whenever I fall in love."

He nods.

I turn sideways to look at him. "When I met you, I thought I was frigid. I was so relieved to be attracted to you because it meant I wasn't. I loved Lucas, but wanting you brought me back. Brought my body back. But then, the better it was with you, the worse it got with him."

"What about when we stopped?"

I shake my head.

"That's shitty."

I give him a sad smile.

"I always think about after," he says, and sits up. "After he died."

"What about it?"

"Us," he says. "That we still . . . I mean, how could we? Why did we?"

"An exercise in despair? Or an exorcize *of* despair."

He gives a bleak laugh, gets up and walks into the main room. I follow.

"You met me in my dark places," I say. "Before and after. Only after, the dark was so much deeper and sometimes I couldn't stand to be there alone. Maybe it was wrong, but I figured . . ."

"That the price had been paid already?"

"Yeah."

Erik stares at the floor and plays with an unlit cigarette. Watching him, studying his face, I see the resemblance to Lucas—the call of blood in the line of his jaw, the set of his shoulders, and I also see a different man from the one I knew a few days ago. He is no longer the wall I threw myself against, the hostile thing that I fought—

defied—for so long. Instead he is fragile, is ripped open and raw. Like me.

A tiny shift in his breathing tells me he wants to say something.

"Aside from Lucas, do you think we could have been something?" he says. "Something . . . else?"

"Maybe," I say, and feel an ache spread from my chest to my throat.

"So . . ."

"Oh, Erik. We can talk about it. We can say 'aside from Lucas,' but there is no 'aside from Lucas,' you know?"

"I know, but . . ." He looks away, swallows. "For a little while, could we be just us here?"

"Don't."

He gets up. "I think we could." He stares at me, his dark eyes intense, naked. "I can't help it, I still want you."

And there's that fire, starting in me again.

"Fuck it, we can." He steps over to me, takes my elbow, and pulls me up to stand in front of him. My knees are wobbly.

"Erik, I don't think . . ."

He puts his hands, ever so lightly, on my shoulders.

"Listen," he says. "You came here wanting to talk and we have. It's been good. Maybe from here we're both going to be . . . better. Maybe. But you're still afraid and your body is all fucked up because, basically, you don't feel safe."

I try to look away, but I can't.

"Nobody's safe though, Mara. You realize that?"

"I . . . I guess."

"So we're not safe. Fuck it, I embrace that. I'm going to tell you."

"Tell me what?"

"The truth." He takes a deep breath and says, "I could have loved you."

The words hit me like a bomb going off inside. His hands are on my shoulders and I start to shake.

He continues. "For you, maybe it was something else. It doesn't matter anyway because we can't go back—but I want you to know I could have. I would have loved you— that's what I felt."

This truth, on top of all the rest, is so crazy sad I can barely find a voice to speak with. "I know," I manage to whisper.

"Don't cry," he says.

"Sorry."

"And don't be sorry."

His hands slide down my arms and then he lets go.

We stand close.

"Maybe, for today, it could be all right," he says, his voice hoarse. "Just today. As if—not as if none of it happened but . . ."

"I don't want us to hurt each other, Erik. And I don't want to pretend."

"I don't mean pretend, exactly," he says. "I mean, maybe we would just let ourselves be free to feel . . . what we might have felt. And whatever we feel now."

I know what he means and I know what he wants, because I want it too. And yet I can't seem to move or speak.

"You're still here, Mara. We've talked, we've gone through it all, but you're still here. We're not done."

He comes closer, puts his hands on the sides of my face.

"Please," he says.

"Please," coming from Erik, finishes me.

"Yes," I say and his arms are around me, his mouth is on mine and we are spinning through space.

This time we are naked before we are naked. We are fierce and intense and hot, but for the first time, our eyes are honest. Every touch strips us, makes us raw. And what we have always taken from each other by force, we now offer up and then go deeper and find more.

Later, Erik sets up a mini-barbecue on the fire escape and makes burgers. Freezing January air whips in past him and I notice his nose is turning red.

"You know, I never knew you ate," I say.

He glances over his shoulder and gives a wry smile. "Only on special occasions. Normally I live on weed, Scotch and sex."

"And candy bars, cyberfood, hemp. Illegally obtained of course."

"Of course."

After dinner he pulls me onto his lap.

"So, earlier . . ." he says, "any heebie-jeebies? Any desire to punch me?"

"You'd have known."

"Maybe not. None of the other guys noticed."

"It's different with you, Erik."

"Let's pretend it isn't." He strokes my hair and kisses me.

"Oh, no, I . . ."

"Maybe I can help. What if you think about those heebie-jeebies?"

"Erik, I don't want—"

"And then what if I whisper sweet things in your ear and touch you . . . like this?"

"On no . . . oh shit . . ."

Suddenly I am flinching, cringing, up against the old pain.

If I am running ahead, slamming doors in his face and skidding around corners, Erik is chasing after, blasting through the doors, always catching up. I leap across chasms and find myself in the attic of my mind. I crash into all shapes and sizes of boxes. Images and memories leap out at me. Polaroids and diaries and ugly outfits. Drawings and voices and little sad, weird versions of me. Shorter, sadder me, angry me, hearing-her-parents-holler-at-each-other me, losing-her-virginity-with-no-love me, losing-Caleb me, kissing Bernadette, fucking strangers, laughing with Sal, missing Mom, saving Dad, clinging to Lucas, wanting, oh, wanting Erik, drinking, smoking, fucking, walking hand in hand with Hugo, dreaming of Lucas, painting, making love, making pizza, hiding, hiding, curling myself into the corner, making myself small so no one will yell or say mean things, so nothing bad will happen because I will not really *be* here, not being happy, not being whole because parts of me, if they were seen, someone would hurt them. People are not gentle enough and when you are small, sometimes they don't see you and sometimes they might step on you and crush you, but sometimes if they don't see you, they won't know you are there in the back, in the corner, and then they will leave you there and close the door and you will be alone forever. And safe? No, still not safe.

If you are touched wrong, if you are brought out and touched when you are not strong, when you do not have the dark of the attic corner, the walls at your back to save you . . . anyone who touches you can hurt you . . . unless they hate you. Unless they hate you or you hate them and then even though you are not in the corner with walls to protect you, to hide some part of you, if you don't care, then they can have the outside, they can have it because your walls are now inside, buried deeper. They do not have you because you are deep, low down. But love digs you out, pulls you out and up with your bare skin and soul open to the world, to the harsh everything. To where you can fail and they can fail—because disappointment is inevitable. Failure is inevitable, you have known it forever.

But Erik . . .

Erik is here in the attic with you. He has not dragged you out into the light, not quite, but he could. He has the love and also the touch that in combination are too much. But he is here and the truth is, the truth is he has already disappointed you and you have already failed him. Both of you have done the worst and so to be soul-naked and body-naked is okay.

"You love me?" you gasp, as his hands grip you.

"Yes," he says. "I do."

With the softest words, and the gentlest touches, and the biggest naked soul, he gives everything.

There is a storm in the attic. Memories fly, photos and shoes and specks of dust swirl. Boxes break apart, doors and windows rattle, edges and corners disappear.

I spin upward, naked. We drive ourselves together and whisper beautiful nonsense and hold on tight when the roof explodes and sends us burning into the sky.

Chapter Thirty-six

We sleep.

I wake rested and new.

I wake before Erik and watch the light grow in the morning sky. I hear the city waking. I breathe in the smell of my exploded life and wonder that I am still here and feeling so much better, so much more, than expected.

I tiptoe to make coffee and then check my messages as it brews.

It's been two days, but there are only four.

Mom: Hi dear. I know you're busy, but call me sometime when you get a chance.

Bernadette: Okay, I appreciate that you called to let me know you're all right, but where the fuck are you? Call me. Call me soon, I'm worried.

Sal(!): Yo. Babe. I came by twice and you weren't there. We gotta talk. Call me, or next time I'm gonna break down the door.

Bernadette: Please call me, I need to talk to you. It's important. Jesus, where the hell are you?

7 a.m.: Erik wakes and joins me for coffee on the couch.

7:10: Erik pulls me closer and we hold each other without speaking . . . and without spilling our coffees.

"You have to go, don't you?" he says eventually.

"My house could be falling down."

"That's not really the reason."

"No," I say. "It's just time. Listen, this whole, last night and—"

"Shh," he says.

"Okay."

"It's funny," he says, "I don't even know where you live."

"The Danforth—on Pape."

"We could walk."

"What?"

"I could walk you there. Walk you home."

"You're kidding—it's cold out. And it'll take over an hour."

"Good," he says. "The longer the better."

In the shower I wash his hair.

He holds me and we share the hot water and I ask, "Did we dishonor him?"

"I don't think so," he says. "Not this time anyway."

"I hope not."

As we walk, we hold hands. We stop for toasted bagels with jam and cream cheese and more coffee. I see a dog that reminds me of Pollock and my heart flip flops, but the owner is a young Asian woman, not Hugo.

Crossing the Bloor viaduct, we stop at the center and look down at the parkway.

"Erik," I say.

"Yes?"

"I wish things were different."

"I know," he says. "Another lifetime maybe."

"We'd always be . . . in relation to him."

"I know."

He turns my face to his and presses his forehead to mine.

"It was good to love you," he says.

The ache at his words is deep.

"At least for a few hours," I say.

"You know it was longer than that."

"Yeah. Me too."

Alone in the center of the bridge on a Wednesday morning in January, we hold each other and let our hearts mingle one more time.

"We'd better go," he says, when he feels me starting to shiver.

"All right."

We wrap our arms around each other's waists and stay that way for the minutes it takes to get to my house.

In front of it we stop.

"I like it," he says.

"Thanks."

He pulls me closer, presses his cold cheek to mine and sighs.

"Well," I say, and pull my key out, "this won't get easier, will it?"

"No," he says.

"Do you want to . . . come in for a few minutes?"

"Better not," he says. "I might never leave."

I nod and take a step back.

And he goes.

Chapter Thirty-seven

Knock, knock, knock.

Shh.

Bang.

Bang.

Bang, bang.

"What the—?"

I haul myself out of bed.

Where am I?

Home.

Right. Home.

Oh. Ow.

Home and someone is knocking, which would not make sense except that it is . . . morning? Ugh, 8 a.m. And I have been sleeping, it must be, since sometime yesterday when Erik left and I came inside and threw myself on the bed and . . .

Bang, bang, bang.

Jeez.

In the kitchen I listen and realize the banging is coming from the back.

I open the door to my neglected studio and peer through the window.

Sal.

Shit.

"Yo, babe!" he hollers when he sees me. "What the fuck?"

Last I checked, Sal wanted to kill me, but he seems friendlier now. And really, if I was going to die, it would have happened by now. Sal would probably make it quick anyway, if that was his intention, so what the hell?

I squint out at the morning sun, hobble to the door and open it.

"Oh, babe," he says when he gets a good look at me. "I guess your lesbo buddy was telling me the truth."

"Huh?"

"You got coffee?"

"Yeah, I think so," I say, and shuffle toward the kitchen. "Come in. Uh. You spoke with Bernadette?"

"Who?" Sal says, and lifts his pant legs before sitting at the kitchen table. "Oh, yeah, the cute dyke. She said she's your best friend."

"She is."

"Well, good, I like her," he says. "How's that coffee coming? You look like you could use some."

"Oh. Uh." I cast about for a moment, reorienting myself to the kitchen and trying to wake up. "Yup, just a minute."

I make coffee and Sal talks about the basketball game he won money on last night and the excellent ice-cube blow job his latest girlfriend gives.

"You should try it," he says. "Well, not that you ever needed props, babe, you're pretty good at—"

"Sal."

"Sorry."

I hand him a coffee and sit down across from him with mine.

"You saw Bernadette?"

"Oh. Yeah. She didn't tell you?"

"No."

"She was supposed to tell you."

"She left messages, but I've been . . . away."

"Physically or mentally?"

"Ah, both."

"Okay . . . well."

"What?"

"She came to see me. Didn't like me much at first, but said she needed, well, that you needed my help. That you were havin' some kinda meltdown."

"Oh."

"Man problems," Sal says, and then inhales his coffee.

"Um . . ."

"And mental problems."

"She said I had—"

"Wait, no. Emotional problems—that's what she said. Emotional problems and man problems and a creative breakthrough—but she said you didn't realize that part."

"Oh."

"And she told me about the dead guy, babe," he says. "I wish I'd known that's what you were dealin' with back then, maybe I coulda helped."

"It's okay, Sal."

"Anyways, I wanted to say I'm sorry, and I'm sorry I cut you off. I was just pissed."

"Oh, Sal, it's fine. It's okay. I should have been honest."

"All right," he says. "Then we're clear. We're good."

"Good," I say.

But how will I ever go back to painting circles and rectangles?

"Thing is though, babe, I'm gonna rip up our contract."

"What? Why?"

Uh oh. Wait—I'll take circle painting over a job at Starbucks any day. Did I say I didn't want to do geometrics? I *love* geometrics! Bring back the contract, bring back the parallelograms!

"Well, you see, that sassy red-headed too-bad-she's-a-carpet-muncher friend of yours—"

"Sal! Offensive."

"Sorry, sorry. Anyway, she brought over one of the pieces you've been working on—"

"What? How did she . . ."

"You gave her a key."

"Oh. Right."

"So. She brought it over and said she thought I should try it at some of those Queen Street galleries."

"She shouldn't have done that."

"Well, you might change your mind on that, 'cuz it sold, babe. It sold fast."

"What?"

Sal reaches into his briefcase, pulls out an envelope, and hands it to me.

"Open it," he says.

"Hang on, I'm still back at Bernadette stealing my painting and you taking it to Queen Street . . ."

"Open it."

"Fine, but—"

"Just open it!"

I open the envelope.

Inside is a check for thirty-five hundred.

Thirty-five hundred dollars!

"Holy shit." I feel lightheaded.

"Less fifteen percent, if you agree to let me be your agent," Sal says, grinning like crazy.

"Wow, wow, wow. Okay," I say, still shaking my head and blinking. "Where do I sign?"

"No, no," Sal says, "think about it first."

"Okay."

"And in the meantime, you have work to do, chicky, so whatever's got you looking like something somebody barfed out, you better get over it."

"I'm fine, Sal," I tell him. "Or I will be soon."

"How many new paintings you got?"

"How many new . . . ? I don't know, ten? Minus the one you sold, so that's nine. And a couple of those are ones I put aside half-finished, so it's probably more like seven. But there's no rush, this money—less fifteen percent—will last me a while as long as Bernadette doesn't hit me up for any charities." And I can pay her back, I think.

Sal does his knee-slapping thing and then points his index finger at me.

"Listen, there's something else," he says. "And I hope this doesn't disturb your mental state, but . . ."

"Yes?"

"At the gallery where I sold the first one, it's nothing fancy, but they like your stuff. They want to exhibit you—a small exhibit—and I told 'em we'd have twenty canvases for March first."

If I'm not drooling or falling on the floor, it's only because I'm too stunned to move.

"Are you crazy?"

"Well, I didn't sign the contract for you, I thought you'd want to do that yourself. Besides, you work fast, right?"

"Sal . . ."

"Here it is: Oz Gallery requests the artist Mara Foster provide . . . etc, etc. Have a look."

An hour later, I've signed the contract, left a message for Bernadette, had a shower, and am sitting, terrified, in front of a fresh, blank canvas, in my studio.

There were two other people—Erik and Hugo—that I wanted to call to share the good news with, but I didn't.

Erik is still fresh—on me and in me, and calling him would violate our unspoken promise.

And being home brings memories of Hugo. I feel a little sad that he hasn't called, but maybe it's for the best.

Before he left, Sal and I counted the canvases, and I actually have eight. That leaves at least another twelve for me to complete in the next few weeks. I might be screwed, but at least I'm busy.

I look at the time.

10 a.m.: begin.

I close my eyes and pray for the creative channel to open.

Paint to brush, brush to canvas . . . and breathe.

I am home.

⸺

Love might be good for art after all.

Even if it is lost love, confused love . . . dead love.

I pour forth all of it, day upon day, and soon I have my twleve canvases.

Bernadette is giddy with excitement and I have forgiven her five times over for running off with that first painting.

The new-new stuff is odd—dark and weird like the old-new stuff, but with an added element that Sal calls "quirky" and Bernadette calls "spiritual-slash-whimsical."

A week before the show goes up, a van pulls into my driveway and Sal and I crunch through the snow to load up the paintings.

"What are they going to do with them all week?" I ask as we lurch through traffic toward the gallery.

"The guy's gotta pick which ones he wants, and then—"

"Wait a sec, I thought he wanted twenty?"

"Twenty to choose from, babe. It's a boutique gallery, not the fucking MoMA, ya know? You didn't think he'd want all of them, did you?"

"You said twenty, so I thought twenty. It's not un-heard of."

"Sure, but you're not famous yet and we're not sellin' to furniture stores anymore, babe. These people are Artsy, capital A," he says. "And so are you, for that matter."

"All right," I say. "I've never done this before. And I haven't been leaving my house much the last couple of years, remember?"

"Yeah, I remember," Sal says and pats my leg. "Anyway, he picks what he wants and then they gotta, you know, set the scene, decide where to put what, how to group shit together, that kind of thing."

"I didn't realize I'd have to sit there while somebody picked my work apart."

"Welcome to being an artist, babe. Wait till the reviews start to come! Maybe not on this show, but it'll happen. Reviewers can be brutal."

"Sal, I'm not feeling better, if that's what you're working toward."

"Don't be nervous, this guy knows talent and he likes the digital prelims I've e-mailed him. It's gonna be fine."

By the time we've unloaded the canvases and walked up two dingy flights of stairs to put them in the back room of the gallery, Sal, the assistant and I are pouring sweat, even with our coats undone, not to mention I'm having a heart attack about this whole thing.

The co-owner, a skeletal goddess named Michelle, seats us in a makeshift office with bottles of water and goes to find her partner.

"Maybe you could handle the rest?" I whisper to Sal. "I don't like this part. I could just take the streetcar home and you can tell me later which ones he's chosen."

"You don't know that you don't like this part—you've never done it," Sal reminds me with a smirk. "Sit the hell down and relax with Uncle Sal."

I groan. "I'm not going to call you Uncle, Sal. That's creepy."

"Suit yourself, but you're stayin' right here. The guy specifically said he wants the artist here when he looks at the work."

"Fine."

"Here you go," Michelle says, floating in with a file under her arm. "I've paged Mr. White and he should be here any—ah, here he is! Mara Foster, Sal Angelo, may I present Caleb White."

It would be so wrong to faint. Of course, that means I can't stand up to shake his hand.

Caleb.

Caleb White.

Oh wow.

Fortunately Sal has me by the elbow and is hauling me up.

"Nice to meet you," I croak.

His eyes fasten on me and he gives me that strange old smile that looks like he's standing on broken glass.

"Lovely to . . . meet you too."

His voice is lower and he has the slightest trace of a British accent now.

I have the wild urge to say things like "Small world!" and "Hey Michelle, you're the only person here I haven't had sex with!" Instead I open my water bottle and gulp some down, spilling on my already sweaty turtleneck.

Sal is talking and now Caleb is talking, and then Sal again.

The rest of the meeting is a blur. I sit back, keep my mouth shut and observe.

Finally it's over. Caleb and Michelle both shake my hand and I hold tight to the railing as I walk back down the stairs.

Sal drives me home.

"You gonna send out any of those invites he gave you?" Sal asks.

I look down at the stack of platinum vellum in my hand and think about the e-mail I received from Hugo last week.

"Checking in" was the subject line, and he'd pasted a picture of Pollock unraveling toilet paper to the body of the text. "Wondering how you are and where you are," the message said.

I didn't know how to respond and I still had ten paintings to finish, so I figured it could wait.

Now I don't know what to tell him, how he'll react to what happened with Erik and me, whether or not I'll ever feel ready to be in love again . . .

But I laid awake thinking of him that night and wished I had him to cuddle up to.

And then, imagining me cuddled up to Hugo made me think of Erik, alone in his bed across the city and the heavy, sad truth of never seeing him again.

"Maybe a few," I tell Sal, and then head inside.

Later I address envelopes to Dad and Shauna, Mom, Bernadette, Faith, a couple of old professors and then, with my hands shaking, to Hugo.

At the bottom of Hugo's card I scrawl a short note: "Hope you can come. Mara."

All I can do is open the door, right?

In the morning, I walk to the post office unmolested by gruesome daydreams and mail the invitations. Back at home I make a phone call.

By the time the courier arrives, I've triple-bubble-wrapped a small painting, one that Caleb didn't want, and tucked a copy of the invite inside with "FYI" written on it.

In the other lifetime, that parallel lifetime where Lucas is not part of us, Erik comes to the opening and stands by my side. In this one, he will at least know I'm all right and that I'm thinking of him sometimes. Perhaps he'll read the reviews online, if there are any, and smile when he thinks of me. Perhaps he will come to the gallery and look at my work when I am not there. If he does, he will see himself, and he will see Lucas, buried deep but everywhere, in my work.

Chapter Thirty-eight

His hair is silver now and still long, worn in a ponytail. He looks like Vidal Sassoon—all arty European, lean in a crisp, collarless shirt and pleated linen pants.

His eyes are the same.

"Good morning, Ms. Foster," he says when I show up to inspect the layout the day before the opening.

"Hi, Caleb."

His eyes hold mine for what seems like forever.

"Hey, Sixteen," he says, and his face breaks into the old grin. "It's good to see you."

"You, too, actually," I say. "Now that I've recovered from the shock."

"Sorry about that," he says. "I could have warned you, but then you might have declined my offer."

"Probably not," I say.

"So . . . how has life treated you? You look wonderful—hardly a day over seventeen."

"You got charming, huh?" I say. "That's new."

He chuckles, runs a hand over his hair.

"Life's okay," I say. "I keep learning, which must count for something. And I've tried to take your advice."

"Ah?" he says.

"'Work hard and become brilliant. Try to forget about me.' You remember that?"

"Yeah," he says. "I suppose you've looked back on me as a heartless bastard."

"Sometimes."

"But you did become brilliant, Sixteen," he says.

"Don't take too much credit," I say, then soften it with a smile.

"I don't," he says. "And did you forget about me?"

I laugh. "Well, you made a strong impression."

"You too, Sixteen, you too."

He clears his throat, steps back and gestures at the walls where my paintings hang. "Do you like how we've hung them?"

I take a moment, then say, "Yes, it makes sense. I didn't realize they were so . . ."

"Good?"

"No, I mean, thanks. I was going to say intense."

"Ah."

"But I don't really look at anything again once it's finished—I just move on."

"Interesting," he says.

"So . . . are you still painting, Caleb?"

"Of course. The gallery is Michelle's mostly, except when I take an interest in someone."

"Like me."

"Yes, like you."

I hesitate, then ask, "Did you know it was mine? That first one Sal brought?"

"Not until the day we sold it. But there was something in it—it spoke to me, gave me a déjà vu, you could say."

"You did teach me a lot."

"Good. Good luck tomorrow night, Mara. I hope you'll allow me to feel just a little bit proud."

Bernadette and Faith force me to buy high heels and a new dress. It's red, and very short, and I'm trying to ignore it. I'm also trying to remember not to scrub my hands through my hair, which has been styled, with lots of product, to stand up on purpose.

Sal whistles when he comes to pick me up.

"You don't think I look conspicuous?" I ask.

"Babe, you're supposed to be conspicuous. You're hot and scary looking at the same time."

"Oh, yay."

"It's good, it's good," he says. "Now, let's go."

It's not the entire art world of Toronto there, but still, the opening is surreal. Michelle and Caleb propel me around and I shake hands and smile and try to answer questions about my style, my techniques, and my influences.

"Vestiges of minimalism."

"Interesting use of blue."

"Obvious commentary on the politics of our time."

"Gritty."

"Rich."

"Sparse."

Can I be rich and sparse at the same time?

This crap cracks me up.

I also overhear the less positive comments and try to keep the same sense of humor.

"Gross."

"It doesn't speak to me."

"Derivative."

"Indecisive."

"Inaccessible."

"Melodramatic."

"Cold."

"Overwrought."

And so on.

Bernadette, resplendent in pink vinyl and see-through knitwear, circles the gallery hand in hand with Faith. They walk up beside people and make loud, positive comments. I take them aside and ask them to stop, but Faith just giggles and Bernadette winks at me and wanders off.

"Can you do something?" I ask Faith.

She shakes her head.

Later someone asks me if it's true that I've been contacted by the Whitney, and I see Bernadette giving me the thumbs up.

"No," I say, and the poor guy walks off looking confused.

Mom comes, looks at the price list and nods her head in approval before taking a call on her cell and disappearing.

Dad and Shauna come later and, likely at Bernadette's provocation, contribute further to the ridiculous Whitney rumor.

"Deny it all you want," Bernadette says, "it's all about spin—it's marketing. And who knows, the Whitney might call you."

"Sure."

Sal keeps me in diet soda and I find myself glancing at the door and feeling disappointed as the hours pass and Hugo doesn't come. Maybe I should have called him to invite him personally.

Should have, should have, should have. I have drunk too deeply of "should have." Perhaps it is time to banish "should have."

And there's that stupid ache for Erik again.

The crowd, which seems large mostly because the gallery is small, thins eventually and I have time to breathe and be with my paintings. Not that I've ever found them great company, but these particular ones on this particular night are different.

I send my thoughts out to wherever Lucas may be. I wonder what he would think of me tonight, and whether he would see himself here, all over the walls. Perhaps he would be happy for me. Perhaps he would want me to let him go, to let time heal the mess we all made. Or perhaps he wouldn't.

Perhaps I will accept that I'll never know.

And I will start to think about what I want.

And then I can begin to deserve it.

Midnight: Michelle goes to lock the front door, but a last straggler is asking to come in.

"Sorry, you'll have to come back tomorrow," she says.

She's about to shut the door when I see who it is.

"Wait," I call out in a strangled voice. "I know him."

She lets him in and goes back to join Caleb for more champagne.

"Hi," I say.

"Hi," he says.

We stand by the door. He shuffles his feet, I pull at my dress.

"I'm not too late?" he says.

"Probably not," I say. "Why don't you come in?"

"All right."

I would have been fine to do this alone.

But perhaps I won't be.

The end